MW00458875

WEIGHTS OF WRATH

CIPHER OFFICE BOOK #4

M.E. CARTER

COPYRIGHT

Made in the United States of America

Print Edition
978-1-949202-59-5

DEDICATION

To the ladies of Smartypants Romance:
You got lucky this year but I haven't forgotten.
We're coming for you, tattoo parlor!

CHAPTER ONE

JOEY

We need to talk.

That's all the text message says. No name. No indication of who it is or who they're trying to reach. Hell, it could be that automated chick Michelle Warren trying to trick me into talking to her about my federal student loan again.

Joke is on her. I don't have a federal student loan. I have an associate's degree from Downtown Chicago College and half those credits came from dual credit high school courses. In the case of my education, thrifty was the way to go.

All I ever wanted was to be a personal trainer. I fell in love with weightlifting in high school. I love the burn of my muscles and pushing my body to its limits. The eight-pack I'm sporting isn't a half bad side effect either. More than one pair of panties have fallen in my direction because of it.

Yet another perk of my job at Weight Expectations. Not only am I living my dream, but there is no short supply of women either. Which means Michelle Warren and her student loan can fuck right off.

"That depends on who is asking and if it's really me you're looking for," I quickly type out.

Muting my phone now that I've sent my reply, it's time to get back to work. With a full-time job and the local Strongman competition only about six months away, my plate is full. I have no time for random games from random texters.

But first, I need to get my favorite group of dames through their class.

"Okay, ladies," I say with a clap of my hands. "How are we doing? Feeling good about pushing ourselves to the limit?"

A chorus of groans, mutters, and a grumble that sounds suspiciously like an "Up yours" comes from my 65-plus fitness class. Not that I'm surprised. They love me when they first get here in the morning but always threaten to cut me by the time it's over. I refer to it as their little love dance.

Never in my wildest dreams of having this job did I anticipate teaching a bunch of elderly women how to be fit would become my favorite time of day.

"I can't do so many overhead presses. It activates my arthritis," one of my regulars complains.

"We discussed this, Harriet. You have to do the modifications. And why are you using such heavy weights?" I ask, pulling them out of her hands.

She shrugs. "I like the color orange."

"Again, orange means they're ten pounders. You need five-pound weights at the most. Those are purple."

"Purple is so cliché for a woman to use," Harriet says with a roll of her eyes.

"No one is judging the color of your weights." I hand her the correct dumbbells despite her scowl at me.

"Edna is."

"You're damn right I am," Edna yells from where she's sitting, doing a really bad rendition of bicep curls. "Purple is for wienies!"

"I'd much rather someone be a wienie than in the hospital, so let's stop looking at the color of the weights, okay?" It's a weak attempt at getting them back on track, but it's all I've got with these firecrackers.

Edna hrmphs and drops her weights on the ground, slowly pushing herself up to move to the next station. At eighty-seven, she's my oldest client and also my grumpiest. There is not one exercise she enjoys, not one person she cares to talk to, not one situation that has ever made her crack a smile. She's a hoot. And frankly, I think it's her bad attitude that keeps her so healthy. She's wildly motivated to come in every day, even if it's just to insult us all.

If only she did the exercises correctly, she could be one of those success stories we read about every once in a while, like, "Ninety-two-year-old woman starts working out and becomes Olympic gymnast five years later."

Okay, that's a stretch, but we've all seen those wild stories before. Unfortunately, the only success story I'll probably see with Edna is that she outlives us all out of spite.

"Careful with your arm placement, Edna. Control your kickbacks a little more. I don't want you to throw your shoulder out."

"And I don't want you to throw your neck out carrying that stupid man bun around, but we all have our crosses to bear."

I could respond, but instead, I chuckle. All I want is Edna to control her movement a little more, which she is. If she has to insult me to get it done, so be it.

"Okay, ladies. Just a few more minutes before our cooldown. Give it your last push."

"I'll give you a push," Edna grumbles, but keeps moving.

I just shake my head and grab my phone, still curious about who's texting me. From the indicator at the top of my screen, it looks like I'm about to get my answer.

It's Cherise from The Pie Hole. We had a one-night stand a couple months ago. Like I said, we need to talk.

Cherise. Cherise… I rack my brain trying to remember which one she was.

Oh yes! Tiny little thing with big boobs. Hot little tramp stamp at the base of her spine that got me in the mood. Flexible and feisty, that one. We had a good time. I could go for seconds.

"Oh dear," mild-mannered Marcia blurts out. "Did someone break wind?"

That's my cue to get these ladies finished. Once bodily functions start going out, it's downhill from there.

"Nice job, everyone," I call. "Grab a chair and let's do some stretches."

I used to try and stretch them on the floor, but too many of them couldn't get back up. It was funny the first time, but after a while, they started to get discouraged. That was one of my first lessons on lowering my expectations with my clients. To meet them where they're at and go from there. Since then, they've all come back almost every day. Lesson learned—I'd much rather have clients who consistently work on their health despite their barriers than clients who can get up and down off a yoga mat.

Speaking of yoga mats, I wonder what kind of exercise Cherise does to stay in shape. She was fantastically muscular on that pole…

Me: Hey Cherise! Nice to hear from you. I take it you're in the mood for a round two? We can try that handstand position again. I promise I won't drop you this time.

That sounds worse than it was. How was I to know she was going to try to reverse cowgirl me while upside down?

Her reply is almost instantaneous.

Cherise: No, you idiot. I said we need to talk. That's not code for another round on me.

Gotta give it to her—that answer makes me chuckle. I like a woman who's feisty.

Me: Remains to be seen. What would you like to "talk" about?

Cherise: The fact that I'm pregnant and it's yours.

My eyebrows lift to my hairline, and I'm sure my face is ghostly white.

Looks like I'm not getting a double dip. I'd have to find my balls first. Pretty sure they just shriveled up and ran away.

CHAPTER TWO

CHERISE

I get off in three hours. Where do you want to meet?

Joey's response to me dropping the "p" bomb on him is running a continual loop in my brain. Even as I strut around the pole, gaining speed before wrapping my legs around the bottom and allowing myself to spin.

"I hope you're working on some new moves," my boss Bennie yells from across the room. All the lights are on since it's the middle of the day and we aren't open for business yet. "I've seen the same routines a few too many times lately, Cherise."

I roll my eyes and ignore him. He's all bark and no bite anyway. Besides, I'm not really working out. More letting my mind drift as I try to decide how to respond to Joey. Easy answer is where and when to meet. The right answer doesn't feel that simple, though.

The tone of his texts changed the minute I told him I was pregnant. I admit, I'm a tiny bit impressed that he didn't immediately demand to know how I knew it was his. But I'm also conflicted about my decision to contact him.

Part of me is grateful he isn't dismissing me as some kind of slut right off the bat. Maybe he'll be open to the idea of co-parenting with me.

The other part of me is flat-out terrified. Telling him was more a formality so I would know for sure that door had already closed. I'd never have to wonder if things could be different because he would know about the baby and have already made the decision to leave us alone. Instead, he wants to meet. Why? Is he going to pressure me to get a paternity test? Does he want me to get rid of the baby? Or worse, will he try to make me give up custody?

My brain is a jumbled mess and I can't seem to land on one way to feel. Reality is, beyond the initial impressions he made on the one night we were together, I don't know who Joey is and that's probably the scariest part of all. I know nothing about him. Sleeping with him was fine but bringing an innocent child into the situation means a whole new level of safety I have to be aware of. Hell, he could be a sociopath or a child abuser. What if he's a horrible person to co-parent with and is a danger to our child?

I'm trying not to get stuck on those thoughts, at least not until we have our sit-down. My gut says he doesn't have ill intentions, but how the hell would I really know? Our one-night stand was supposed to remain just that—one night. Saving his number in my phone was solely for the purpose of tracking him down if we got separated on our way out of the club that night. If Joey had been any good in the sack, I would have used said number to extend our soiree into another night, but he wasn't a great lover. Not that I expected much from what was supposed to be just scratching an itch with a stranger. But falling on my head wasn't even a thought I had when we stumbled back to his place that night.

All I did was bend over and touch my toes. It's a good angle for me. But that idiot thought I was trying to do some sort of circus trick and suddenly, my legs were wrapped around his waist and my head banging against the wall.

It was weird. And pretty much cemented that our one night together would be our last. It ended up being my last night with anyone at all. There was no particular reason for my sudden celibacy, except maybe a bit of PTSD from my near concussion. More likely, though, I just didn't meet anyone who caught my eye—not that I have time to date when I work the kind of hours I do. Nor do I meet many quality candidates in the audience of The Pie Hole. Usually, it's drunken frat boys who are barely over age, guys old enough to be my dad, or an honest-to-goodness pervert who sits by himself, trying to hide the fact that his hand is stuck down his pants for most of the night.

But Joey was different. I don't know if it was the dirty blond locks held up in a disheveled man bun or his vibrant green eyes. Hell, it could have been those impressive guns he calls biceps. But really, it was probably because he didn't look at me like I was a piece of meat on that stage. He looked at me like I was a person. A person who deserved respect.

Okay, okay. That's taking it a bit too far. He still leered like everyone else, but at least he didn't try to tweak my nipple when I got close to the end of the stage. Instead, he very carefully tucked a twenty in my thong. And yes, I know how cheap that makes me sound to be impressed by someone keeping their paws off of me as he shoves a Jackson at me. But seriously, have you been to a strip club before? It's not like these guys have tons of boundaries. The wedding rings half of them sport are proof of that.

So as a reward for both of us, I went home with him for the night. I had a... *decent* time once he finally got me off and thought I'd never see him again. Unfortunately, his swimmers had other ideas. How those little shits got through a condom and my birth control pill, I will never know. But I'm preparing myself for a toddler who runs across parking lots the second I take my hands off him. He or she is already proving himself to have some sort of super speed.

Dropping down off the pole, I sigh. "Hey, Bennie?"

"Yeah," his voice calls from somewhere behind the bar.

"How many pregnant girls you have working here over the years?"

His head pops up, a startled look on his face. "None that I know of. Why are you asking? You got yourself in a bad way?"

I cross my arms and prepare for the worst. That response alone pretty much cements my concern that I'm about to be out of a job.

I don't even have to answer his question before his face completely changes. "Aw shit, Cherise. You're my best dancer. Why'd you have to go and do that?"

"Boredom," I retort nonchalantly.

"Seriously?"

"No." I sigh again and plop down on the end of the stage, careful not to poke myself with my stiletto. "It was an accident."

"Told the daddy yet?"

I hold up my phone and wave it at him. "Just did."

"And how'd he take it? Do I need to kick someone's ass?"

I snicker. Bennie may be the proprietor of a shady establishment, but he still does his best to take care of his girls. It's an odd dichotomy. Like that phrase, "honor among thieves." He doesn't steal anything except maybe some of our dignity as far as I know, but he always makes sure we're at least physically protected.

"He doesn't seem too upset about it right now. I don't know." I absentmindedly run my thumb over the screen, still considering my own feelings on this whole mess. "I guess it's early enough that anything could happen."

Bennie rounds the bar and comes to rest next to me against the stage. "How much longer do you have before you start showing?"

I know where this conversation is headed, and it makes me oddly sad. Stripping was never my dream, more something I decided to do because of the money with the added benefit of pissing my mother off. But I hate that I'm about to be forced out.

"No idea. I've heard first-time moms go longer without showing. So, a month? Maybe longer."

Bennie crosses his arms and legs but doesn't say a word. He doesn't have to. We both know I can't work a pole for much longer. Even if Bennie catered to a fetish like that, the liability would be too much. The kinds of moves I do wouldn't be safe for me or the kid.

The baby.

It seems so surreal at this point. I have to keep reminding myself that there's a real live baby inside me. Maybe eventually, it'll feel real.

"Well, you know there's always a place for you here once you have it."

A sad smile crosses my face. "Thanks, Bennie. For everything."

He nods once and pushes off the ledge. "Just make sure you have a good babysitter when you do. This is no place for a baby, and lord knows, I'd be terrible at watching it."

I huff a small laugh. No way would I bring my kid here. It's been fine for me and the money has been great, but my mother is already going to kill me. No reason to make my death more painful.

Once again, I consider how I need to respond to Joey. More than anything, I just need to get through this meeting. Knowing if he's in this for the long haul, or if he's just trying to take advantage of the situation to get into my pants again will go a long way to help me figure out my next move.

Might as well show him who he's really getting involved with and find out what kind of guy he really is before this goes much further, I think as I type out my reply.

Me: Do you know where Blessings Chicken is?

Joey: I don't eat fast food.

Me: I don't care. I have a craving and as your baby mama, you need to meet me at Blessings Chicken.

The three little dots populate and then disappear, populate and then disappear, populate and then disappear, before I finally have an answer.

Joey: I'll meet you there at five.

Hmm. No denial. No arguing. Not even conflict over my choice in food. Maybe Joey isn't as selfish as I thought.

CHAPTER THREE

JOEY

Pregnant.

Knocked up.

Bun in the oven.

Not at all what I was expecting Cherise to say when I replied to her text. And yet, here I am, walking down the street to Blessings Chicken to meet my baby mama. Part of me wishes Michelle Warren really did have some student loans to collect. That would be a much quicker issue to solve.

But a baby? How did this even happen? I've gone through my memories about a hundred times in the last couple of hours, and I'm positive I wrapped it up tight that night.

Regardless, I know life takes you by surprise sometimes. Like when my parents decided to up and move to Florida the minute I got my own place. (Kind of rude to take the washer and dryer with them, if you ask me.)

Or when my work buddy ended up happily shacked up with a supercute cougar within a few months of his divorce. I admit, Abel and Elliott are a perfect match, but it was still an unexpected pairing. I thought he would at least sow some wild oats for a while, but nope. Now I'm my own wingman.

Speaking of wings…

"Welcome to Blessings Chicken," an employee says from behind the world's oldest cash register as I walk in. Her voice sounds dry, monotone, and like she's been here way too long. Her tone is also oddly familiar, but I can't put a finger on where I've heard her voice before. So, I give a small wave in response, praying I never hooked up with her. Then I glance around the room, looking for the woman supposedly carrying my child.

Despite having not seen her in two months, and with her wearing more clothes in public, I spot her immediately. Her hair is longer, and her face is clean of makeup, but she's still just as beautiful as she was that night under mood lighting and a cloud of cigar smoke.

I'd forgotten how stunning she is. The little man in my pants kicks up as he remembers, too.

Sauntering over, I approach the table she's sitting at and flash her my brightest smile. "Is this seat taken?"

Slowly, she looks up at me, beautiful brown eyes staring—no, wait—*glaring* in my direction. "Really? I text you because I'm knocked up, and you greet me with an opening line like we're at a club?"

Generally, I'm a happy person and try to see the bright side of situations, even if it means starting off on the wrong foot. I'm a nice guy. I have a decent job and have some great friends. And don't get me started on my great head full of hair. The kid could do worse in the daddy department. So yes. Yes, this is my opening line.

"Is there something different I should be using?"

That glare is back. It's actually more like a weak attempt at intimidation. That's another thing I had forgotten—the cute way she tries not to smirk when she's trying to be a badass but is having a hard time trying to pull it off. I actually find it kind of cute. Like a feisty little kitten. Her snarky attitude is a strange turn-on right now. "I was thinking something along the lines of 'how did this happen?'"

I'm pretty sure that's actually the question running through *her* head. I already know that answer. A night of dirty, dirty sex.

Sliding into the seat, I don't let her bitterness faze me. I may be blindsided by the situation, but I'm not the one who is dealing with the physical ramifications while making most of the hard decisions here. "I admit, I'm as surprised as you are, but we all know the risks when we hook up. It's not ideal, sure, but I'm trying to see the positive in all this."

"Which is?"

"Dinner with a beautiful woman."

Her eyes narrow, and I know she's assessing me. It's hard for people to grasp that I'm truly an even-keeled kind of guy all the time. Nothing ruffles my feathers. Well, except that time Elliott sent me a fake article encouraging me to masturbate three times a day for testicular health. I was irritated—figuratively and literally.

But for the most part, I just go with the flow. I focus on silver linings. Seeing Cherise again under these circumstances has definitely got me concentrating on the shiny side of the situation. She's a cool chick. I'm kind of excited to get to know her again.

"This isn't dinner," she finally says dryly. "This is a conversation over food."

I raise an eyebrow at her because that sounds suspiciously like my definition of a dinner date.

She rolls her eyes harder than anyone I've ever seen before. It's actually pretty impressive. "You know what I mean. We need to figure out how to handle all this."

Leaning my forearms on the table, I clasp my hands together. "I guess the first thing I want to know is how are you? Are you healthy? Is the baby healthy?"

If I'm not mistaken, I see a tiny chink in her invisible armor. "We're fine. A little morning sickness but nothing to worry about at this point."

"Good. So how long do we have to prepare? When is the baby due?"

"May fourth."

"That's a great day for this Star Wars fan." Baby names start running through my head immediately. I wonder what she'd think of Han for a boy and Leia for a girl. Hmmm….

Cherise seems completely indifferent at having the best due date a George Lucas fan could ever hope for, instead reaching into her purse that's sitting on the chair next to hers. "That's what the doctor told me yesterday. Here."

She slides a row of black-and-white pictures over to me and my breath hitches as I take in what I'm looking at. "Holy shit. It's… it's…"

"A weird-looking blob. I know."

"But it's a beautiful blob," I breathe as I run my finger over the pictures.

"The doctor pointed out the head and legs or whatever, but I still can't see anything."

I have no idea what I'm looking at either, but I don't even care. "Cherise, this is… it's just amazing."

Looking up at her, I catch her fighting a shy smile. She doesn't want to be happy that I'm happy, but I can tell she is. "Yeah, it is kind of cool."

I'm glad we agree on that, but it doesn't mean we're on the same page for the future. I know what I hope for in this particular scenario, but I also know it's not my choice. I helped get her into this mess, so I have to help her out of it as well, whatever that ends up meaning. "You know I'll support you no matter what you choose to do."

Her answer comes quick and final. "Oh no. I was born and raised a good Catholic girl. There is no getting rid of anything, I don't care what kind of blob of cells it is right now. The worst thing that could happen to me is not being pregnant out of wedlock, it's my mother finding out I had an abortion and her praying directly to the Virgin Mary about me instead of the saints she regularly calls upon. The two of them would get together to put some sort of hex-y thing on me."

"I don't think hexes go along with Catholicism."

"You don't know my mother. She has a hard enough time with me being a stripper. Between her and my aunt, there are so many candles lit for me, it's a wonder the church hasn't burned down yet."

Good to know. Now that we've covered the biggest decision, I suppose it's time to move on to the next difficult topic.

"I don't want to sound like a dick, but I wanna make sure what I'm getting into is real. I don't want to fall in love with this baby, only to find out later it isn't mine." I hold by breath because as much as I hate having to ask, let's be real. I don't know Cherise all that well.

"That's… oddly sweet." I shrug and smile. She's not the first one to say that to me. "But I haven't been with anyone else after you. And not for weeks before. I was going through a bit of a dry spell."

This causes me to sit up straight in the booth. She's young, single, beautiful. I'm surprised she hasn't been playing the field. "How come?"

"I sleep during normal business hours. And quality men are few and far between in my line of work."

"Aw. Did you just call me a quality guy?"

"Don't flatter yourself. You haven't seen your competition."

The same employee who greeted me when I got here drops a tray of food on our table. I guess Cherise didn't wait on me to order.

"Can I help you with anything else." She doesn't actually ask a question. She just dryly tosses out the statement, making it very clear that it's too much effort to actually help with anything else.

"Nope," Cherise replies, pulling the tray closer to her. "This is all I need."

"Enjoy your meal."

Finally, it hits me.

"Aha!" I snap my fingers, as the proverbial lightbulb goes off over my head.

Cherise mumbles, "What?" around a bite of food.

"You ever watch the movie *Monsters, Inc.*?"

"Yeah. It's my favorite. So?"

"She sounds like Roz. The secret agent who pretends she hates everyone."

Cherise gets a delighted look on her face that she quickly schools as she glances over at the employee and nods slowly. "That's it. It's been driving me crazy since I got here, but you're right."

I pat the table and throw my hands up. "Look at us. Already figuring stuff out. We're going to nail this parenting thing."

It's her turn to quirk an eyebrow. "Knowing the voice of an animated character is different than knowing how to change a diaper."

"But it's a starting point."

"No. A starting point would be me finding some gainful employment."

That's not what I was expecting her to say. "What do you mean? Are you not at The Pie Hole anymore?"

"Yes, but not for long." She gestures down her body as she chews and wipes her mouth. "Not a huge market for pregnant strippers."

"Are you sure? It's a fetish." I've seen something about it online before. Not that I go looking for pregnant porn but running across it wasn't a surprise either.

"One that I don't particularly care to engage in. Nor does my boss. Especially since neither of us does online work."

"So, what now?"

"No idea. The only job I've ever had is stripping. Well, unless you count that one time I tried to help babysit in the church nursery."

"Maybe you could work at a daycare?"

She looks at me like I've lost my damn mind. But is it so unrealistic to have a former stripper as your babysitter? I think not.

"They kicked me out early when we all discovered the hard way I don't actually like kids."

Okay, so that could be an issue. "I can see how that would be a problem. Do I want to know how you figured it out?"

"Short answer, it involved boogers and me rocking in a corner." Cherise tosses an empty bone on her plate and grabs another piece, booger talk not deterring her appetite at all. Damn. Is this how pregnant women eat all the time? Is this what they mean by eating for two? I'm starting to worry that maybe she's having twins with the way she's going at it.

"It doesn't help that my options are limited. I dropped out of high school, so no diploma."

"Why did you do that? Trouble at home?"

She purses her lips. "It depends on what you mean by trouble. Were my parents abusive? Not even close. But my mother and I have butted heads for as long as I can remember. The minute I turned eighteen, I went out and found a job that I could live off of and surprise! There's not a lot of demand for teenagers with no education. Besides, stripping is good money, and I don't really give a shit who sees my boobs. It also fed my habit for all things extravagant, Gucci and Prada included."

"Seems like such a drastic move at a young age has been working for you so far."

"In hindsight, maybe I should have waited that last semester to leave like my mother begged me." She grabs the last piece of chicken and begins picking at it. "No sense in crying over it now. I've got a job to find. My biggest issue is I don't want to work in fast food or retail. The pay sucks but the hours are worse. And I don't know how my nose would handle the smell of that much grease." She says it while shoveling the world's greasiest drumstick in her mouth. I wisely keep my thoughts to myself.

"What about working at the gym?"

"What gym?"

"Weight Expectations. I'm a trainer there."

She looks at me like that's the dumbest thing she's ever heard. "I can't be a personal trainer. I don't even know how to exercise without a pole and some five-inch heels."

"Well, that explains your kick-ass calf muscles."

She glances at her legs under the table and bites back a smile. "I do have nice calf muscles, don't I?"

"You have nice everything. That's why I liked watching you so much that night. You could compete on the pole. Did you know they're making it into an Olympic sport?"

"Really?" Cherise sits up straight, eyes brightening. I guess she enjoys her work for more than just the money. "That's really cool. I hate the pervs that come into the club, but the actual dancing is so fun. I could do it all the time."

"Maybe after the baby's born, you could get some certifications and learn how to teach pole classes."

Her chewing slows as she thinks through what I just said. "You really think the gym would let me?"

"I don't know for sure, but they're always trying to shake things up. If it really does go to the Olympics, you know it'll make an even bigger comeback as an exercise plan than it already has. Might as well be prepared. What's the worst that can happen? You work at a different gym teaching classes instead?"

Her entire demeanor changes. Gone is the guarded woman who was lobbing insults at me as she felt me out. For the first time since our night together, I'm seeing glimpses of a woman on a mission. Like her passion has more opportunities than she originally thought.

"Well, I'll have to look it up but I guess I have some time now that my current employment is about to end. For now, what kind of job were you talking about at the gym?"

"I know we have a housekeeping position open."

She groans. "Seriously? I hate cleaning my own place, let alone a sweaty, stinky gym."

"You're in luck. Weight Expectations doesn't stink, and since we have housekeeping on site at all times, it's more maintaining the cleanliness than deep cleaning."

She chews on a fry and thinks. "Do they pay well?"

"Not what you're making now, but they're not cheap either. They like being a premier facility, so they expect everyone to work hard, but they pay you appropriately for it. Plus, full-time employees get benefits, and we could use those with all the doctor's appointments coming up."

Nodding, she replies, "You make a good case for it."

"It'll buy you time to look into getting certified to train. Maybe get your GED if it's a requirement. And it gets your foot in the door at a really good place of employment."

"Okay. You've convinced me. How do I fill out an application?"

I mentally pat myself on the back for how easy it was to get over that first major hurdle as a parent. I'm better at this dad thing than I thought I was going to be.

Now, I just need to figure out how to cook.

CHAPTER FOUR

CHERISE... ER... ROSALIND

I had forgotten how sweet Joey is. And caring. And attractive.

But the second he slid into that booth at Blessings Chicken, my hormones reminded me that he may have gotten a little overzealous in the bedroom, but he didn't leave me hanging. He made sure I was good and finished off that night before kissing me thoroughly and telling me how amazing I was.

Joey is the kind of man women dream of.

He is also a big, fat liar.

Not that I have any room to talk since he still doesn't know my real name. I've almost told him several times, but then I made a wager with myself on how long it will take him to figure it out and it makes me laugh. With my budgeted play money stripped down to almost nothing—pun intended, I have to find some way to entertain myself.

But still, omission of the truth is way better than his flat-out lie about my new job. Working in housekeeping is definitely not just "maintaining cleanliness" like he claimed. It's picking up dirty towels and cleaning toilets and hauling an ancient vacuum around. Frankly, it's kind of gross. And Joey's nasal passages must not be working, because the men's locker room smells so much worse than he thinks.

I guess I should have expected as much. I've never heard of a gym smelling like roses. And truly, the benefits that come from spraying showers with anti-fungal cleaner outweigh how much filth is in that same shower. Barely, but it does. Besides, I need to keep my eyes on my future. If Joey's right and I can do what I love in a place like this after the baby is here, it would be like hitting the jackpot.

Not that I felt down and out working at The Pie Hole. I liked my job. It made me feel happy. Or at least, what it could buy me made me happy. I make no apologies for liking the finer things in life—designer clothes, a large one-bedroom apartment in Hyde Park, regular hair/nail/massage appointments—and I liked providing them for myself. Stripping can pull in some big money if you do it right. That is, if you can get past the whole getting-topless-for-strangers part. It never bothered me. They're just boobs. Okay they're fabulous, perky boobs, but they're not *that* big of a deal. Very soon, milk will be shooting out of them and they'll be covered in baby drool. I doubt the pervs at the club will think they're very sexy then.

I think what kept me there so long, besides a job that paid for more than just the bills, was the challenge of the dance. I like working hard to perfect a move that takes strength most people don't possess. I like coming up with a routine that will wow my audience for its skill, not just its skin. I would spend hours practicing a new trick until I could do it without a second thought and revel in the achievement. It was the best kind of high.

If I can do that same kind of job in a respectable and hoity-toity place like this, my mother would be able to stop praying to the Patron Saint of Dance to break my pole and toss some clothes down my direction. I'm sure she'll still be lighting candles for my indecent soul, but any progress is a step in the right direction.

I pick up yet another wet towel off a chair in the locker room and toss it in my huge laundry basket on wheels out the door. It's actually a repurposed garbage cans with wheels attached to the bottom. Whoever engineered it probably did so after discovering people go through more towels here than necessary at this place.

The squeaky wheels announce my arrival in the treadmill area so everyone can stare at me a little too long. I'm sure it's because I'm new and they don't know who I am yet. Or maybe they're annoyed by the squeak. I don't blame them. Someone needs to WD-40 the crap out of that soon.

Pushing it into the large storage area where it waits for pickup from the laundry company we contract with, I grab the basket of clean towels and switch them out to fold. Making sure all towel areas are stocked is an essential part of my job, according to my new boss Christina. "We're one of the only gyms in the area to provide towels to our customers. It's why we're a premiere facility."

Sounds like justification to charge the members more money to me. But admittedly, it's not hard to fold a bunch of towels, and now I have insurance, so she'll have no complaints from me.

I shut the door behind me and turn, only to barrel right into a solid wall of man.

"Rosie?"

Looking up, my eyes widen at the sight of my favorite cousin. "Abel!"

"Holy shit, I haven't seen you since… well, Christmas probably!" He pulls me into a tight hug. "How are you? What are you doing here?"

"I work here now. Just started a couple days ago."

Abel pulls away but keeps one hand on my shoulder. I can tell he's confused by my presence. For years, he just assumed I worked in customer service. Technically, it wasn't a lie. "In housekeeping? How do you like it?"

I shrug nonchalantly. "Eh. Beats fast food, ya know?"

"I do, I do. How's your mom?"

"She's good. Finally over that pneumonia she had and still doing her thing, shopping for her grandbabies and volunteering at the church."

I can see the cogs turning as he counts in his head. "How many grandkids does she have now? Three?"

"Four. Timothy and his wife had another one."

He snaps his fingers together. "Oh, that's right. Man, I can't believe that pussy grew up to get such a hot wife."

I laugh because he's not wrong. He may be my older brother, but Timothy has always been a wuss.

"Yeah, but Mom's about to have a fifth grandchild she doesn't know about yet." I smooth my hand down over my staff shirt to show off my barely there baby bump that popped up some time in the last week or so. It's actually more like a pooch that no one can see except me, and maybe some of my regulars who sit on the front row.

That doesn't stop me from rubbing it, though. It's like an automatic reflex or something.

Abel's eyes widen and his mouth drops open. "You… Rosie, wow."

I smile shyly and ignore him calling me by the nickname I hate with a passion. Instead, I'm ready to give him my spiel about how I'm okay with being an unwed mother and this baby isn't a mistake but an unexpected gift—all that bullshit you have to say so people stop judging your choices—but Joey comes out of nowhere and interrupts us instead.

"Hey! Abel! I see you finally met my baby mama!" Joey puts his arm around me, not noticing that Abel's face just hardened into someone who's ready to kick a dude's ass.

Crossing his arms slowly, Abel's eyebrows rise. Oh shit. This isn't good. "Say again?"

"Abel," I warn, but he's not looking at me. He's staring at Joey, a murderous look in his eye. I've seen it before. In the past, it's usually ended with Timothy in a headlock. Somehow, I think Joey won't be getting off with just a noogie though.

Joey, on the other hand, still seems oblivious. "This is Cherise. I told you about her. We only spent that one night together, but I think this is going to work out well. Abel is a great dad, so I'll learn everything I need to know from him," Joey says to me. All I can do is shake my head. This is about to get really ugly.

"Who the hell is Cherise?" Abel asks. I grimace, knowing I'm about to be called out by both of them. Awesome.

Joey furrows his brow and points at me. "She is."

"No. Her name is Rosie."

I roll my eyes because we've had this conversation many times before. "No one calls me that except you, Abel."

"Because they call you Cherise," Joey tries to explain.

"No, because Cherise is my stripper name," I finally fess up, cheap fun finally over.

Abel's face turns bright red, his anger toward Joey temporarily forgotten. "Stripper?" he exclaims a little too loud. "Since when are you a stripper?"

I purse my lips and try to come up with some sort of alternative explanation, but nothing comes to mind. "Since I dropped out of high school?"

I swear his eyes almost bug out of his face. "You've been stripping for *eight years*? Does Aunt Mona know?"

"Please. You think my mom didn't figure it out when I started making more money than my dad? Of course, she knew. I can't believe you never noticed the holes in the knees of all her pants. She and your mom have been trying to pray me out of that job for forever."

"My mom knew and didn't tell me?"

"I know, right? You'd think the entire family would whisper about me by now, but it's the tightest kept secret in the DiSoto family line. For once, the shame I will bring on the family worked to my benefit." I force out a laugh to lighten his mood. It doesn't work.

"I'm serious, Rosie."

I throw my hands in the air, getting irritated by this whole thing. "Why? You needed to know for what reason? So you could go watch me dance?"

He grimaces. "Oh, hell no. I don't need to see my baby cousin naked. Maybe she should've told me to make sure I stayed away from your place of business."

"Wait," Joey interrupts, finally catching on. "You have a stage name?"

As if he finally remembers the original issue at hand, Abel turns menacingly toward Joey. He takes one step forward, but Joey doesn't seem fazed. "Her name is Rosalind. Rosalind Palmer, but we call her Rosie."

"No one calls me Rosie, Abel," I say for the second time in this very weird conversation.

He ignores me, of course. "And she's my baby cousin. So, I hope I didn't hear that correctly when you said she's your baby mama. The one you got pregnant after a one-night stand. Whose name you don't even know."

Joey pauses for a second before turning to me and saying, "Your last name is Palmer. You didn't think Rosie Palm might be a better stripper name?"

Abel visibly inflates and grumbles, "I'm gonna fucking kill him."

"No, really," Joey continues, either oblivious to Abel's distress or just uninterested. "Rosie Palm is a great name for a stripper. You could do a whole routine and call the background dancers your five sisters."

"Someone better stop me," Abel says while pacing and taking obvious measures to breathe slowly through his nose.

I put my hand on his chest. "Cool it, DiSoto. Give me a second." Then I turn to the man who hopefully passed on his sexy hair and not his IQ genes to my baby. "Joey. I didn't use Rosie Palm because I was trying to keep my work life and personal life separate. Clearly it worked."

"But it's so clever."

"Agreed. It was also totally overused by the time I got to eighth grade. Now if you can please give me and my cousin a minute, I need to talk to him before his head blows off or he decides to go one round with you, mixed martial arts-style."

For whatever reason, that's when Joey finally seems to notice his best gym buddy is in the process of losing his shit. And yet, he still doesn't seem afraid. "Dude. Man, I thought you'd be happy for me. I'm gonna be a dad. And we're gonna be family."

I can't help it. The joy on Joey's face makes me melt just a little. Not enough to show it outwardly, of course. But for that split second, I feel like I'm making some good decisions with the best partner possible. The way Abel's body relaxes just a bit, I think maybe he knows it too.

Dropping his chin to his chest, Abel mutters, "Dammit."

"Go, Joey. Give him a minute to process."

He finally takes the time to really look at Abel before acquiescing. "Okay. I'll go. I need to talk to Keely about some ideas to drum up some new clientele anyway. I'm not gonna screw this up. Not for either of you."

I'm pretty sure he says that last part for Abel's benefit more than mine, but I appreciate it, nonetheless.

"Good idea. We'll see you later."

Joey walks away with no more fanfare, and fortunately, no bloodshed. Of course, that still doesn't mean Abel is going to walk away without a bit of commotion. But I'm not afraid of him. He might be a hothead sometimes, but he's not the only one with a full-blooded Italian temperament. With my pregnancy hormones, the one in real danger here is him.

Grabbing a towel out of the basket, I begin to fold. "I'm sorry you had to find out this way."

Abel nods once, his hands on his hips. "That's… a lot of big information to process."

"Which part?"

"All of it." He looks around absently, trying to process how he feels. "Rosie…"

"Rosalind," I correct.

"… if you needed money, why didn't you come to me?"

I look at him with confusion. "Needed money? I didn't need money. I *wanted* money. Lots of it."

"Oh, you're gonna tell me you were dancing for… for strangers, and it never bothered you?" His hands move around rapidly like his words can't come out fast enough. "No one dances naked because they like it. Or like money that much."

So much for giving him time to process. Now, he's just pissing me off.

"First of all, you can keep your holier-than-thou attitude over there away from me. My mother has berated me for years about my job choices. She never lets me forget what a disgrace I am, so I know what a *shameful* thing it is, okay?" I make sure to air quote "shameful" in case he doesn't catch my sarcasm. Just because I disagree doesn't make it any less painful to hear regularly, though. Hence, why I never fully trust what people think about me and why I have such anger toward him now. "You don't know why people dance for a living. Some people actually like stripping. The lack of clothing might not be their favorite, but they like something about it. Whether it be the money, or the feeling of being powerful, or the beauty of the dance."

"Beauty of the dance? Get outta here."

"Yes. The beauty of the dance. Pole dancing might be an Olympic sport. I bet you didn't know that, did you, Mr. Judgey Pants?"

"It is not." He has the audacity to roll his eyes at me, which only makes me angrier. Fortunately, I have a towel to snap in place of his neck.

"It most certainly is. Right now, it's recognized as an international sport, which means it could be included in the future. The industry is already pushing for it. You can look it up if you don't believe me." Like how I researched it after Joey told me, but Abel doesn't need to know that part.

"So, you're telling me you enjoy being a stripper because you're an athlete?"

I narrow my eyes at him before turning away to grab another towel. "You sound really condescending, you know that?"

"Maybe because my baby cousin, whose diapers I used to change, is dancing naked for strangers and having my best friend's baby."

"Topless. Not naked. And all of that affects you how?"

"Because you're my family."

I toss the towel down, sick of this conversation. "So, it embarrasses you that you have a cousin who strips for a living?" Out of the corner of my eye, I see someone stumble on the treadmill as I say this, but I can only focus on one person's judgement at a time.

Abel takes a step back now that I've called him out. "That's not what I mean."

"It's not? The only thing you've done since I told you I'm pregnant is threaten to beat up Joey and insult me by insinuating my chosen line of work isn't good enough for you. Which, incidentally, is why I didn't tell you in the first place."

His face falls and his whole demeanor changes. I know what he's about to say. It's what everyone says. Everyone except Joey. And isn't that an interesting revelation to have at this exact moment.

"It's not good enough for you."

And there it is.

"You don't get to decide that. I decide that. Whether I want to fold towels"—I snap it his direction for good measure—"take off my clothes, or even sell my body on a street corner has nothing to do with you. But thanks for doing a damn good job of making me realize what a failure you think I am."

I throw the folded towels back in the basket, making them unfold and undo all the work I just finished. I hurry to push the basket into the one place he can't follow me

—the ladies' dressing room. I like folding out in the open where I can get more interaction, but suddenly, the company isn't that interesting to me.

"Come on, Rosie," he pleads behind me.

I whip my head around, long dark locks flying so fast they hit the cheek on the other side of my face. "For the last time, no one calls me that!"

And I storm off to do my job away from his judgey little eyes.

CHAPTER FIVE

JOEY

My favorite hour of the day is over, and those ladies kicked my ass. Things were going well until Edna accused Harriet of hiding the purple weights so no one could use them. Not sure why Edna wanted them since she used the gray ones this time, and in her words, purple is a wienie color anyway.

Nevertheless, I haven't heard name-calling like that since I once had an actual sailor for a client. It was entertaining in an "I wonder if Edna used to mud wrestle in her day" kind of way.

No blood was shed—except for when Marcia broke a fingernail—and now that they're gone, I need to take a piss.

As I round the corner into the locker room, it becomes clear I'm going to have to wait a little while longer for some relief. Abel is at his locker, probably getting ready to pick up the girls from school. As soon as he sees me, he crosses his arms and goes into a bouncer stance.

"I'm not sure it's a good idea to kick my ass while on the job, do you?" I say by way of greeting, reminding him that violence is never the answer.

"I'm not sure I care right now." His tone is menacing, which is a bit discombobulating. I've never seen Abel angry like this, not even when May left him and their daughter to fend for themselves. I may need to warn Elliott so she can prepare well in advance for the girls' dating years.

But first, back to the conflict at hand.

"You'll care after HR fires your ass and you're trying to figure out how to provide for your family."

His arms uncross and he takes a step forward. "Really? You want to lecture me about providing for a family?"

"No. I don't want a lecture at all for either of us. But I'm not sure why you're so pissed, either."

Abel scoffs. "We've already established that. You knocked up my baby cousin."

My head falls back and I look at the ceiling. Its exasperating being the voice of reason. "You're looking at this the wrong way, Abel."

"Because I don't have your positive, sunshiny attitude?"

"Well, yes. But also, she's not your baby cousin. She's your adult cousin who makes her own life choices. One of them just happened to result in a pregnancy. You should be happy the second person involved in this is me and not some asshole who is either going to let her go it alone, or use the kid as leverage to be a douchebag to her." I take a step closer. "This is *me*, man. You saw my reaction after she sent that first text, remember?"

His jaw twitches as he considers my words, and I know he's remembering my reaction when he asked where I was going.

"Dude. I think I'm going to be a dad."

The words don't sound like much, but I know I was smiling when I said it because I could feel it. I could feel the joy of all the possibilities for my future. Our future. I knew she was in control of it all, and I was scared, but I also knew what I was hoping for—our baby to be born and to raise him or her to be the best little person they can be.

Abel sighs deeply before speaking. "Come on."

"Where are we going?" I raise my hands up to stop him before we go. "Remember any bloodshed has to be mopped up by Cherise—"

"Rosie."

"—so it would be really rude to make a mess. She shouldn't be doing heavy lifting in her condition."

He shakes his head, a common reaction when we talk. "No bloodshed, I promise. Maybe some boogers, though."

"Ew. What?" I scrunch my nose in disgust. "Maybe I'd rather you punch me."

"Just come on."

I follow behind him, close enough to keep up but far enough away to run for cover if I have to. I'm not at all surprised when he takes me to the childcare center, seeing that's his favorite place to visit now that he's bumping uglies with the afternoon manager.

Fine, so she's his live-in girlfriend and so much more than that. I'm still going to make fun of them any time I can. Elliott's embarrassed blush is so endearing it makes me laugh.

I wonder what Rosalind would look like if I made her blush. Would it stop at her cheeks? Would it creep up from her ample chest all the way up her neck?

"Hey!" Elliott greets us with a huge smile on her face, bouncing a toddler on her hip. Now may not be the most appropriate time to be thinking about Rosalind's chest. "I hear congratulations are in order."

My turn to blush, only it's not embarrassment as much as excitement. I can feel by the heat in my cheeks. "Yeah. Thanks. You may be the first one to have said that to me. Everyone else seems to just give me lectures." I turn and glare at Abel.

Elliott, on the other hand, gently pokes the toddler in the tummy, making him twitch. "It takes people time to figure out what they need to say about an unplanned pregnancy. Give them a couple months and they'll be excited with you." She turns and shoots her own scathing look at Abel.

He ignores both of our obvious attempts at inducing guilt. "How's it going, babe?"

Elliott sighs. "It's been rough today. Is there a full moon? We've had two poopy diapers in a one-hour period, an injury from a thrown block, and this little guy"—she tickles the toddler on her hip again, but he just scowls—"is having a tough time being away from his mama."

"He looks okay to me," I say.

"It's deceiving," she replies. "Watch."

Elliott bends over and places the kid on the floor. He immediately starts screaming, the shrill of his voice just about blowing my eardrums out.

I put a finger in my ear and yell, "Good lord, make it stop!"

She smirks and picks the child back up. He immediately goes silent, scowling like the world has done him wrong.

I'm still fidgeting with my ears, pretty sure I just lost about ten percent of my hearing. "Holy shit, that was loud."

A hand smacks the back of my head. "Watch your language in here," Abel bitches.

"Not like anyone can hear me now that we all have blown eardrums." I open and close my mouth a few times trying to clear my ear canals.

"And that's what being a parent is like, Joey," he lectures. "Blown eardrums. Drool on your shirt. Snot on your pants. Not sleeping through the night. Every single priority you have is blown to bits. It's all about someone else. You want to train for Strongman? Not if your baby has a fever. You think it's bad to be in here for four seconds? What makes you think you can handle the next eighteen years?"

"Because I didn't make that one," I say, pointing to Mr. Ear-Breaker. If only he knew these are actually the best years of his life.

Abel throws his hands up in exasperation. "What does that mean?"

"Look, I get it. This pregnancy wasn't planned, and it's not ideal. But it's happening. I have a lot to prep for and even more to learn. But I have the best examples to learn from right here in this room."

"If you think flattering me is going to make me remotely okay with this, you're wrong."

"Good thing I wasn't talking about you. I was hoping to pick Elliott's brain for parenting advice. I'm not going to let my baby suffer just because you won't get over yourself and help your best friend and your cousin navigate this new lifestyle." I turn to Elliott who seems oddly delighted that I'm standing up to him. "I already wrote down a list of questions about what to do with a baby. Do you think we could get together so I can get some information from you?"

She nods in agreement. "Absolutely. I'm glad to see you're already planning ahead."

"I'm going to bring Rosalind with me. I know she's a little freaked out too."

Elliott switches the baby to the other hip but keeps swaying. "That's normal. We're all a little freaked out in the beginning. But it gets easier. And I'm here to help however you need."

"That's really nice of you, Elliott. Thank you."

"You're family, Joey." She says it to me, but she gives Abel a pointed look at the same time. "And not just because of Rosalind. It's always been that way, and we'll do what we can to help you however you need."

I narrow my eyes slightly. "You're not going to send me fake articles about sewing my own organic baby clothes to reduce allergies or something are you?"

Elliott laughs out loud, startling the scowler who seems to make an even more menacing face. I make a mental note to keep my new baby from this potential psycho. He may be little, but I've seen *Boss Baby*. You just never know.

"Joey, I have no problem screwing with you all day long. It gives me immense joy."

"So I've seen," I grumble.

"But I will never, ever do anything to drag your baby into it," she promises. "Kids are off-limits."

"Really?"

Elliott purses her lips and thinks for a second. "Let's see how it goes when he or she is a teenager. If they have your personality, I retract my promise."

"If my baby has my personality, I'll retract it myself."

Elliott smiles at me and opens her mouth to say something else when a wail comes from across the room. "Sounds like I'm being summoned. You two better leave before the chorus joins in."

Sure enough, someone else also decides it's time to scream.

I back away slowly, trying to not make any sudden movements while all hell breaks loose, but as soon as my ass hits the door, I bolt.

I only make it a few feet before I hear Abel calling after me.

"Joey."

I glance over my shoulder but keep moving. I have one more client and my own workout to get in before leaving for the day. Plus, I still have to pee. The last thing I want is yet another talking-to.

"I've got a class, Abel."

"It'll just take a second."

I continue to walk, not necessarily ignoring him but not making it easy for him either.

"Joey, stop." His hand lands on my shoulder, forcing me to just give in to his request. Doesn't stop me from shrugging him off, though.

Quickly stepping in front of me—either to make sure I can't go anywhere or to make eye contact—Abel runs one hand over the top of his head while the other rests on his hip.

"I'm sorry, okay?"

When I don't say anything, he's forced to continue. To grovel, if you will.

"I'm just… it all just shocked me. I didn't even know Rosie—"

"Rosalind."

He ignores my correction. "—was working at a dump."

I raise an eyebrow in defense. "It's not a dump, Abel. It's a regular bar-like atmosphere that happens to employ women to get topless while we drink."

"And one of those women is someone I love. That's a hard pill to swallow."

"Why? You didn't make her do it. She voluntarily does it because she likes it."

Abel throws his hands up. "Why do people keep saying that? No one wants to be a stripper for a living."

"Says you. Abel, I've seen her dance, and she's incredible, with or without clothes on. The upper body strength she has is beyond anything I've ever seen. It's just…" My thoughts get lost as I think about the first time I saw her and how she was able to hold her entire body out sideways before cartwheeling off the bar into a full split. In heels. With her boobs bouncing. I better keep myself on track. "It's incredible."

Snapping my eyes back to him, I re-center my thoughts. "But that's not even what's important here. She and I are having a baby together."

"But are you together? Like a couple?"

"It's too early to know, but I like her, Abel. I like her a lot. She's tough and secure in herself. She's a ballbuster even when she's secretly amused. She's an athlete, even if you don't think so. She's cool. And regardless of what you think about it, we're going to do this together. So, you can either help us both through it, or you can move out of my way."

His head hangs low, both hands on his hips. Either he's considering my words or he's getting ready to clock me. I'm hoping it's the former since I don't have a spare t-shirt in the event this one gets bloody.

Finally, after what seems like an awfully long time for him to decide how to proceed, he looks up at me. "You're right."

I cup my ear with my hand and lean in. "What was that? I think I misheard you."

He punches my shoulder lightly. "I'm not saying it again. I'm doing my best to wrap my brain around everything, but I promise to let it go and help you out more. You've always been a good guy and she's a good girl."

A smirk and raise an eyebrow at him. "Well, not always."

The punch that lands on my shoulder is harder this time.

"Ouch, you dick. That hurt," I whine as I rotate my shoulder to work the pain out.

"I don't want to know anything about Rosie except that she is a nice Catholic girl who loves her new job and is having a baby with you. That's it. The end. Don't tell me anything else beyond that."

"I'm disappointed in you. You've always loved hearing about my sex-capades."

"No. No, I have never loved it. In fact, I've told you to shut up more than once over the years. Now would be a great time to actually listen to me."

"We'll see." I push past him but turn to walk backward toward the locker room and get some relief for my bladder. "But I'm glad to see you finally on board with my new family. Did you hear your girlfriend back there? We're family now, man! You're never getting rid of me now!"

He rubs a hand down his exasperated face. "Believe me. I've already thought of that."

I point two fingers at him. "Christmases are going to be amazing!" Then I turn around to finish out my day while he groans behind me.

The unexpected benefit of all this, I have now been given unlimited access to torturing Abel during the holidays. Awesome.

CHAPTER SIX

ROSALIND

I'm utterly and completely wiped out. I want to blame my new job, but I'm not sure folding towels and vacuuming take more energy than using my entire core to spin around a pole while sporting five-inch heels and not fall on my head.

I could blame it on watching Joey train. My whole body felt hot more than once as I tried to hide the fact that I was watching him. Who can blame me? No gym shorts can hide the tree trunks he calls thighs. I'd notice how thick and powerful they are and then I'd remember what else he has that's thick and powerful and my mind would replay our night together. Well, it made some alterations to the actuality of the event, but still left me hot and bothered.

That was only for about an hour or so, though, so that means my exhaustion must be the pregnancy. I hate these hormones and all the issues they're having on my body. Twice today, I had to run for the toilet, so I didn't spew all over the floor. Call me considerate, but it was for purely selfish reasons that I didn't just go for the nearest trash can. As the newest member of housekeeping, it would have been up to me to clean it, and I wasn't feeling up to it.

I'm not enjoying pregnancy like I assumed I would. I've always heard about the glowy feeling and my hair getting thick and luscious. It's still early in this process, but neither of those things have happened yet. Mostly, it's been lots of vomiting and wishing for naps.

Admittedly, there has been one benefit of my changing body—my boobs are getting bigger. I had a decent amount before and quite enjoyed showing off my cleavage. But now, I look pretty damn amazing. Too bad my newfound pooch takes attention away from the favorite parts of my body. I don't mind my growing belly. It's kind of fascinating. It's just unfortunate it has to grow faster than my fab boobs.

I sigh. Nothing about this pregnancy is like I imagined my first one would be.

A knock at my apartment door has me wondering why someone is showing up at this hour, and I silently curse whoever is trying to force me to get off my couch. Maybe. I haven't decided if I'm going to answer.

The second knock has my temper rising as I realize they aren't going away. "Hold your horses. And if you're selling something, you better run, or I'll kick your ass for making me get up when my feet hurt."

My words are more bark than bite. I live in Chicago. I'm not opening the door for anyone I don't know. Peeking through the peephole, I see the last person I expected. "Why are you here so late?"

Flinging open the door, a white plastic bag is immediately shoved in my face. "Thought you might need some protein after a long day at work. Also, it's seven thirty."

I take the bag from Joey's hand with a "yeah, yeah" and try not to smile at his offering. It's sweet, but I'm not sure he needs to know I think that. So far, he's lived up to every one of my minor expectations, but if he's in this for the duration, he needs to prove himself a while longer. Call it the curse of my mother's constant reminder of what a disappointment I am, but trust doesn't come easily for me. It would be so much easier if it did. But if I've learned anything from her continual scoldings, it's that love doesn't always mean support. And *like* is a step below that to start with.

"Thank you. Blessings Chicken is the only thing I crave these days." As soon as the smell of dinner hits my nose, I know I can't wait any longer to eat. Me and this baby may starve to death if I don't get a drumstick in my face ASAP. I wave Joey in and head back to the couch. Not concerned about what he's doing, as I am hyperfocused on food I just pull my legs up underneath me and begin digging through the goodies. "How'd you know where I live?"

"Abel told me."

That catches my attention. "Abel?" He nods. "My cousin Abel?" Another nod. "The guy who was going to flatten you in the front of the lady that runs weird on the treadmill?"

"That's Bambi, and yes, your cousin Abel who wants to rip my dick off. But I think he's over his animosity now."

I go back to my bag. "Impressive. How did you manage that?"

Joey plops down next to me and puts his feet on the table—a huge pet peeve of mine. I give him the evil eye, but he doesn't seem to notice. "Abel is loyal to a fault when he loves someone. I reminded him that he doesn't just love you, he loves me too, and his little hot head just deflated in front of me." Joey chuckles. "It looked like a hot air balloon when you turn off the fire."

"Joey."

"Hmm." He turns to look at me, a content smile on his face.

"Get your feet off my table."

Without one shred of guilt or embarrassment, he removes his feet and sits up. "Are shoes okay in the house or do I need to remove those too?"

It's weird how he just asked without getting derogatory or pissy. I'm used to people, mostly family, rolling their eyes and thinking I'm ridiculous. But Joey just asks an honest question and wants an honest answer. There wasn't even so much as a flicker of concern. It's the strangest thing. And yet, it's kind of nice. He doesn't need me to pussyfoot around things to protect his feelings. There's no pressure to make him feel better. It's all just matter of fact. I don't really understand it. I was raised in a household full of passionate debate and manipulative expressions. This "even keel" is taking a bit to get used to, but I admit to liking it. To liking him.

"I prefer shoes by the door. Keeps the floors from getting dirty."

"Done." He gets up and does as instructed, removing his shoes and laying them on the tile by the wall. "I'll make sure to bring an extra pair of socks next time for maximum cleanliness."

Hmm. He has a point. Fresh socks would be a good idea when I walk in the door. I'll have to see about getting one of those cute baskets for the shelf right there and stock it with some bootie socks before the baby comes and does tummy time. Well, when I have the money to buy one. In hindsight, having a savings account for things like an unexpected pregnancy would have been a good idea.

"Back to Abel. So, has he forgiven you?" I take a bite of my favorite, a fried chicken drumstick, and moan at the juicy goodness. Joey doesn't answer me, so I look up to see why he's distracted. Turns out, it's me and my fabulous boobs. We may have only had one night together, but Joey is a virile guy. I'm surprised people moaning in pain at the gym don't turn him on. I never thought about how many people make sex noises during their workouts until I started my job.

What am I thinking? That's probably why he works with old ladies. Easier to keep the beast in his pants under control. Not that I want him to necessarily restrain himself right now. We may be only getting to know each other, but I have eyes. Eyes that keep trying to peruse his body because they like what they see. Never thought I'd stop thinking about the bad sex but here we are.

Pull yourself together, Rosalind.

It takes him a few seconds to refocus and I admit feeling a bit empowered by the fact that he still finds me hot. I feel so gross these days, it's good to know I haven't turned into a complete troll.

Finally, he answers my question. "Uh... yeah. I mean, not yet. I mean…" He takes a deep breath and focuses. "I wouldn't say he's forgiven me yet, but he apologized for being an asshole, which means he's considering it. He can't stay mad at me forever. Especially when his girlfriend is giving him shit."

"What's she like, anyway?"

"Elliott?" I nod because, while I've met her in passing, I haven't actually talked to her since the baby bomb dropped on Abel.

"She's great. Supercool lady. Keeps Abel on his toes."

"Good. He needs someone like that. His wife was such a bitch."

"May? She wasn't that bad."

"Letting you stare at her boobs when she talks doesn't make her not a bitch."

"What? Who would do such a thing?" I quirk an unconvinced eyebrow at him knowing full well he just did a long, lingering perusal my way. "Fine. At least she never slapped me," he grumbles.

He's got an odd point. She was a piece of work. I know I love attention and the finer things in life, but even May has me beat with those qualities. She isn't just a princess; she's completely wrapped up in herself too. Case in point, leaving her daughter behind for her job. Granted, I'm not a mother quite yet, but I already can't imagine leaving this baby behind for anyone or anything, and I'm barely even showing.

That's part of why I'm still freaked out by Joey being so excited to co-parent with me. I know he wants the baby, but what if he doesn't want *me?* We're doing all of this backwards and that rarely ends well. What if we end up in a massive custody battle and I'm given supervised visitation only? What if he moves to Canada and takes the baby with him?

I'm fully aware that these are very irrational fears, and I'm almost positive Abel would never be best friends with someone like that. But the stress of all this hasn't exactly had me thinking rationally lately. My protectiveness is in full swing.

Wait. Is that the maternal instinct everyone talks about? The need to protect your child at all costs? I had no idea that would show up. I thought I wasn't wired that way. I assumed I'd act just like my mother. Cool.

"Small mercies." I take another bite, this time being aware of what noises I'm not going to make if I want to hold a conversation with someone other than myself. It may be too late though. I glance up, and sure enough, all the boob talk has him looking right at my chest again. "So, what are you doing here, anyway?"

Shockingly, he looks away from my chest to focus on my words. "I just wanted to check on you."

"Check on me? Why?"

"Because you're pregnant, and I know you've been throwing up a lot lately."

I narrow my eyes. "Who told you that?"

"Every one of my clients when they come out of the locker room. They don't know it's because of my seed growing inside you. They assume you're sick."

I roll my eyes at his ridiculous use of the English language. At least he's entertaining.

"They all tell me some lady is throwing up and unless half our clients have a stomach bug, I assume that's you."

I shrug. "I hear it's normal to have morning sickness all day long."

"So do I, but it still sounds like it sucks."

"I'll manage."

He looks around my supercute living room taking it all in. I love this part of my apartment. It took me a couple years to get it decorated exactly the way I wanted it, but it's my favorite place to be now. I have a bad feeling Joey isn't going to ask me about the paint color, though, and this conversation is headed into territory I don't want to be in yet.

"You gonna manage with this apartment?"

My hackles immediately rise. For years, I've fought with my mother about my independence and being able to provide for myself. It's a touchy subject for me because I have no desire to be dependent on anyone else for my survival. Maybe I'm just strong-willed but relying on others hasn't always ended well for me. It's part of the reason I had to get out of my parents' house so soon. Relying on them to pay the bills meant pretending to be the person they thought I was. I don't want to go back to that.

So Joey, ready to ride in on his high horse and save me from my mistakes, isn't going to end well if I don't keep my DiSoto nature under control. I may be a Palmer in name, but that maternal gene pool is strong.

"What's it to you?" My tone is laced with unnecessary anger. Not only is this a sensitive topic for me, after today's events at work, I'm kind of sick of the machismo getting thrown around. "Don't think I can take care of myself?"

"I know you can take care of yourself. I also know you don't have to."

Well, doesn't that just deflate my own hotheadedness. I wonder if he's envisioning another deflating balloon right now.

"Cheri— wait… what do you want me to call you?"

I can't help my smile. It's funny that we're having a baby together and he doesn't even know my name.

"Rosalind. That's my preferred name. Roz is okay too since my name is kind of long. Do *not* call me Rosie. Abel got away with it this time, but he won't for long. With my mood these days, I have no problem kicking him in the nuts if he doesn't quit."

"Noted." Joey tries to discreetly cover his junk, but I catch the movement. You have to be slicker than that on my watch. "So, *Rosalind,*" he says making sure to accentuate my name, "how long did you go without working before you started at the gym?"

I take another bite of the world's best chicken, stalling for time. No, that's wrong. I'm truly enjoying the greasy goodness. But I'm also trying to avoid talking about my dwindling finances. Turns out Joey is as stubborn as I am when it comes to gathering information. I didn't see that coming.

"I didn't. Worked right up until the job change. I still paid all my bills."

"You gonna be able to keep doing that on your new salary?"

I purse my lips and glower in his direction, but for whatever reason, it doesn't faze him. He's been hanging out with Abel too long. He's apparently immune to the Palmer intimidation tactics, not to be confused with the DiSoto temper. That comes from my mom's side. Still, it's not his business. I think. I suppose it's partially his business because I'm carrying around his child, but not totally.

"I'll be fine. I always figure it out."

"Rosalind."

"Joey. I've been on my own for a long time. You may have gotten me knocked up, but that doesn't mean you get to come in here and get all up in my business."

He raises his hands defensively, and I tuck back into my food. The minute I start chewing, my mood gets better.

Shit, am I going to be hangry like this for the next six months? I had heard pregnancy hormones are a bitch, but I didn't expect to feel defensive over every little thing. I'm going to have to keep myself fed regularly just to stabilize my moods.

"I'm not trying to get in your business," he continues, and my irritation starts ratcheting up a notch just at the sound of his voice, which makes me feel a twinge of guilt. These pregnancy hormones are no. Fucking. Joke. "I just…"

"You what?"

He sighs deeply, like he's feeling discouraged. I stop chewing and watch him closely. "I'm trying to say this without it sounding like it's going to sound."

I start chewing again but drop the bone back in the box and wipe my hands. I've been trying to dissuade him from this serious conversation, but it's a losing battle. Might as well get it over with. "Say it anyway."

"It's not about you. Hell, it's not about me. It's about this little blobby-looking thing inside you."

I want to stay mad, but his words take some of my anger away. "Blobby-looking thing?"

"I have looked at the picture you gave me a million times, and I still can't figure out what I'm supposed to be seeing. It looks like—"

"A blobby thing."

"Yeah."

I sigh and think through my words. It's admirable that he wants to make sure his child is cared for. But it also stings a bit that everything he does, everything he says, none of it has to do with me. He doesn't want me. He wants the baby. And I don't understand why that hurts.

"So, you're not here because of me. You're here because you want to take care of your baby."

"Yeah. Taking care of the baby means taking care of you, too, to an extent." I cock an eyebrow at his terrible answer because we both know that part is only through default. "Or at least helping you take care of yourself." Much better answer. "And I know this apartment has to be really expensive. I don't want our baby to have to uproot later or something because we're too busy being independent to help each other out."

I turn away, not able look him in the eye. He's right, and I'm not sure how to feel about that. Here he is trying to plan for the future of our child, and I'm picking fights with him because I don't want to think about the reality of my dwindling bank accounts. I feel like I've already failed as a mother, and I haven't even given birth yet.

Leaning over, I put the remains of my dinner on the coffee table and turn back around, crisscrossing my legs. I take a deep breath and prepare myself for one of the hardest conversations I've ever had—one where I let my guard down, listen, and give total honesty.

"Tell me what you have in mind."

"Really?" Joey looks at me, delight written all over his face. It makes me roll my eyes.

"Yes, really. Don't make a big deal out of it. I can't be held responsible for my weird mood swings right now. What plan did you come up with?"

He looks around my living room again before turning back to me. "You have a really nice apartment."

"Yeah."

"And it was probably not hard to afford on a stripper's salary."

"Nope."

"And you and I both know you aren't getting paid nearly the same at the gym. None of us do."

I wind an errant piece of hair around my finger and look down, not exactly embarrassed by my lack of income, but definitely uncomfortable talking about my finances with someone I've only had a handful of conversations with. Weird that this feels intimate but reverse cowgirl didn't.

"So, I was thinking you could move in with me."

My eyebrows shoot up and I blink more times in a row than normal. Pretty sure it's an acceptable reaction when your baby daddy springs something like this on you.

"Um… we're barely friends. Don't you think that's moving this relationship a little too fast?"

"I don't mean as boyfriend and girlfriend. It's not like that."

I'm glad we're on the same page. But still… ouch.

Joey turns and props his leg up on the couch so he can face me fully. "I got a sweet deal on a two-bedroom apartment a couple years ago. It's owned by this little old couple who live below me. They love me, because what's not to love"—another eye roll from me—"so they don't raise my rent whenever I re-sign my lease. The neighborhood isn't as swanky as this one, but it's nice. Real family friendly. Close to work. And it's affordable."

Still feeling the sting of his dismissal, I opt for some pushback. "But you're a stranger."

He scoffs and waves his hand dismissively. "This stranger is going to be in your life for at least the next eighteen years and beyond, so we're about to know each other really well. Besides, even with all his agitation, has Abel warned you off of me?"

I have to think about that. Abel has been angry. He's been shocked. He's been way too mouthy for my taste, but he has never once said to watch my back because Joey would hurt me or this baby.

"Fine. So, I can trust you not to steal all my money or whatever. But how come I'm the one who has to move? Why don't you just move in here?"

"Because even if we combine resources, there is no way we could afford a place in this neighborhood for long. And from what I've been told, you grow out of a one-bedroom apartment quickly when you have a kid."

I hate that he's right. I really don't want him to be because I love this apartment. But he is. I've known since the minute that stick popped a plus sign that I wasn't going to be able to stay here for long, but I was avoiding reality, hoping for a miracle that I already knew wouldn't come. I guess it's time I suck it up and face the truth.

"Fine. As much as I hate that you're right, you are."

"I am?"

"Don't look so surprised," I say with snark. It only makes his smile grow.

"I just thought I was going to have to work harder to convince you."

"Don't flatter yourself. This is something I've been thinking about for a while. I just hadn't figured out the logistics of moving yet."

"But you would have eventually."

"Of course, I would have." I pause to backtrack. The goal is to be honest with Joey and that wasn't totally accurate. "Okay, fine. I might not have had a solution I could live with without your help."

"Wow." He sits back slowly, as if he's totally stunned. "I wasn't expecting that."

"One step at a time, buddy. I'm used to being independent, so let's do this as a hypothetical for now. When are you wanting me to move in?"

He rests his back into the couch, hands crossed over his chest, that damn man bun which both turns me on and pisses me off bobbing as his head moves. I hate that I'm so attracted to him right now. I want to blame the hormones, but he's just so damn sexy when his arms flex like that.

"When does your lease run out?"

"I'm actually going month to month."

His head whips over, eyes showing more shock. He's easy to get a reaction from. "Rosalind Palmer. You already had a plan in place, didn't you? Were you just hoping for a better offer?"

I shrug because the thought may have crossed my mind. "Coincidentally, I was supposed to re-sign my lease the same week I found out I was pregnant. I figured paying the extra month-to-month fee would be cheaper than breaking a lease when I moved home or something."

He crinkles his nose, and it's oddly cute. I have the fleeting thought that it might be fun if our baby has his nose.

"Were you really considering moving in with your parents?"

"If it came down to it, what other choice would I have? Why? You don't think it's a good idea?"

"It just didn't end well for Elliott."

"Sounds like there's a story there."

"Oh, there are many stories there. Most of them ending with the same lesson—don't move back in with your parents unless you want to end up in the looney bin."

"Any of these stories end with promoting the idea of living with your baby daddy that you only met once before being tied together forever?"

He looks up at the ceiling, and I can practically hear him thinking. "I'm sure there's a random eighties movie about it."

"Eighties movie?" I ask with a laugh. "Where'd you come up with that?"

"It's history, baby! A sexual revolution like no other. George Michael's *I Want Your Sex*. Madonna's *Like a Virgin*. Teen pregnancies skyrocketing. Safe sex discussions implemented in health classes. Public fights over condoms being available in high schools."

"That is possibly the weirdest random fact I've ever heard."

"You're still getting to know me. It'll get worse, I'm sure."

That may be the first thing he's said to me that I don't doubt at all.

We sit in comfortable silence for a few seconds, Joey resting his head again while I pick at my nails. I'd really like to get them done again, but unless I can barter for something, a trip to the salon may be out of my budget now. That reminds me, I need to figure out how I'm going to afford to get waxed on the regular. Having a baby doesn't mean I can let the upkeep of my hoo-ha go.

"So," Joey says after a minute, "that means your lease is technically up at the end of the month?"

"Yeah, I guess."

"So, if we get you moved next weekend, that'll give us a few days to clean this place and get your deposit back." I shrug because that sounds about right. "Great. Then I'll put the date on my calendar to help you move."

I have no response to that. Looks like I need to find some moving boxes.

CHAPTER SEVEN

JOEY

"How do I—" I huff and take another breath. "—always get suckered into moving furniture?"

I brace myself, trying to balance the dresser while standing five steps below Abel. A normal dresser isn't heavy. Hell, Abel and I can each bench-press four hundred pounds. But I swear this antique piece must be made of concrete. Not to mention, it's a weird, bulky shape to carry up to the third floor.

"Quit your bitchin'," Abel puffs out, giving away that he's as winded as I am, which makes no sense since I'm the one doing all the pushing. "You're the one that asked her to move in. If anyone should be complaining, it's me."

"You'd never not come help your favorite baby cousin."

"It has nothing to do with my cousin. It has to do with the favor you're going to owe me when we're done." He leans against the front door temporarily. "Get ready. I'm opening the door. One, two, three—"

I groan, lift, and push on his mark, glad to finally be inside the apartment. Hopefully, this is the heaviest thing Rosalind brought with her and the worst of it is over. It was so much easier moving things out of her ground-floor apartment—no stairs involved.

Since it was a last-minute decision to move, Rosalind didn't have time to downsize. Not that there was much. Her apartment wasn't all that big, so there wasn't a whole lot of furniture, thank God. But until she decides what she wants to keep, all of her furniture is coming here. I have a feeling it's more of a strategic move on her part so she can convince me to redecorate. As long as she lets me keep my supercomfortable oversized chair, she can do whatever she wants in here. Clearly, she has a better eye for decorating than I do.

Apparently, she also has figured out how to swindle us into doing all the work, too.

"What the hell, Rosie?" Abel yells, dropping his end of the dresser, making me cuss as I almost lose a finger.

"No one calls me that!" she shoots back, not even bothering to look away from the television while she munches on some Bugles. The lack of movement makes him even more irate.

I, on the other hand, find it weirdly cute. But what's not to like? The Cherise I knew at The Pie Hole was all big hair and long eyelashes, strutting around in her glamorously naked glory. But Rosalind is fresh-faced and relaxed, her long dark waves secured on the top of her head as she watches Dr. Phil give some random advice on saving a toxic relationship, while she licks Bugle dust off her fingers. She also shoots me a flirty grin that basically has me like putty in her hands. I know she's about to milk this situation for all it's worth, but the clever way she does it keeps me on my toes. I like it. Life will never be boring, that's for sure. A man like me could get used to this.

"Why are you sitting on the damn couch while we're moving your furniture?" Abel challenges.

"Because your dumb ass keeps calling me Rosie. I didn't know you were talking to me." She pops another Bugle in her mouth and I can't help feeling amused by this whole exchange. It appears there is one other person in this world who enjoys giving Abel shit as much as I do. This may be the beginning of a beautiful and ornery partnership.

"There are still more boxes in the U-Haul," Abel suggests with just a hint of demand. "If you get bored, you could always help bring them up."

Her head turns slowly, her eyes wide in fake shock. Then she rubs her hand over her belly. "It's not good for the baby for me to lift things."

He points right at her, anger flashing on his face. "That is a load of crap."

Geez, man. Is this how all cousins fight all the time? I'm an only child with one cousin living three states away. These family dynamics are so weird. I hope our kid has a high tolerance for noise.

"You haven't gone to my doctor," she says sweetly. "You don't know what's good or bad for me."

Abel narrows his eyes, and I can see him getting ready to try a different tactic. He gives me the same look all the time. It's usually followed by a low blow. "Hey, have you told your mom you're pregnant yet?"

Yep. Called it.

Rosalind's jaw drops open. Her eyes are almost as wide as her mouth. "Abel Anthony DiSoto, I swear on Nonna's grave I will rip your nuts off if you tell my mother before I do."

"Nonna is alive!"

"All the more reason to keep your trap shut."

"Then get your ass off the couch and help."

Rosalind slaps her hand down on the cushion. "I am a princess, Abel. I pay people to move furniture for me."

"You aren't paying me."

My eyebrows shoot up in surprise. "Great! Does that mean I don't have to spring for pizza and beer?"

"No, it does not." Abel turns his annoyance on me. He's probably just hangry. "In fact, you better get me stuffed crust with extra toppings after all this bullshit."

"Like I said," Rosalind interjects, "I'm paying you to move my stuff."

"No. Joey is paying me to move your stuff."

Rosalind rubs her still mostly flat belly again and gives Abel a sweet smile. It's totally fake. I love it. "He and I are a team now. What's his is mine. What's mine is mine. Therefore, *we* are paying you to move furniture while I sit on the couch and feed the baby."

I laugh at her logic and obvious attempt at claiming rights to literally everything. Abel is less amused, which makes the whole thing even funnier. "You are a bigger pain in the butt than if I had a sweltering boil on my ass."

"Watch your language in front of my kid."

"It doesn't even have ears yet!" Abel yells, completely flustered at this point. Hands down, Rosalind has won whatever weird competition they have going, and I am having the time of my life just watching. How he lives with three women with no problem, but immediately gets flustered by his cousin's quick wit, is beyond my understanding.

"Okay, okay. Enough." Elliott walks in from the kitchen. "Jesus, Mary, and Joseph, I hear less bickering from the two nine-year-old girls that I live with. Rosalind, do you want to at least start putting stuff away? No lifting, just organizing?"

Ah, Elliott. Always the voice of reason. It's probably the natural parent in her. I should be taking notes right now.

Rosalind thinks on it and puffs out a breath before looking at me. "Did you bring the box of my winter clothes in yet?"

"I think those were the first boxes we carried up. They're on your bed."

"Okay," she says with a shrug. "I can help." Without another word, she pushes off the couch and saunters to her new bedroom, winking at me as she walks by. I have a feeling she's just going to watch TV in there out of Abel's eyesight. Grabbing the Bugles bag was a dead giveaway.

Speaking of, Abel turns back to me, a mixture of irritation and concern all over his face. "You sure you want to live with that one?"

I smile and clap him on the shoulder, moving past him for one of those beers I already mentioned. "I like her feisty attitude. Keeps things interesting."

He follows me, stopping only to give Elliott a quick peck on the lips. She mentions something about taking a potty break, which only makes me wonder if I should start using the word "potty" now. Pee? Urinate? Tinkle? Good thing I have a while to find some kid-friendly words about bodily functions.

"How old will this baby be before we need to start toilet training?" I ask Abel, because there's no harm in finding this stuff out early.

"*Toilet* training? What are you British now?"

I push a couple of boxes out of the way so I can grab two bottles from the fridge. The whole room is cluttered with containers of all shapes and sizes, but at least half of them are empty. Thank God for Elliott and her willingness to help unpack. If it was left up to me and Rosalind, we'd probably live like this forever.

I toss the bottle to Abel and he catches it, twisting the top off and taking a quick swig before I can answer his quip.

"I couldn't think of a family-friendly way of expressing myself. Seriously, though. When can I stop shelling out money for diapers?"

"I don't know." Abel shrugs. "I guess it depends on if you have another one anytime soon."

The sip I just took gets caught in my throat, and it takes all my effort not to spray beer all over him while I choke on his words. The fucker laughs at my plight and drinks with ease, not even bothering to pat me on the back.

Wiping my mouth with the back of my sleeve, my cough finally tapers off. "Why would you even say that? I'm thrilled about this first one, but let me get through having it first, would ya?"

"You know twins runs in the family, right?" he shoots back, clearly amused at the panic he's instilling in me.

"Why are you getting such enjoyment out of giving me anxiety?"

He laughs lightly and lifts the bottle to his lips again. "Same reason you enjoy Rosie giving me shit. Besides, you seem to be taking this whole situation in stride."

"What else am I supposed to do? Be pissed off? Nah, man. That baby didn't do anything wrong. Not his fault I have great aim."

"I have to admit, you've impressed me with your desire to do the right thing."

Setting my bottle down on the counter, I lean back and rest my hands on the ledge behind me. "It's not doing the right thing. That's the bare minimum. Like giving her money every month and showing up every other weekend. I can't imagine only putting in that kind of effort and not being there for them. Having a relationship with both of them. It's just… I can't… I mean…"

"It's love, man."

The thought has crossed my mind, but it's so early in our relationship, I don't want to get ahead of myself. So I make sure to look at him like he's crazy. "Rosalind? We're just getting to know each other."

"No, you dickhead. The baby. That's exactly how I feel about Mabel and Ainsley. The thought of being away from them makes my heart physically hurt."

"Yeah. That's it exactly."

It's also not what I expected from myself so soon. Sure, I always envisioned having a family someday, once I was done sowing my wild oats and found someone to settle down with. What I wasn't expecting was how quickly my protective instincts would kick in. How quickly I could say with absolute certainty I would die for my child. It was almost immediate from the time Rosalind sent me that first text. The idea of being a caring, doting, involved dad just seems normal.

Chalk it up to having really good parents who taught me what it meant to be loved through and through, I suppose. Of course, they could have loved me a bit more by not ditching me for the warmer temperatures of South Florida, but I suppose I can't hold that against them. It's their retirement. Besides, vacationing on the beach is a hell of a lot cheaper when you have a free place to stay. My mother reminded me of that as she drove off in the moving van.

"You think it's bad now. Wait until you see your baby's face for the first time." He throws his head back and laughs. "Oh man, I hope they take pictures when you start crying."

I push off the counter and down the rest of my beer, dropping the now empty bottle in the recycling container. "You better believe I'll be boo-hooing all over that hospital room. I'm not ashamed. Hey, speaking of the girls, where are they anyway?"

"Elliott's mom has them for the day."

My eyebrows shoot up before I can stop them. "*Elliott*'s mom?"

He chuckles lightly. "It surprised me as much as you the first time she offered. But I guess Rosemary has decided we're a real family now and has taken to my girl. I'm not complaining. It's kind of nice. The other day she was out shopping and picked up matching jammies for the girls just because she thought of them."

"Did they have pink ducks on them?"

"What? No. Why would they have pink ducks on them?"

"No idea. Elliott's mom strikes me as the kind of person that doesn't care if something is butt ugly. If it makes her happy, she's going to buy it for you and make you wear it."

"Because she got me that White Sox jersey? I told you, I didn't want to offend her by telling her that team was created straight from the pits of hell."

"You're a wuss. I'll give her that she tried hard, but did she really?" I propose. "Red Sox and White Sox aren't even close on the color spectrum. I still think she did it on purpose to make you look like an idiot."

He rolls his eyes before finishing off his own beer. "It wasn't that bad."

"I have pictures that say otherwise."

"Pictures that better not ever see the light of day."

"No guarantees. Piss me off enough and I might forward them to Rosalind. I'm sure she'll have something to say about your betrayal."

"Hey, Joey." Elliott interrupts my empty threats. Or maybe they aren't empty. We. Shall. See.

"How many baby books do you plan to read before yours gets here?" A sudden feeling of shyness takes over as she holds up the two books I've been reading, one by some guy that may or may not have been in Star Trek and *Pregnancy Sucks*.

"Did I get the wrong ones or something?" I rub the back of my neck, trying to get rid of the heat I feel trying to climb up to my face. I hate blushing. It makes me look blotchy. "Are those not good to read?"

"No, they're great." She flips one of them over and reads the back. "This *Pregnancy Sucks* book sounds kind of funny."

"It's not bad," I admit. "Way less boring than the other one."

Abel takes one of the books from her and starts flipping through it.

"Dr. Spock has some good information, but he's definitely drier in his presentation," she agrees.

"Did you find these in the bathroom?" Abel asks her, a shit-eating grin on his face.

"In a little basket by the toilet."

I shrug with indifference. "What else am I going to do when I take a dump?" I ask him before Elliott can say anything. Good thing, too. Her response is a gag that makes me laugh.

"You two are so gross." She slaps the other book into Abel's hand and turns back to one of the almost empty boxes. "Don't you have some more furniture to carry or something?"

"I think that means we've been kicked out of the kitchen." Abel pushes off the counter and kisses Elliott on the neck before disposing of his own empty bottle.

It's sweet the way they're so comfortable with each other. I wonder what it's like to interact so effortlessly with someone else. As if you almost share the same thoughts. A part of me has the weird hope that someday Rosalind and I will be the same way at some point.

Nah. More likely she'd kick me in the shin if I came up behind her and startled her like that. From the beginning, she's struck me as the type who doesn't want to be touched unless she initiates it. I'm okay with that.

"Alright. Second wind, dude." Abel claps me on the back, trying to drum up my motivation. I'm not fooled. He's actually trying to motivate himself. "I think we've got the bulk of it already, so let's try to get this done quick."

"That stuffed crust is really calling your name, huh?"

"I'm a growing boy."

"Just don't grow too much. I don't need my training buddy to wuss out on me. Strongman is five months away. I'm the one who needs to start bulking up."

"Sucks for you," he says with a grin and runs his hand over his washboard abs. What a dick.

We head down a bazillion stairs to the street where the truck is parked. Fortunately, the dresser was the heaviest thing Rosalind seems to own, so except for the whole two-flights-of-stairs thing, it doesn't take much effort to finish up. What does take effort, however, is Abel deciding what type of pizza to order. After a solid hour of debating himself, he finally gives up and lets Elliott decide. I'm not convinced she didn't somehow work that to her benefit because who the hell thinks pineapple is a pizza topping? Elliott. That's who.

Looking around the living room, I realize the one person we're missing is the same one we're all here for. "Have you guys seen Rosalind lately?"

Abel gives me a halfhearted "nope," but he and Elliott are too busy canoodling on the couch. At least, I think that's what they're doing. I'm not positive what "canoodling" actually means, but I assume that giggly, snuggly thing going on is it.

Deciding I'd rather not be here for this and more than curious where my baby mama disappeared to, I turn tail and follow the sounds of some crazy catfight on a television down the hall.

Sure enough, my prediction was correct. An empty Bugles bag is lying next to Rosalind as she relaxes on the bed. The smile on her face makes my heart stutter. Maybe it's the pregnancy glow or maybe it's because she has so many people on her side, but she looks beautiful like this—totally peaceful.

I'm glad to see her feeling so rested. I'm sure the closet still empty of any hanging clothes is part of her serene demeanor.

"Pizza's on the way," I say with a smile, leaning against the doorjamb. I don't want to invite myself into her room without her permission, no matter how badly I want to go sit next to her and lose myself in whatever mindless crap television she's watching.

She doesn't even blink. "What kind?"

"Extra meat on two of them and Canadian bacon with pineapple on a stuffed crust."

That grabs her attention. She crinkles her nose in disgust. "Whose dumb idea was that?"

"Elliott's."

"I like Elliott. She's really nice. But her pizza choices leave some room for improvement."

"I agree," I say with a chuckle and gesture at all the boxes still sitting around unopened. "You haven't made much movement on unpacking."

"You didn't bring me my box of hangers."

I drop my head to my chest and smile. This girl has a quick comeback for everything. I find it incredibly sexy.

"I didn't realize I needed to, but I'll keep my eyes peeled for it. In the meantime"—I point into her room, requesting entrance—"may I?"

"Sure. It's your apartment too."

"I don't want to invade your privacy."

Rosalind scoffs, that tough exterior on display like always. "You've seen me naked, Joey. And not just at work, but with my legs wrapped around your head. I think we passed the point of privacy a long time ago."

I climb onto her bed and settle in next to her. "I'm not going to make any assumptions about boundaries because we slept together once. I may be a selfish idiot, but I'm not an asshole."

"No, it doesn't appear that you are," she mutters under her breath, but I hear it loud and clear. And what she's said without words is she appreciates that I'm doing right by her in more ways than one. Message received.

We fall into an easy silence, which seems to be normal for us. I don't hate it. I spend so much of my day interacting with people and schmoozing clients, it's kind of nice to just be with her without having to do anything other than just be.

It also helps that whatever she has on the boob tube is like watching a train wreck.

"What the hell is this crap we're watching?" I finally ask, not able to take anymore without getting a little background information. All I can figure so far is whoever this woman is, she hates everything and everyone in the entire free world.

Rosalind laughs and I think it's the first time I've heard her make that sound. It's kind of loud. Kind of obnoxious. And kind of makes me feel like I want to hear it again because it means she's well and truly happy. It's also really weird for me to be having these girly thoughts. Must be pregnancy pheromones rubbing off on me. One of my books says that's a thing.

"It's my favorite gossip show."

"Why is the host so angry?"

Rosalind shoves me lightly. "She's not angry. She's opinionated."

"She hates everything. That's not opinionated. That means she needs therapy."

"Maybe. But I like her. She says what everyone else is thinking."

"Ummm…" I cock my head as the host makes a quip about the length of some celebrity's dress at a red-carpet event. "I don't think everyone was thinking that a hemline makes someone automatically look like a whore."

"Okay, fine. You got me there. I think that dress is pretty." She doesn't laugh this time, but she's still smiling. "I don't know. She's just unfiltered. Makes me feel like it's okay that I say what I think too."

"Who says you can't?"

She shoots me an incredulous look. "Pretty much everyone my entire life."

"And how many of these people are actually important to you?"

"Let's see… Abel, my mother, all the nuns at St. Martha's Academy where I got most of my education, every boyfriend I've ever had—"

"Okay, okay." I hold up my hand to stop her. "Everyone you know wants you to conform to their version of normal. Got it. You win."

"Good." I watch out of the corner of my eye as she bites her lip to fight off a smirk. This is good. It means she doesn't hate my forthcoming nature any more than I hate hers.

"You know I like you just like you are, right?"

She doesn't respond with words, but her smile finally breaks through. That's all the response I need.

We get sucked back into whatever interview is happening. I have no idea who the celebrity is. There are so many these days I can't always keep up with who is a runway model versus an Instamodel versus a model by default because their TikTok video went viral or whatever.

Plus, I'm too busy concentrating on the woman sitting next to me and what she smells like (lavender and some fancy lotion), what she sounds like (quiet breaths with the occasional deep sigh of contentment), and what her body feels like next to mine (exactly where it's supposed to be). With as much as I'm trying not to watch her, it shouldn't come as a surprise when she grabs my hand and places it on her belly, but it does.

Despite my shock, I use all my muscle control to keep from looking over at her. Somehow, I know she won't like it if I act on my feelings. And I have a *lot* of feelings right now.

Instead, I settle my hand on her stomach, overly satisfied to get this close to my child even with the negativity blasting through the television. Abel can get the door when the pizza gets here. I'm busy bonding with my new family.

CHAPTER EIGHT

ROSALIND

I'm not sure what wakes me up bright and early this morning, but the pain in my back might have something to do with it. I desperately need a new mattress, but I don't have the money for one right now. It's not like I can find a comfortable position anyway. I'm normally a stomach sleeper, but that makes me even more uncomfortable. It feels like I'm lying on top of an egg, so I've been lying on my side which sucks. And the shitty part is, I'm not even all that pregnant yet! I don't want to imagine how this is going to feel when I'm finally showing to the rest of the world, not just myself.

Groaning, I roll out of bed and try my best to stretch the kinks out of my body. I could really go for a spin around my pole, but the only one I've ever used is currently sitting idle inside a strip club a few miles away. Actually, based on the time, it's currently in use by someone who probably isn't as athletic or agile as I am. Was. Whatever.

I wish Bennie would let me in just to get a good workout, but that's unlikely. Not that it's a smart idea in my condition anyway. I'm already starting to feel a little off-balance from everything protruding out my front these days. At this point, mostly it's my boobs, even my larger knockers are making me feel out of whack.

I sigh deeply and look out my small window. It's not terrible living here. I miss my old place, but Joey's apartment is nice, and he's an okay roommate. He's a little bit of a slob, but he's always cracking jokes and is interested in my day. He isn't into decorating, so he gave me free rein to change whatever I wanted to make me feel at home, which made me feel good. The only weird thing is he orders a lot of takeout. Considering what he does for a living and what he's training for, I thought he'd be cutting every additive, preservative, GMO out of his body, especially with the competition that he won't stop talking about coming up. I'm sure it's coming. I suspect that will change since we'll probably have to do more cooking if we're going to save money for the baby.

Truly, I got lucky. As leery as I was at first, Joey is turning out to be the best kind of man. Not only is he ridiculously hot, which my body likes to remind me of nightly, he's just kind. And he loves this baby already. That's what every mother-to-be wants.

Unfortunately, I'm also hyperaware that it's going to suck the first time he leaves to go on a date. I have to prep myself for that moment, though. Our living together is about taking care of our baby, not being romantically involved. And I know a man like him has more options than he can count. I just have to keep reminding myself that couples co-parent while dating other people all the time. I could have it so much worse than feeling jealous over whoever he decides to date. I'll just have to focus on the good parts of our situation.

Overall, things seem to be shaping up nicely. The worst part of my new living arrangements is walking up two flights of stairs. I will never take an elevator for granted again. Even one of those scary ones that goes really slow and creaks the whole time.

The biggest problem on my plate right now…

I still haven't told my mother. With Thanksgiving next week, I should probably let her know now. I could try to manipulate the situation and tell her this important information in front of others to help eliminate her making a scene, but I know my mother, not to mention the rest of the family, and it wouldn't happen that way. The exact opposite is more likely.

Basically, my aunt Lucia and my nonna will join in as my mother rants about living in sin, and before I know it, they'll be spraying me with holy water someone inevitably has stuffed in their giant purse, and then everyone will hit their knees with their rosaries in their hands. It sounds exhausting.

No, it's a much better idea to do it by phone.

I pad my way through the living room, listening for any sounds of my new roommate. He mentioned something about going to the gym this morning to help set up some new equipment he was all excited about. I wasn't paying much attention. My eyes started to glaze over when he started spouting off rotations and weight numbers. But that's probably where he is.

I don't mind the quiet. Joey doesn't hover, but I wouldn't be surprised if he wanted to make me breakfast instead of letting me do it on my own. He's really nice that way. Or maybe he's just trying to be heavily involved with this pregnancy. Either way, his chivalry is welcome. I've always said I'm a princess who deserves to be waited on, so I won't complain if he's decided to be my personal cabana boy, minus the cabana.

A large box with the local grocery store's name printed on the side is sitting on the table. That's curious. I didn't think he had time to go shopping this morning. Peeking inside, I find a mostly empty box except for some dried foods, lollipops, and a bottle of prenatal vitamins.

Picking up a small sheet of paper, I read the note.

Joey,

I know you can't cook and don't have a lot of time anyway, so there are enough premade meals here to last you a couple of weeks, I hope. They are high carb, high calorie like we discussed for your training.

The ginger lollipops are NOT FOR YOU! They are for Rosalind. My new friend Vonda's daughter is an ob/gyn at a fancy hospital in NYC and she says they help a lot of new moms through morning sickness.

Ohmigod. Is this from his mother? He told his parents about the baby? And they're sending me gifts? My heart starts pounding as I continue reading.

The prenatal vitamins are also for her, which I shouldn't have to tell you, but you are your father's son, so I better make that clear. They're the top-of-the-line brand with lots of folic acid and vitamin B, just like Vonda's daughter recommended.

Good luck with your training. We're so proud of you. And we can't wait to meet Rosalind. You treat her like a princess, you hear me? Pregnancy is exhausting and she is the mother of my grandbaby!

Love you,
Mom

I drop the note, stunned at how kind her words are. I blink back tears as I think about how supportive she is. The woman doesn't even know me, has never met me, and is already going into grandma mode. My hand instinctively covers my abdomen as I process this. This is what kind of mother I want to be. One that is encouraging and loving. But I fear I'm destined to be critical like my own mother. I know she loves me; she just has a hypercritical way of showing it. I can never meet her demands for perfection, and she has no problem reminding me of that regularly.

Then again, I don't know what Joey told his parents. It's possible he made me sound better than I am. Did he tell them how we met? Do they know this baby is a result of a one-night stand?

All the insecurities I usually push aside come rushing in as I take in this new information. It's hard to digest that Joey's family will do more than just tolerate me as the mother of this child. After all, when anyone else in my life has found out about my job, the judgement was pretty clear. Why would they be any different?

I do my best to dismiss the negative thoughts and focus on what I can—eating and calling my mom. If Joey's parents know, it's time for me to suck it up as well.

After a hearty meal of dry toast, which seems to be the only thing I can hold down these days, I realize I can no longer put off the inevitable. It's time to call my mother.

I try to slow my breathing as the phone rings, just to keep my heart rate down. But I only have a couple of seconds before my time is up.

"Thank the Lord you're okay. I have been praying for your safety every morning for the past week."

I can't help the snicker that comes out of me. "You always pray for my safety, Mom. Why is this week so special?"

"Don't laugh at my beliefs, Rosalind. Someday you'll get yourself right with God and have to spend way too much time in the confessional for it."

Good thing she can't see my eye roll.

"And don't roll your eyes at me either."

I look around the room, a little creeped out that she called me out. How does she do that?

"I've been trying to reach you for a week, but you suddenly stopped answering your phone."

This is it. The moment I've been waiting for. Time to spill the beans. But I'm going to start with the good news first. "Sorry about that. I've been busy settling in at my new job."

The phone goes quiet. It's so silent I'm not sure if we got disconnected or she passed out.

"What do you mean by that?" she asks quietly. It's like she's afraid to use her normal volume for fear she'll shatter the illusion of her dreams for me coming true.

"I mean I quit working at The Pie Hole."

"Can you stop saying that name?" she interrupts, like I knew she would. Mona Palmer isn't known for holding her tongue. "It's so crass."

"I didn't name the place, Ma. Anyway, I'm not working there anymore. I'm doing housekeeping at this fancy gym. You probably heard of it. It's called Weight Expectations." I laugh lightly. "I'm actually working with Abel, which was a surprise to both of us."

"Is this an April Fool's Day joke?"

"It's November, Mom."

"You're telling me you quit your job as a stripper and are now gainfully employed at a swanky exercise place, working alongside your favorite older cousin, who can keep you on the straight and narrow?" The Chicago accent is coming through loud and clear as she tries to wrap her brain around my news.

"That about sums it up."

Things go silent again but not for long.

"Oh, thank the sweet baby Jesus! My prayers have been answered!" Her celebration is so loud, I have to pull the phone away from my ear to protect my own hearing. "Do you know how many candles your aunt Lucia and I have lit on your behalf?"

"I know. But there's more."

"I can't even count how many. But it was so many Father Thomas had the fire department on speed dial."

"That's just nine-one-one, Ma."

"He was considering buying some fancy non-toxic brand of candles to eliminate fumes, so he doesn't get cancer."

"Candles don't cause cancer."

"And a braided wick so it's harder for them to catch the building on fire."

Ohmygod she's going to keep going forever.

"Mom!" I yell. "There's more!"

Her rambling finally stops as she refocuses. "More than just a new job?"

I take a deep breath now that I feel like I've just run a race to stop her from going off the deep end. There's no telling how it's about to go once I tell her the rest.

"Yeah. I moved into a new apartment."

"But you loved that little place in Hyde Park."

"I know. But I got a sweet deal on an apartment owned by an elderly couple who lives on the first and second floors." I haven't actually met them yet. I waved once, but Joey has told me all about them, and I know it'll endear my mother. "Plus, it's closer to the gym and it's got two bedrooms."

"What a wonderful blessing! I hope you're helping out those people as much as you can. You know Nonna can't get around very well anymore. You could be very useful to them, especially if they don't have any family nearby."

"I will. They're good people." Or so Joey's told me.

"And such a big place for just you."

I grimace knowing it's now or never.

"Well, it's not just me."

"Do you have a roommate? Oh no. You didn't let one of your stripper friends move in with you, did you? You know old people aren't as understanding of that kind of lifestyle as I am."

It takes everything in me not to laugh out loud. I would hardly call her tolerant of my former job. But she's still my mom and even if we don't agree on, well, basically anything, I know better than to disrespect her like that.

So, I take a deep breath, blowing it out slowly and brace myself to pull the phone away from my ear as soon as the shrieking begins again. "I'm living with a man."

"You're what!?!"

Yep. Just like I expected. Her question is more a demand to explain myself, so I do as quickly as possible.

"His name is Joey Marshall and he's really nice, Mom. He's a trainer at the gym I work at. Oh! He's Abel's best friend."

"And Abel knows about this?"

Oops. I didn't mean to throw him under the bus. But since she already knows… "He helped me move in."

"What!?!" And the shrieking continues. "How could Abel do this to me? Helping my baby girl move in with a man!"

"Calm down, Mom. He did it as a favor to me."

"And you better believe I will be having a conversation with his mother as well. Helping you live in sin! What a horrible thing for him to do."

"Abel's living in sin, too, Ma. I don't think she'll care."

"He is a *boy*, Rosalind. You have virtue to protect."

"And here we go," I mutter. "I was a stripper for years, Mother. Pretty sure the virtue is gone."

"Which is why you need to do everything in your power to protect what little is left. You don't have any to spare."

She continues to blather on about my soul needing cleansing and where she went wrong as a mother. I realize now is probably a good time to rip the final Band-Aid off. This conversation is giving me a migraine. "My virtue doesn't matter anymore, Mom, because I'm pregnant."

Her rambling dies off quickly and ends in silence. It's eerily quiet. I don't like it.

"I'm not sure I heard you correctly. Can you please repeat that?"

Oh shit. She turned on her customer service voice. I'm in so much trouble.

"I'm close to sixteen weeks pregnant. Due May fourth. We don't know what we're having yet and don't know yet if we want it to stay that way. We'll see. And I know it doesn't thrill you that I'm an unwed mother, but it's happening, and I need you to be happy for me. But if you can't, at least don't be sad because I could have had an abortion, but I didn't." I probably shouldn't have thrown that last bit in, but what does she expect? I've spent my entire life with her making me feel the wrath of Catholic guilt. It rubbed off on me.

"My baby is having a baby?" she says softly. Does she sound... *excited*?

Bewildered by her initial response, I can only think of one way to counter. "Uh, what?"

"My baby is having a baby!"

This is not what I was expecting at all. My mother, the first one to get to mass and the last one to leave, is excited and squealing and happy about this turn of events. I did not see that coming, and I admit, I'm a bit perplexed.

"Oh, Rosalind, I'm thrilled. Obviously, I need to pray for you to repent for having unwed sex, but babies are innocent of their parents' sins and are a blessing no matter how they come into this world. Are you going to bring your new beau to dinner next week?"

I could correct her about Joey being my "beau," but this is already going better than expected. No reason to jinx it. "I hadn't planned on it." For his own protection.

"No. That won't work. You need to bring him. He's part of the family now, and we need to get to know him. Make sure he's going to raise this baby in the church."

I hold up my hand even though she can't see me. "Why do you need him for that? Can't you ask me all those questions?"

"No. Because I usually don't like your answers." She's got me there. "Bring your sweet Joey so he can get to know his new family."

I snicker. "First, if I had to describe him, I'd say ornery is more accurate."

I'd also say sexy-in-a-boyish-charm kind of way, but no way are those words coming out of my mouth right now.

She tsks. "Don't speak of your child's father that way."

"And second, we're not his family yet. The baby isn't even viable at this point."

"Rosalind! What a horrible thing to say about your child!"

"It's science, Mother. It's… you know what? It doesn't matter. I'll talk to Joey about coming for Thanksgiving, okay?" Not because I think he needs to be there. But because I'm going to enjoy all the focus being on him instead of on me. If he's going to be part of this family like my mother says, he can suffer like the rest of us.

"And tell him to bring something for our potluck."

"Negative. The man doesn't cook. But explain to me why we're doing a potluck for Thanksgiving?"

"Oh pish. Only a few of us have done all the Thanksgiving turkey for years. It's time to share the duties with the rest of you moochers. I'll add you to the Google Form so you can decide what to bring."

"There's a Google Form?" No, really. This conversation went from being painful to downright strange. What is happening here?

"Really, Rosalind. It's the twenty-first century. You should be more tech savvy by now. Why I even bothered paying to send you to that fancy private school, I will never know."

"Me neither, Ma."

We chat for a few more minutes about my pregnancy and things I should expect before delivery. I had no idea my mother had gestational diabetes every time she was pregnant, so that's one more fun thing I get to tell my doctor about at my next appointment. Who knew growing a kid would wreak so much havoc on my body? They never tell you that part when they're doing DNA tests on Maury.

Overall, the conversation goes better than I expect. As a mom, she's happy about my new job. As a pending grandma, she's probably already spending money. And as the host of this year's holiday festivities, she's eluded all of her responsibilities by passing the cooking on to the rest of us.

Yeah, she has no reason to complain.

I, on the other hand, have to prepare to bring Joey into the DiSoto fold next week. But first, I need to find this Google Doc before the easy stuff is taken.

CHAPTER NINE

JOEY

I am not the guy who ever gets nervous. It's just not in my nature to get flustered over things I can't control. Even as a kid, when everyone else was anxiously trying to plan out the first day of school, I was just ready to make new friends and see what cute girl I could finagle into sitting next to for the year.

As an adult, I'm still the same way. New job? Cool. Can't wait to expand my knowledge. New friend? Great. Let's find something fun to do. New baby? Awesome. I'm going to learn everything I can about being a good dad.

I'm not sure where I got the personality trait, but I assume from my father since my mother has always playfully bitched about how he could go with the flow, even in the middle of a damn blizzard.

Still, for all my calm, today I'm experiencing something brand new—nerves. This isn't excitement. It isn't anticipation. This is flat-out fear of what will happen when Rosalind and I walk through her mother's front door for the first time with the fruit of my loins presenting themselves inside her daughter's slightly swollen belly.

If Rosalind's bristly attitude is any indication, I really should have worn my cup.

We get out of my truck in front of a brownstone that looks an awful lot like Abel's. We actually may be on the other side of his neighborhood. I wasn't paying much attention on the drive over, too busy following Rosalind's directions and reminding myself to not drop any f-bombs today.

I take a deep breath and follow Rosalind up the steps, doing my best to avoid staring at her ass. But let's be real—her backside has always been fabulous and has been the visual image of too many intimate moments with myself lately.

"Are you sure they're going to like me?" I ask, trying to remove the fear from my voice.

"Nope."

My jaw drops and I nearly stumble on the step in front of me. "That doesn't make me feel better."

"You're not supposed to feel better," she retorts. "You're supposed to be prepared for anything. It's easier that way."

"What does that mean? What could possibly happen?"

Rosalind snorts a laugh and puts her hand on the doorknob, only stopping to turn around and finish this conversation. "Anything. Anything could happen, Joey. My mother could slap you or she could kiss you. Nonna might hit you with her purse or drill you on Catholic traditions. Hell, my pops could make you his new best friend or he could pull out a Glock. Honestly, my mother threw me for a loop when I told her about you and the baby, so I have no idea what we're walking into."

"At least Abel will be here to protect me," I grumble like a child.

"Don't count on it. When my dad asks for his gun, he expects my cousin to be the one to find it, so he doesn't have to take his eyes off the target."

Great. Should have worn my cup *and* my bulletproof vest. And don't ask why I have a bulletproof vest. It involves a very detailed story that includes an illegal round of poker with a guy who used to work on a SWAT team.

"Deep breaths, Marshall. Don't let them see fear." I do as she instructs, all the while praying I don't pass out. "You ready?"

I half-heartedly nod, not sure I am in fact ready to meet her entire family at once. I might be walking into a mob of angry people. Either way, she notices my hesitation and gives me an extra moment for one last deep breath.

"Let's do this," she says with a quick fist bump and pushes the door open.

I stay close behind her as she steps foot through the front door and announces our arrival. "We're here!"

The room is packed with people of all ages, all genders, possibly one priest—everyone turning to look right at us. What was a loud and joyous occasion, suddenly goes completely silent.

Rosalind waits for a few seconds before gesturing to me with her thumb and saying, "So this is Joey."

All at once, as if they have been practicing to get the timing right, all hell breaks loose.

You know that scene in National Lampoon's Christmas Vacation, the one where all the relatives show up and Clark can't do anything while his mother inspects him like he's at a doctor's appointment? That scene is vivid in my mind for two reasons.

First, because I did my yearly Thanksgiving watch of the classic Christmas flick while waiting for Rosalind to finish trying on eight different outfits before we drove over. On a side note, she ended up in jeans, so I'm not sure why it took so long, but at least I got a few Griswold laughs in.

And second, it's exactly how I feel right now as I get poked and prodded and slapped on the back. I'm surrounded by people I've never met, who are peppering me with everything from kisses to questions on my religious beliefs and who I voted for. If I weren't such a personable guy, it would make me wildly uncomfortable. Fortunately, I'm a pro at fitting in, so I smile back and reciprocate hugs, trying to avoid any politics and religion talk with a standard answer of "Let's save those topics for dessert. We can't start throwing punches until after we've eaten. Hahaha." The men, at least, seem to find that response acceptable and maybe even smart.

Finally, the crowd parts, a stern-looking woman making her way through. It's as if everyone knows a queen is in our midst. Her dark hair is held up on top of her head in a fancy bun. She's wearing a brightly colored blouse and dark pants. Her jewelry is significant, yet not gaudy. She sashays toward me, scowling as the crowd quiets. She stares me up and down and up again before speaking.

"I am Rosalind's mother. You may call me Mona." Unsure how to respond, I say nothing, do nothing, barely breathe. She finally throws her arms out wide and yells, "Welcome to the family!" before grabbing me and hugging me tightly.

The room erupts into cheers as Mona guides me through the sea of people into the kitchen where food is already being set up. There are at least three good-sized turkeys, two hams, and all the side dishes I could imagine. It looks and smells fantastic, and I thank my lucky stars carbs are a required part of my diet these days. Strongman might still be five months away, but I need to build my middle to help stabilize my core during the heavy lifting. I'll miss my eight-pack, but by midsummer, it'll be back. That's the height of bathing suit season anyway.

Everything on the counter is clearly homemade with a lot of love. I'm not sure where we're going to put the Tupperware I have in my hands. I guess Mona will figure it out. She looks like she's done this hosting thing before.

Handing the container to her, I say, "We brought deviled eggs."

She takes it from me with one hand and cups my cheek with the other. "Isn't he sweet? He made us deviled eggs."

More murmurs from the crowd that seems to be following us around. I suppose I am sort of a sideshow attraction right now—the first man to come home with the stripper relative. Although Rosalind swears it's the best-kept secret in the family. Still, I'm a novelty and I know it.

"Actually, I'm a horrible cook," I admit. "Rosalind made them."

"Oh," her mother says, a look of disappointment on her face. The expression changes quickly when she announces, "Isn't he sweet? He brought us Rosalind's deviled eggs!"

The crowd erupts in cheers again, and I'm starting to wonder how long they've all been hitting the sauce. This isn't just a family meal. It's almost like a sporting event. I wonder if they give out ribbons for best food and if Mona wins all of them because family politics.

When she steps aside to put the Tupperware down, another family member takes her place.

I'd say she's elderly, but she doesn't seem to believe so. The way she carries herself, the way she's dressed, the way she looks me up and down while she licks her lips reminds me of a darker-haired Blanche from *Golden Girls*. She'd probably fit right in with my 65+ workout class. Once she stops eyeing me like a piece of meat, I should offer her a free trial.

I bend down anticipating a hug, but instead she reaches her hand up, because physically boundaries seem to be absent in this room so far, and pulls the band out of my man bun, making my hair fall around my shoulders.

"Look at all that beautiful hair," Italian Blanche breathes seductively while she runs her fingers through the golden strands. If I didn't like head massages so much, I might be uncomfortable. But her fingers are magical, so I'll deal with the unsolicited flirting. "You look like a younger, more handsome Fabio."

And my comfort level comes to a screeching halt. I have been compared to Brock O'Hurn and Jason Momoa before, which is flattering. But I've never been compared to Fabio, and I'm not sure I like it. The last thing I want to remind people of is the guy who got his nose broken by a bird when it flew into his face while he was riding a roller coaster. The video was pretty brutal. And oddly amusing, although I feel a tiny bit of guilt for laughing at that man's pain.

Abel may be right—it might be time to get rid of the man bun.

Before I can respond, Italian Blanche is manhandled out of the way by an older gentleman, his dark hair is thinning on top, stomach rounded with a potbelly indicative of age.

"Keep your hands to yourself, Aurora," he demands, and I can already tell in his younger years he was probably terrifying. Hell, he's intimidating now, and I've got at least fifty pounds of muscle alone on him. Strength means nothing if I'm swimming with the fishes.

I stand stock-still as the man assesses me, the entire room dead silent once again. While I'm not uncomfortable being the center of attention, being the star of what may or may not be a mob drama is admittedly a little nerve-wracking.

The man takes his time walking around me, as if I'm a steed whose worth he's determining based on pedigree and athleticism. He ends up in front of me again, shrewd eyes never glancing away, holding my gaze in a power struggle I'm determined not to lose.

"I… am Rosalind's father, Lorenzo Palmer." His appraisal makes more sense now. I'm more confused on how I should respond, though. Do I hold eye contact and win this game? Or do I give up as a sign of respect? I didn't watch the *Godfather* movies. I don't know the right way to proceed. Maybe having Fabio hair is a good thing right now. It'll be easier to change my appearance if this all goes south.

After a few more seconds of uncomfortable and intimidating silence, Lorenzo speaks again. "You are the man responsible for getting my Rosalind in the family way. What do you have to say for yourself?"

I swallow hard, buying time before deciding to just go with the truth. "Rosalind is a fantastic woman. I'm really excited to be a parent right alongside her."

His jaw twitches but he says nothing. "So, you will take care of my daughter and my grandchild."

I don't even have to think about my answer. It's automatic. "I would die for them."

He stares for a few seconds more, until suddenly he throws his arms out, smiles and yells, "Welcome to the family!" The room erupts once again as his beefy arms come around me and he hugs me tight, kissing me on the cheek.

I am again passed around from person to person, each one welcoming me like I've always been part of the family. I have no idea who anyone is, as names are thrown at me left and right, but the whole thing is kind of fun. My family is so small, I've never been welcomed into anything like this, so it's an experience I'll never forget.

So far, Thanksgiving is a success. Fingers crossed the food makes it even better.

CHAPTER TEN

ROSALIND

I am officially stuffed. I indulged in Nonna's Olive all'Ascolana before eating anything else, and I ate pretty much everything else. But those went first. I'd be highly disappointed if I didn't have enough room for her stuffed and fried green olives. She only makes them once a year, and I spend the three hundred sixty-four days in between waiting for them again.

I wonder if I can get her to make them a few more times, claiming the baby is craving them. I make a mental note to call her next week and try it out. She doesn't know how to make single servings of anything, and a family-sized portion will hit the spot.

Sitting on the couch, rubbing my swollen belly, I watch Joey engage with the family. The nerves he was sporting on the way here have more than disappeared. He's actually enjoying himself. He's so intriguing because it's the exact opposite of my personality. Where he chats with everyone, I feel like I'm always assessing people and their motives. Where he smiles, I have a severe case of resting bitch face. Where he has never met a stranger, I have a hard time making friends. It's so strange to me that he "peoples" with such ease. I have such a hard time with it; most people just write me off as a bitch, which I'm not. I don't think. I may need to examine myself more closely on that one.

Abel plops down next to me on the couch, stretches his legs out and sighs deeply. Gesturing to the crowd gathered around my baby daddy, he asks, "Did you know this was going to happen?"

"What, that the family was going to love Joey more than they love me?"

He chuckles. "I guess that's an accurate way to put it."

"Nope. It's completely unexpected."

Abel watches for a minute before declaring, "It's weird."

"You're telling me. I honestly expected Mom and Nonna and all the aunts to add him to their rosary or something. Instead, Mom got all excited about having two new members of the family."

"When you guys came in?"

"No, last week when I finally told her. Oh, also be forewarned," I add smacking his thigh, "she's pissed at you for knowing all about my business and not telling her."

He gasps. "Dammit, Rosie, why did you bring me into the conversation?"

"I didn't do it on purpose." Although maybe I should have since he keeps using that damn nickname. "I was trying to make her feel better by telling her you had already assessed the situation and approved. She didn't buy it. She started droning on about how mad she was you didn't tell her."

He groans and drops his head to the back of the couch. "Shit. I was wondering why she gave me the evil eye when I walked in. I hope the gnocchi she gave me wasn't poisoned."

"Oh! Gnocchi!" I exclaim, my mouth suddenly watering. "I forgot about her gnocchi! Is there any left?"

"Doubt it," he says, crushing all my hopes and dreams. "Pretty sure your boy toy over there ate most of it while you were sucking down Nonna's olives."

"Don't judge me. I'm growing a real Italian baby over here."

Just then, Joey raises a glass and yells "*Opa*!" before taking the shot of whatever liquor my dad just gave him. Probably Johnny Walker Black.

Abel and I both watch the scene in utter confusion as all the men laugh and clap Joey on the back. "Joey knows *opa* is Greek, right?"

"I highly doubt it," Abel says. "Your Italian baby is going to be awfully confused."

Based on this whole day, he's not wrong.

We watch as Joey continues making conversation with just about everyone. He fits in so naturally here. Don't get me wrong—physically he stands out. Compared to the potbelly on my dad and all the uncles, Joey looks like a supermodel. Not that he doesn't always look like he should be in pictures. It's just more pronounced with him being taller than anyone else, with long hair and wearing a tight sweater that shows off the cut of his shoulders.

No, even with the physical differences, it's as if he's been part of the family for years. This is good. He just blends in seamlessly. This is good. Joey fitting in and not being intimidated by my weird family will make it easier for the baby. And me. But mostly the baby. I think.

It's really confusing to be hot for the guy who knocked you up when you're almost positive his only interest in you is what you're growing for him.

Abel nudges me before my thoughts go too far off the rails. "You know I'm happy for you, right?"

I turn to my favorite cousin and smile. "I know."

"You know I'm still going to give you shit, though, right?"

"I would expect nothing less," I say truthfully. "It just means I'll be giving you shit right back."

"Ah, I have trained you well, young Jedi," Abel mumbles making me groan at his use of a *Star Wars* reference.

"Not another May the fourth joke!" I protest.

Able just laughs. "Joey won't let the *Star Wars* baby names go, will he?"

"I have no idea what to name this kid, but I can tell you no child of mine will be named Anakin. I don't care what my due date is."

Abel continues to laugh while I close my eyes and press down on various parts of my stomach, not positive if I'm feeling the baby or my digestive system. I'm choosing to believe these are little baby movements and not gas.

Feeling the couch depress next to me, I roll my head to the side and open my eyes. It's Abel's sweet little girl. Well, sweet might be stretching it. Mabel is sassier than anything, but she has her moments of sugar and spice and all things nice.

I've always been a sucker for this kid. She reminds me a whole lot of me at that age. So, with her looking at me with giant puppy dog eyes, I know I'm not going to be able to resist giving her whatever she wants. "Rosalind, can I touch your tummy?"

That's an easy one to answer anyway. "Sure, sweet girl."

Mabel resituates herself on the couch and her knobby knees poke me in the thighs. "Ouch. Let's sit crisscross applesauce okay?"

She nods enthusiastically, readjusts her body to a less dangerous position. I take one of her hands and place it where I can feel the baby the most. Or at least, where I hope it's the baby I'm feeling.

"You can't really feel him right now, but maybe we'll get lucky," I warn her as I press her hand deeper into my tummy and wait.

"Him?" Abel asks.

"Or her. I don't know. It's just easier for me to say him for some reason."

Concentrating on feeling for movement, I finally feel just a tiny press. Moving Mabel's hand over a bit, I press down again. "You feel how hard that is?" She nods. "The baby is inside that lump." Or it's a food baby, but her toothy grin gets so wide I refuse to burst that bubble.

Ainsley, Abel's stepdaughter for all practical purposes, is standing off to the side watching with interest. "Ainsley, you want to feel?"

Her eyes get wide and she nods.

I nudge Abel with my shoulder. "Move over. I have some little girls to entertain."

He scoffs, but scoots for Ainsley to sit, putting his arm up on the couch behind her. I love that he treats Ainsley like she's his own. Every man should be that way. I hope Joey is, but I've watched him interact with both girls today, and I'm pretty confident I have no cause for concern.

Ainsley, who apparently has been watching me for a while, and is way better than Mabel at following instructions, immediately crisscrosses her legs. Taking her hand, I put it in a similar spot to Mabel's and press down. "You feel that?"

She nods, her eyes wide. "It feels like… like… a rock."

"Or an egg," Mabel chimes in.

"I guess it's about that size right now," I mention.

Just then, he kicks. I gasp, my eyes wide.

"Did you girls just feel that?" I whisper.

Ainsley shakes her head. "What? What was it?"

"He… he kicked."

Mabel begins bouncing in her seat. "He jumped!" Mabel says excitedly. "Daddy, the baby jumped!"

Everyone in the room goes quiet as they register Mabel's words. I catch Joey's eye across the room and smile.

"Did you…" he starts and then pauses to lick his lips. "Did you just feel the baby kick?"

I nod, never taking my eyes off his. "I think I did."

Joey rushes over and the entire room breaks out in chaos, which has always been the DiSoto way. Joey barely gets to me, drops to his knees, and places his hands on my stomach when my mother pushes him away so she can talk to the baby. It doesn't last long. She's immediately accosted by Aunt Lucia and then Nonna, who doesn't hesitate to use her cane as a weapon.

As Nonna whispers a blessing over me for a healthy baby, I look behind her to see Joey frowning in the back of the crowd. Poor guy thought he'd gotten off easy with this family. I guess he hasn't yet figured out that you have to learn to be pushy around here if you're going to get gnocchi or your turn at rubbing a baby bump.

Still, it is his child, so he probably deserves to be next to me more than Nonna and her weapon. Turning to Abel, I ask sweetly, "Would you please let my baby daddy sit next to me, so he can be near his child before these women scare the baby away?"

Abel chuckles and signals Joey to push through the crowd. They quickly change spots before anyone else can slide in like the asshole that always steals a parking spot someone is waiting for. Ainsley stays where she is because like I said, Joey seems comfortable with Abel's kids and reaching around her doesn't seem to bother either of them. Even when he leans over and puts his hand on my stomach right above hers.

Almost exactly when he presses, Baby Marshall decides to pole vault across my uterus again.

Joey doesn't feel it, but I do. My gasp is almost inaudible, but he hears it, and dammit if the look he gives me in response doesn't make my insides melt.

Leaning over Ainsley and into me, he whispers, "I guess this is really happening now."

I bite my lip and nod. "I guess it is."

"You ready?"

"Nope. You?"

"Not even close," he says and kisses the top of my head, something no one except my dad has ever done. I like it.

"Good. Then I guess we're in this together."

When Ainsley bounces away at the insistence of her mother who recognizes Joey and I are having a moment, I lay my head on his shoulder. This whole day has me exhausted but feeling thankful in a way I never have before. Even if I did miss out on those gnocchi.

CHAPTER ELEVEN

JOEY

The month between Thanksgiving and Christmas is a fantastic time of year. The festivities and food make up for the fact that the weather is shit.

The only thing that breaks my mood every year is how the number of paying clients tanks. Not only do half my regulars take time off for family time—the slackers—getting new clients is almost impossible.

Sure, traditionally we see a spike in January, but my goal isn't to get fair-weather clients, so I'm constantly recruiting. I want solid clients I can rely on, who will give me a steady income. It's always been my business plan, but I can't seem to figure out how to get it done.

Damn me and my lack of a business degree.

"I think you're setting your goals too high," Abel says with a shrug, as he pops a baby carrot into his mouth and wipes his hands with his napkin. "This isn't the time of year to snag new clients. People are busy. Everything slows down. And they want to eat at all the holiday parties without you reminding them of their gluttony. Didn't you plan for this lull?"

"Of course, I planned for it," I argue and toss my pen down on the counter to stretch my back. The smoothie bar is our go-to place to congregate between clients since it's inside the building and has food. It's the best place to eat while crunching numbers, and Tabitha tosses in her two cents as she has time. Every business has that one person who knows everything about everything. For us, that's Tabitha. Usually her advice is spot on. I have no idea if she's mature and wise or if she's just supersmart, but I'll take her suggestions any day. Hell, I wish she would quit doing inventory in the back and come help me out right now.

"My beefed-up savings just didn't include two extra mouths to feed. And one of them eats a lot right now."

"Oooh, you better not let Rosie hear you say that," he says with a chuckle. "She'll have your balls."

"You better not let her hear you call her Rosie for the same reason."

"Touché." Abel chews and swallows his last carrot before wiping down his eating space. "I get it. Money is going to be tight for the next month or so. But it's not forever. We're talking six weeks, tops."

"It's not just the next month, man." I rub my hand down my face as my thoughts swirl around my brain. I hate math. Figuring this shit out is my nightmare. "I don't know how we're going to do it once the baby gets here. We've got two salaries, but you know how little Rosalind makes at her job. That's not enough to cover daycare, let alone everything else. Man, I wish this place was licensed as a daycare facility so we'd get more than three hours of childcare a day."

"That's not going to happen and you know it. You're just going to have to cut out unnecessary expenses. Like eating out."

I cringe at the thought of the last time I made spaghetti while babysitting his kids. It ended with pasta sauce on the ceiling. Elliott was less than thrilled. "You know I can't cook, man. I try but it doesn't happen."

"You don't follow the directions. That's why it never works."

"I follow them. Enough of them, anyway."

"That last sentence is why it never works," he says with a finger pointed at me in victory. "But you need to figure that shit out soon or you're never going to make it. Not on your meager salary."

"Excuse you. My salary is not meager. I am a well-sought-out personal trainer."

Abel scoffs. "Yeah, who had half his clients quit after this place burned to the ground last year."

I bob my head. "Minor setback. And at least we got brand-new equipment out of the deal. All I have to do is build up my clientele again and I'll be golden. Why do you think we're sitting here? You're supposed to be helping me with my marketing."

Abel barks out a laugh. "Good luck, brother. I've been trying to alter my own marketing plan for months. There just aren't a lot of new clients signing up to be members right now. Unless some hardcore gym rats come walking through that door, you may need to come up with a different plan, like taking a cooking class."

He grabs my pen and worksheet, looking over the notes and details I have written down so far. While he critiques, I absentmindedly stare at the front door, wracking my brain on where the best place is to find new people who have an interest in getting healthy.

The produce aisle in the grocery store? Soliciting at another business is probably frowned upon.

Put out an ad on Craigslist? Frankly, I never trust anyone I meet there. Don't get me started on the personals section and the twenty-five-year-old woman I found on that site. Newsflash: She was neither a woman nor twenty-five. I still can't figure out why a seventy-year-old man spends his time catfishing people. Dude needs a real hobby. Although I'll give him that his fishing tips were bang on. I should message him again and ask about getting some new lures.

Maybe I should take out an ad on social media or something. Surely, I wouldn't be the first one to try it. It could work. Or it could be a waste of money.

I shake my head in disappointment. Abel's right. Unless some random bodybuilders just walk through that door, hustling is going to be the story of my life.

The door swings open and my eyes widen. A couple of giant men who clearly work out come barreling through the door. Holy shit, my prayers have been answered.

"Quick," I hiss, punching Abel in the shoulder. "Tell me tonight's lottery numbers."

"What?" Abel is still looking at the worksheet, having made a couple notes already. "And why are you hitting me?"

"You spoke it and it came true," I whisper yell. "Now give me the lottery numbers."

Abel looks up in confusion, but I see it on his face the second he realizes he has psychic abilities. "Holy shit. How did I do that? Am I a witch?"

"You'd be a warlock. But either way, it worked. I'll be back. This baby daddy needs to make some money." I clap him on the back, thrilled that my luck is starting to change, and head toward the beefy bodybuilders.

These dudes are huge. Both are taller than me, but what I lack in height, I make up for in muscle. They clearly hit the gym often, but I can already see where I can help them increase in bulk. I'm suddenly excited about the prospect of not just training these guys, but maybe even working out with them. Abel may be the strongest trainer by traditional standards, but I'm training for the Strongman competition. It's a completely different kind of strength. I like it because every day is a different kind of training. No standard squats and push-ups for me. Well, not very often anyway.

"Welcome to Weight Expectations, gentlemen," I interrupt Natalie, who is obviously getting her flirt on. "Looks like you guys ventured into the right place."

Natalie glares. "Can you wait until I'm done getting them all signed up?"

Ah, Natalie. Never one to pass on the pretty boys. Too bad for her I've got bigger problems than scoring a date. "As much as I appreciate you pitching in and helping out with my responsibilities, I'm finished with my lunch break now, and there is a line of patrons ready to check in." One of our regulars rolls her eyes. Not at me. This isn't the first time Natalie has ignored paying customers to woo a pretty face.

The larger of the two men turns to see the line and quickly moves out of the way. "Oh shit. Sorry about that. I didn't realize we were taking up your time."

"No! No. It's no problem." Yet another flirty smile crosses Natalie's face. Even as she continues to ignore everyone else. "You're not bothering anyone. I'm happy to help."

"Don't worry about it, Nat." I purposely use the nickname she hates, just to see the scowl she gives me. "It's part of my job description, but I appreciate you stepping up and helping me out while I finished up lunch."

Her eyes narrow as she slaps the clipboard into my outstretched hand with a huff. I'd feel bad for ruining her chances of getting laid, but most of the time Natalie acts annoyed when people walk in. Unless they're hot. And these guys are definitely hot. Why does our boss keep her around? Oh yeah. Nepotism or something.

"My name is Joey Marshall, and I'm one of the trainers here at this fine facility," I say and reach out to shake both their hands.

"Stan Willis," the bigger one says, his giant hand engulfing mine.

"I'm Nicolas Leday." The smaller guy isn't small by any means, but leaner for sure. He also has a bigger smile and seems a little more outgoing. Maybe it's because he smiles and nods at just about everyone who he makes eye contact with.

"Can I entertain you boys with a tour of our facility?" I give my most inviting smile, hoping they're interested in more than just a facility to base out of. I'm sure there's more dudes where these guys came from, and I intend on wooing them all.

Stan, who has dark hair and a more reserved demeanor, shrugs. "Sure. This is where we'll be for a while, so why not?"

We start our trek around the gym, me quickly looking around to make sure Rosalind is nowhere to be found. It's the same tour I've taken hundreds of people on. Basically, it's a giant circle route to show off the facilities in an attempt to convince people to sign on the bottom line. That means there's no reason to give these guys a chance to hit on our newest employee. It's a given that they'll see her and immediately go gaga over how beautiful she is. And lord knows I don't need her to be tempted by them when I'm trying to build a solid foundation with her.

Yes, I admit to acting like a jealous idiot. I have no shame. But dammit, they're mine and I don't want her with anyone else until I have a chance to prove my worth. Besides, I need to lock in this commission. Not that it will be hard. I get the feeling these guys are ready to join, and I'm mostly selling my stellar personal services at this point. The best way to do that is with small talk. "Did you guys just move to the area?"

They glance at each other in confusion. "What makes you think that?" Nicolas asks.

"You don't get shoulders and biceps like you guys have by staying home. I just assumed you're new to the area and looking for a home base for your workouts. Or maybe you got tired of your current gym."

Nicolas snickers. "Actually, we've been here for years. And you're right. We work out practically around the corner."

Hmm. Gym hoppers. Interesting.

"So, what made you decide to check this place out?"

Stan eyes the track above us that encircles the open basketball court area. The way his eyes move makes me feel like he's assessing all the exit points. Weird. "Our friend Carlos Davies comes here."

I snap my fingers in recognition of the name. "Oh yeah, he's my buddy Abel's friend. Good guy." And also explains why Stan is probably looking for vulnerabilities in our security. Not that we have any. But with his physique and demeanor, my money is on him being some kind of security guard to the stars. I bet he could tell some interesting stories.

"He's a little batshit crazy now that he's a dad," Nicolas mutters.

Even Stan chuckles at that. "How many times did they call 'Code Pink' at work for a while?"

"Oh man, Quinn was so pissed when he found out what that meant." Nicolas bends over, holding his gut as he laughs. "I thought his head was gonna explode."

I'm completely lost in this conversation, but if they're happy, I'm happy. Because happy people sign contracts with trainers and spend money before the sad feelings hit.

Nicolas wipes the tears from the corners of his eyes. "Those two are the best birth control I've ever seen. Going certifiable seems to come with the territory of fatherhood."

"I hope not," I interject, not because I am any closer to understanding their conversation, but because I don't want them to forget I'm here. Plus, they may have me wigging out just a bit.

"What?"

Welp, Stan just confirmed that they were well on their way to losing focus on why we're all standing in the middle of the weight room.

"My girlfriend is pregnant," I admit. Is she my girlfriend? I haven't kissed her in a really long time, but she's having my baby, so that counts for something, right? Also I really need to kiss her again. "I hope I'm holding it together okay. That 'Code Pink' shit sounds awful."

The two of them give me their congratulations and claps on the back—all that stuff that goes with finding out someone is having a kid. The whole time I'm accepting their praise, I'm wondering if I've been acting loopy lately too. I'd ask Abel, but he'd take the opportunity to give me shit.

"Listen," Nicolas says, as if he just read my mind and my concerns. "So far, you haven't tried to show us a baby picture, nor are you glued to your phone searching up baby gear while holding a half-ass conversation, so as of now, you're doing way better than Carlos is."

Wait... baby gear? Do I need to start looking up baby gear? Oh shit. I thought I had a few months. Am I supposed to start ordering it early? Does Rosalind know where to find whatever baby gear even is?

I push my pending panic attack away. There won't be any purchasing of anything for any child if I can't bring in some new clients. Back to small talk it is.

Guiding them upstairs to show them our yoga and Pilates room because hey, they may need some vinyasa after a hard day of protecting the stars, I keep the banter going. "Since Carlos is a regular here, I guess he's the one who recommended us?"

"Sort of. The gym at our office flooded, so we need somewhere to work out while it gets renovated."

I stop and turn to stare at them both. Having just gotten back in our facility recently, I know firsthand the nightmare a complete renovation can be when you're trying to keep working. "Oh shit. The whole gym? Equipment, flooring everything?"

"The whole thing," Nicolas says, exaggerating his words for effect. "Thank God it was contained to the gym only. The boss man was in a rage when he found the mess at something ridiculous like five in the morning, but then the plumber came in and found the source of the problem. It was an unfortunate incident with a clogged toilet that somehow led to a massive pipe burst."

I grimace. I don't even want to know how a bunch of shit ended up busting a pipe open. It's no wonder the place has to be gutted. No one wants to work out in a place that smells like a sewer. Men's locker rooms smell bad enough as it is.

"I told them the plumbing wasn't designed to handle that many of us in one office. Water-saving toilets don't work on man-sized shit," Stan finally adds. "I warned but no one listened."

Nicolas rolls his eyes. "People need to be going home to take a shit. Not using the office facilities."

"Not gonna happen," Stan argues with a shake of his head. "Not with the amount of coffee we drink. And I'm not driving home to take a dump when I'm in the middle of working a case. If nature calls, I'm answering."

"Working a case?" I interrupt, not that they're paying much attention to my tour anyway. We seem to be getting off track a lot today. Eh. It's fine. It's not like they need to know how to work the equipment anyway. "I thought you guys worked at Cipher Systems with Carlos."

They look at each other and smirk before one of them says, "We do. In security."

"No shit. I figured that part out already. But you downplay it like you drive a golf cart around the mall, never leaving the premises. I call bullshit."

Nicolas chuckles. "My Mercedes isn't a golf cart, that's for damn sure. No, it's high-end security which almost always requires extra effort and investigation."

My eyes widen in excitement. Now we're getting to the good stuff. I wonder if they know Demi Lovato. She's hot. "Like for celebs and stuff, right?"

"And stuff. Not so much celebrities."

Well, that's a disappointment.

"So, you can see why we don't have the luxury of getting lazy and taking time off from hitting the weights."

"For sure," I agree and turn back to the room, gesturing to top-of-the-line equipment we boast. "As you can see, we're fully stocked with all the basics. Free weights, machines, treadmills, we even have a track that goes around the perimeter of the building."

"Nice," Stan remarks. "I hate treadmills, but it's almost too cold to run outside."

Nicolas punches him in the shoulder in response. "Wimp. The chill is good for the lungs, man."

"Speak for yourself. I know you hated the heat in Arizona, but I could go for a little Southern weather when the snow starts falling around here," Stan retorts. "Besides, I'd hate to waste office money by not using the facilities, since they're paying our membership fees. In fact"—he looks over the edge, the noise from Tabitha's blender catching his attention—"I'm gonna charge one of those smoothies to my account. They look really good."

"Ooooh, boy." Nicolas laughs. "Carlos will be so pissed when he sees that."

"Carlos won't notice because he's distracted with everything baby Evelyn Rose Davies."

"Can't say I blame him. That baby is pretty damn cute. But forget that. You may be onto something. Suddenly, I'm feeling a little faint. I think I might need to get some sustenance in me." Nicolas pats his flat abs, a conspiratorial grin on his face.

"Tabitha makes the best smoothies. That's not me bragging." I hold my hands up defensively. "If I didn't work here, I'd still come in at lunch to get one."

Nicolas shakes his head, like I just reminded him of something important. "Oh man, I haven't had lunch yet either. That would hit the spot."

"Come on. I'll introduce you to her."

We make our way back down the stairs, chatting about nothing and everything related to weights, smoothies, and even the Strongman I'm training for. I'm beginning to like these guys a lot. Even if they don't become clients, they're going to be some fun members to have around. It's also going to be entertaining watching how many of our gym rats fall all over themselves trying to get their attention. My money says Bambi finally stumbles off that treadmill at least once.

Abel has already left the counter by the time we get there, but Tabitha is hard at work as usual. She's on her computer, so I guess she's done with inventory and is ordering supplies or something. She's deep in concentration, dark curly hair pulled high up on her head, and the purse of her lips means she isn't too happy with whatever she's seeing. Lucky for her, I'm about to make her day a little bit brighter.

"Tabitha, I'd like to introduce you to some of our newest members."

She slowly tears her eyes away from the screen, lids heavy like they always are when she's concentrating. I sense her interest the second her eyes finally make contact with my new friends because she freezes. Well, except for her eyebrows, which make minuscule movement in the upward direction. I'm sure they don't see it, but I do. I know Tabitha well enough to know that she is already looking forward to their daily trips to her bar.

"Welcome, gentlemen." Tabitha puts her hand out to shake theirs, which is weird because she never does that. I guess that's as close as she can come to copping a feel.

In her defense, I wouldn't mind getting a hand on those rock-hard guns either. They are that impressive. "Are you new here or just looking around?"

Nicolas jumps right in, smart enough to know flirting with the smoothie lady could work to his benefit. "It's our first day, but Joey here has been singing your praises. Thought we'd come over and try one of your famous drinks."

She flashes him a flirty smirk. "Well, you've come to the right place. A man of your" —she doesn't even try to hide that she gives him the once-over—"physique would probably enjoy an Ultra Protein Banana Mint Shake."

"I'll take whatever you want to give me," he says with his own playful grin.

"Oh Jesus," Stan grumbles, and I know there's a story there, but it's their first day. I'll pry later.

I've got other things to worry about—like making these guys my new regular clients and making it to my next appointment on time.

CHAPTER TWELVE

ROSALIND

Flipping through the stupid pregnancy-slash-motherhood magazine in my hands, I'm getting more and more irritated. I'd blame hormones, but this time I'm actually justified in my anger.

It's our first real ultrasound since the blob turned into more of a human and Joey's late. Not just a few minutes, but really late. At first, I tried to give him the benefit of the doubt, but then I waited in an uncomfortable chair in the lobby for thirty-five minutes before having to pee in a cup and change into a paper gown, just so I could sit on more paper in a freezing cold exam room waiting for *another* thirty-five minutes. Still no doctor and no Joey.

I get it. The doctor had an emergency delivery or something. But geez, are all babies so inconsiderate with other people's time when they decide to be born?

"Listen, I know you're a little baby and you don't know better yet," I say to my ever-expanding stomach, "but I swear I will make your father feed you his cooking when you get teeth if you pull this shit on me. Okay? Let's find a time that works and stick to it."

A small nudge in my belly is the response. Good thing it's still little. I'm almost positive it was aiming for my ribs.

Sighing out of boredom and annoyance, I toss the magazine onto the counter. It immediately slides to the floor. Typical.

I know I shouldn't be angry. Things happen and Joey probably has a good explanation for being late and not letting me know. But being mad feels better than the emotion I'm trying to ignore—sadness.

There, I said it. I'm sad. Sad that this is probably not the only time I'll have to do something important like this on my own. Because as much as Joey is making a massive effort to have us do this together, and really he's pulling out all the stops, as long as we're not a couple, we're still just two single parents who work really well together. And that makes me sad.

Having kids wasn't on my radar yet, but I always knew eventually I'd want a family. I just wanted to fall in love with an amazing guy and run away to elope to my mother's chagrin before having them. Instead, my mother seems delighted and the one person who could be the man of my dreams doesn't seem anywhere close to thinking of me as more than just a friend.

The door suddenly flies open and, for a split second, I feel relief that maybe my appointment is about to begin and I can pull out of my pity party. But no. It's my baby daddy-slash-current frontrunner on my shit list. He's out of breath and has clearly been rushing to get here.

I narrow my eyes, pushing the sadness back down and allowing my self-protection to kick in. I'm in no mood to be melancholy or complacent. It's our first appointment together. They better not all be like this. "You're late."

"I'm sorry," he says still out of breath. "I was signing up two clients for a brand-new program I was just given the go-ahead to teach."

"And that's more important that this appointment?"

"No. But we need the money for diapers, so I got done as fast as I could before Abel could snatch them away and took all the revenue for himself."

I scoff. "Abel wouldn't do that."

One of Joey's eyebrows lifts like that is a ridiculous notion. "You obviously don't know your cousin very well. He's my best friend, but we also have a love-hate relationship when it comes to clients. We love to hate each other for having them. And we hate to love each other when we're successful. But trust me, these guys I signed… you are going to love them. They are so ripped, even I kind of want to jump them."

I blink rapidly, making sure I heard him correctly before responding. "That is the weirdest thing you've ever said to me."

"Weirder than when I told you about the time Frank was schooling us in the locker room on proper self-pleasuring?"

"Okay, maybe a close second."

"I will agree with that."

I sigh and try to focus on the fact that he didn't forget me or this appointment. He was trying to pull in money to provide for our child. As much as I hate to admit it, it's admirable that everything he does is with the baby in mind. Besides, the doctor is way later than him, so he hasn't missed anything important.

Conceding the point and letting go of my irritation, I lean back on my hands to try and stretch out my back. "Fine. You're forgiven for being late. Tell me about these new clients you're so excited about."

Joey pulls up a chair closer to the table and makes himself comfortable. "Seriously. They're these high-end security guys. They're huge. Bigger than me."

High-end security? And buff? Now he has my attention. Joey is an impressive specimen of a man. My dreams don't ever let me forget it. But if these guys are even bigger than him, that's… wow. Again, I'd blame the hormones, but really, I'm just a hot-blooded American woman.

"I was talking to them about Strongman," Joey continues, either not seeing the sudden interest on my face, or just ignoring it, "and they want to train with me two days a week. Not to compete or anything, just with the different kinds of exercises. So, we talked to Keely…"

"Wait… we? All three of you talked to Keely? Our head honcho, big boss Keely?"

He shrugs like it's a given. "How else do you pressure your gym manager into letting you start a brand-new training program completely different than any other class we have, than to bring the paying customers with you? I already told you they're hot. How could she say no?"

Sadly, he has a very good point.

"So anyway, she agreed to let us do the class as sort of a trial run. Promote it a little and see how it goes. If we get more interest, or maybe get some of their co-worker friends to join us, it might become a permanent part of our program."

"That is…" I pause to get my thoughts straight. "…pretty cool, actually. To come up with a class idea spur of the moment and get it approved on a trial basis so fast. You think they'll get their friends to sign up, too?"

Joey's eyes light up as he tells me more about some toilet incident, which is why the gym is suddenly being overrun by extra hot men with extra-large muscles. The only part I really hear is that there are lots of potential clients and lots of potential income.

I wasn't stressing about money before I got here. Since my insurance doesn't kick in until I've been working for two months after my start date, today's visit is all out of pocket, though, and when I had to hand over my credit card, that's when my concern began. I have no idea how much money an ultrasound is going to cost, but I can guarantee it won't be cheap.

But these new clients might help with some of the upcoming bills. Even better, maybe a bunch of buff men have wives and girlfriends who might be interested in a pole class in a few months.

What I haven't told Joey yet, or anyone because it feels a little too personal, is that I've started researching how to become a certified fitness trainer and get a pole fitness certification so I can have all the qualifications I need to start my own class. I don't want to walk into Keely's office and pitch the idea of a class like this with nothing to back it up. I know stereotypes can make it a hard sell to begin with. I want Keely to view me as a true expert in the pole fitness arena and see the value I can bring to the gym and our clients.

First things first, though, I need to get my GED so I can even start the training. Once again, that requires money.

Before Joey realizes I'm off in my own little world, the door opens again and Dr. Walters walks in sporting a huge smile. I glance at the clock next to the sink, leaning up against the wall.

An hour and fifteen minutes late. The man is an hour and fifteen minutes late and is smiling like half my afternoon and my freshly shaved legs weren't ruined by sitting in this freezing room for so long.

"Hello! How are we feeling today?" He begins the process of washing his hands, completely oblivious to the daggers I'm staring at him.

Before I can answer with a snarky remark about teaching children early in life how to have some consideration for others, Joey jumps right in with, "We're great! Can't wait to see our little baby."

"You're what, fifteen weeks or so now, Rosalind?"

I nod. "Sixteen weeks, three days."

"Good, good." Dr. Walters grabs a paper towel to wipe his hands off and grabs my chart to flip through it. "Any nausea?"

I shake my head. "Not anymore."

"Spotting?" Another shake. "Both of those things are normal, so just let me know if they come up. In the meantime, your blood pressure looks good, and your weight gain is on track. Okay, let's lie you down and have a look."

We go over some more random questions and he measures my pooch, which isn't painful, but brings home the point that I'm never going to get my figure back the way it used to be. It sucks, but I suppose I shouldn't be surprised.

"Okay," Dr. Walters finally says with yet another huge smile. Seriously. Does the man ever frown? "Who's ready to see their baby?"

"Yes! We're ready!"

Of course, Joey is. Me? I'm nervous as shit. I'd never admit it to either of them but up until now I've just been pregnant. Suddenly, I'm having *a baby*. It's the same thing, and yet it feels totally different. It's hard for me to digest this change in thought process.

The lights dim and Dr. Walters rolls the ultrasound machine toward the exam table. My gown goes up, my pants slide a bit as another paper cover is tucked in low, and some warm gel is squirted on my lower abdomen. Joey grabs my hand, I suspect more for his sake than mine, and we wait for the wand to rub all over me and show us what's hiding inside.

We hear it before we see it. The steady thrum of a heartbeat.

"A hundred thirty beats per minute, which is right where it needs to be," Dr. Walters says absentmindedly as he studies the screen, slowly moving the wand to find what he's looking for. "And there… is… your… baby."

Sure enough, the screen changes from random gray and white colors to a very distinct circular shape. And that bubble is very obviously a tiny human being.

"Holy shit," Joey breathes, expressing my thoughts exactly.

"You can really see this baby's profile. Right there you see its nose and there are the lips."

Dr. Walters points out various parts of our baby's features while I lie there in awe. It's surreal to see that it has hands and feet. Tiny fingers and toes right there on display. And then our baby confirms it is, in fact, our child.

"Look at that! Our baby just flipped us off!" Joey and I both laugh.

"I expect nothing less from a Palmer-Marshall baby," I quip, still giggling and feeling the stress from before melt away. Seeing that alone made the long wait worth it.

"You guys interested in finding out the sex?"

Joey and I look at each other, both of us sporting a surprised expression.

"We can see it this early?" Joey asks, echoing the question in my mind.

"Sometimes. It really depends on the baby and how clear the picture is at this point. It's worth a shot if you're interested."

"I… I don't know," I stumble through my words, my thoughts tripping me up. "What do you think?"

Joey bites his bottom lip before releasing it to answer me. "I know it's supposed to be a fun surprise and all, but I don't know if I can wait until the baby is born to find out, ya know?"

I nod rigorously because that's exactly how I feel. "It would make it easier on my mom to not have to buy double and take half of it back later."

"And we could start coming up with name ideas."

Turning back to Dr. Walters who is still looking at the screen while he moves the wand, we give him the go-ahead.

"Let's do it."

The good doc smiles at me, probably as excited as we are. When your job is looking at lady bits all day, some of them less taken care of than others, I'm sure fun stuff like this is extra interesting. "Okay, let's do it. Any guesses so far?"

Joey shakes his head, eyes clearly focused on the screen. Like he'll be able to tell what anything is without the doctor interpreting for us.

"I don't know that I have any gut instincts about it so far," I say, watching just as closely as they are, without any belief I'll figure it out on my own. "But I do find myself referring to the baby as 'he.' I don't think it means anything. It's just easier to have a pronoun to attach to it, I think."

"That's pretty normal." Dr. Walters continues to move the wand, but now he's pressing down a little harder and his eyes are squinting. "I have a lot of patients who use whatever pronoun pops in their head at the time. He or she, doesn't matter. Depends on the day and their mood, I guess."

"I can understand that." I feel a very distinct flutter in my belly just as there is a jump on the screen. "Holy shit, did you see that?"

"What was that?" Joey asks, just as perplexed as I am.

"That," Dr. Walters says with a chuckle, "is a very ornery baby already. He's moving away from the wand."

"Wait a minute, he's hiding from us?" Joey questions and I immediately start laughing.

"I don't know if he's hiding, but he definitely doesn't want us to see his private parts."

I laugh harder, somehow not surprised. "So, our baby flipped us the bird, is trying to run away, and refuses to show us his gender? Oh yeah. This is definitely a Palmer-Marshall baby."

Joey chuckles and squeezes my hand a little tighter. "We are so screwed when this kid learns how to walk."

So screwed. And yet, in this moment, as I watch the most amazing thing I've ever seen on that little screen, I can't find it in me to care.

CHAPTER THIRTEEN

JOEY

Turning my head, I look over at the clock on the dresser across the room. It's twelve eleven. That means I have less than six hours before the damn alarm goes off. Yet I'm still lying here wide awake.

I've tried everything to fall asleep: watching TV, reading, I even slathered on some lavender oil a former girlfriend left in my cabinet a couple years ago.

Newsflash: it doesn't work on me, and now I smell like I've been taking a bubble bath. Abel's going to give me so much shit about it tomorrow.

Regardless of what I try, my brain just won't shut down. It keeps going back to the appointment at Dr. Walters' office and seeing my baby. *Our* baby. The most beautiful thing I've ever seen, which I don't understand because it was a black-and-white outline.

Still, I've never felt that kind of bond toward anyone before. Not my first girlfriend in high school, not Abel's kids, not even my own mom.

And it's not just the overwhelming love I feel for my unborn child. Suddenly, I want to learn how to cook without blowing up the kitchen. I want to deep clean the house to make extra sure there aren't unnecessary germs around. I want to make enough money for the best daycares and do research on the most absorbent diapers. I want to install a small swing onto the lone tree in the back yard and call Carlos to find out what kind of baby gear he recommends.

What the hell is wrong with me?

All these thoughts are running through my head, keeping me wide awake even though my body doesn't have any desire to move.

My door opens quietly, and I immediately sit up, knowing there's only one person it could be.

"Rosalind? Are you okay?"

Seeing me awake, she quickly slips in and shuts the door behind her. Her long legs are bare, ass barely hidden by an oversized t-shirt that's sliding off one shoulder. Her hair is pulled up so I can see the gracefulness of her neck. She looks beautiful in the moonlight and I can't help wondering if this is a good time to finally kiss her again.

But no. We need to build a solid relationship. I don't want to pressure her into anything she's not ready for.

Gliding up to my bed, she pulls the covers back. "Move over."

"What?" Okay, I don't *think* she's ready for anything sexual, but now I'm not so sure.

She sighs sounding as exhausted as my body feels. "My bed is uncomfortable. And my room has shitty ventilation. I am the baby mama. Move over."

"Isn't it the same bed you've been sleeping on for years? Suddenly, it's uncomfortable?" I poke playfully. Really I don't mind her being in here. I just can't resist the chance to see the fire in her eyes.

"I don't make my body hurt," she retorts as she slides under the sheets. "I just try to accommodate whatever it wants right now."

Admittedly, she's not wrong. I got a preview of her mattress when I flopped down on it after moving it up two flights of stairs. It is pretty shitty. "Okay." I move out of the middle and onto the far side of the bed as she moans her appreciation for a quality pillowtop. I may not be domestic at all, but a man knows the benefit of a good night's sleep after a hard day at the gym. Still, I'm not positive of her intensions, and she's been starring in my dreams for weeks now, so I need to clear something up.

"Does this mean we get to have sex now?"

Rosalind snorts a laugh and punches the pillow as she settles in. "No."

"What? You're moving into my bed, and I don't get any of the benefits?" I joke back.

"You get the benefit of my presence and knowing your baby and I are both getting a good night's rest."

She's got me there. At this point, their safety and well-being are my biggest priorities. I suddenly understand why Abel is such a worry wart when I babysit.

Don't give her too much sugar, Joey.

Don't let her stay up too late, Joey.

Don't burn the house down trying to cook spaghetti, Joey.

One time. It was *one time* that I blew up the spaghetti pot.

I make a quick mental note never to make spaghetti around my child.

"Hey, Rosalind?" I clasp may hands behind my head, staring up at the ceiling again.

"Hmm."

"Are you nervous?"

She takes a deep breath, and I get the feeling she's been up all night, wrestling with her thoughts, too. "About which part?"

"I think… maybe, all of it?"

Rosalind rolls over, putting her hands under her cheek as she stares me dead in the eye. "I'm terrified. What if I'm not cut out for this, Joey?"

"What do you mean? I saw you with Mabel and Ainsley at Thanksgiving. They love you. You're a natural with kids."

"Mabel and Ainsley are easy," she retorts. "I smile and laugh and talk to them like real people. I don't have to keep them *alive*. I don't know how to keep a baby alive."

Shit. She's right. "Neither do I."

We lie there some more, lost in our own thoughts again. I'm so excited to become a dad and I'm equally as terrified, which is such a weird feeling. There is so much that can go wrong. So much I don't know how to do yet. So much to expect that I haven't even thought of. Babysitting Mabel and Ainsley is easy. Pop in a Wii game and let them go nuts. But a baby? That's a whole different thing I've never done before.

"At least my parents are really excited."

"I know. I've read the notes that have come in your care packages." She giggles, probably because I'm a grown-ass man who is still being fed by his mother.

"You think that's funny, do you?" I poke her rib making her squeak. "That my *mommy* is sending me food?"

"I do. I mean, it's nice that she's being so supportive of your training. And it makes me a little less afraid to meet her since she's trying to feed the baby, too."

That stops me. I had no idea she was feeling that fear. "You're scared to meet my parents?"

She nods. It's subtle, but it's there. I don't miss how hard it must be for her to let down one of her walls.

"Why? Your family is *terrifying*. How are my parents, who send you vitamins, scary?"

Rosalind shrugs and bites her bottom lip. "I don't know what they're going to think of me and how we met."

"Why does it matter?"

"I don't want them thinking this baby is an inconvenience you got saddled with because some whore got knocked up on purpose to trap you."

The look in her eyes breaks my heart. This is what she believes others think about her. And now some of her standoffish-ness makes so much more sense. She's afraid the people in my life, the people I love and who love me, are going to judge her for her employment history and how our child came to be.

I grab her hand and intertwine our fingers. I expect her to pull away, but she doesn't, instead letting me hold on to her.

"First, you're not a whore. You never were. You're an athlete."

She huffs a disbelieving laugh.

"It's true. So, you flashed your boobs while you did it. Who cares? I see more boobs at a Mardi Gras parade than I ever did while you danced."

That makes her smile. It's small, but it's there.

"Second, my parents already know how we met."

"What?" She sits up, eyes wide, our hands disconnecting. "You told them?"

"Oh, Rosalind, you vastly underestimate my upbringing."

"What does that mean?"

"My parents are the best people. Except for not letting me live in my childhood home rent-free when they moved. Something about me being an adult and taking care of myself. Totally rude if you ask me, but that's a story for another day." She lies back down, settling into the covers again. "But they are the least likely people to judge someone else for their job. In fact, I'm pretty sure my dad was a bouncer at a club similar to The Pie Hole when they met."

"Seriously?"

"Yep, I don't know the whole story and, frankly, I don't want to. There are certain things I don't need to know about my mother, and her sexual prowess is at the top of that list."

Rosalind huffs another laugh, only this time, it's in amusement. It makes me happy to be making some headway with her insecurities. I suspect she's had them for longer than she cares to admit. Then again, if my mother was Mona Palmer, I might feel insecure, too.

"So, you think she'll like me? Not just because of the baby, but because of me?"

"I don't think so. I know so." Reaching over, I gently stroke her hair, moving a stray piece behind her ear. More than anything I want to lean over and kiss her, but I won't. Not while we're having a tender moment like this.

"Thanks, Joey," she says quietly, the relief evident on her face. I'll probably have to keep reminding her she has nothing to worry about, but it's a start. "But that doesn't solve the problem of how the hell we're going to figure out how to be parents."

"You think maybe we should talk to somebody, like Elliott?"

Rosalind looks up at me again, her dark eyes seeming to glow in the moonlight. I hope our baby has her eyes. "You don't want to talk to Abel?"

"I don't trust him," I say with a chuckle. "He'll think it's funny to tell me I have to get the baby a mohawk for his health or something."

"And you think Elliott won't?"

I think back to last year when she sent me the article about penile health. I spent a long weekend jacking off three times a day to make sure I didn't get backed up only to find out it was a joke. Chaffing is something no man ever forgets.

"Good point. Let's talk to Dinah, instead. She's been working in the childcare area for forever."

"I like Dinah," Rosalind says as she stretches her whole body and rolls onto her stomach. Well, as much as her stomach will allow. I grab an extra pillow off the floor next to me and hand it to her. "Thanks," she breathes as she situates it under her body. "She's always so nice to me and her kids are already grown, so at least she knows how to keep them breathing."

"Wait, Dinah has kids?"

Even in the dark, I can see her brows furrow. "You didn't know that?"

I shrug, feeling kind of stupid for just assuming she was single and childless. "I guess it just never came up."

"You've worked with her for how long and never thought to ask?"

"I make it a rule never to ask a woman if she has kids. That, her age, and her weight are liable to get you punched in the junk."

Rosalind giggles and it's a welcome sound. I like that she's getting more comfortable with me and trusts me enough to let her guard down sometimes. "You got me there. I just think it's weird that it's never come up in conversation. My first week there she mentioned one of them coming home for a visit."

"In my defense," I argue, "the only times I visit the childcare center are when Abel and I are talking, and he has to go make googly eyes at his woman."

She laughs again, probably because she knows I'm right. That man it so whipped. Not that it's a bad thing. Elliott is pretty cool when she's not yanking my chain about shit that makes me yank other parts of my body.

"Maybe we should make a trip in there without Abel tomorrow. To talk to Dinah and pick her brain. Ask questions about what to expect when you're expecting."

I raise my head and stare at Rosalind. "Did you just make a baby book joke?"

"Why, I believe I did."

"Nicely done." I fist-bump her in the dark because I'm pretty impressed. Not only did she make a funny, she did it after midnight when she's falling asleep. "And yeah, let's go see Dinah tomorrow. Maybe she can give us a little more insight into… hell I don't even know what she can tell us."

"That's exactly why we need to talk to her." The words are barely out of her mouth before a giant yawn takes over. She's exhausted and needs her rest.

"Go to sleep," I whisper. "I'll be here if you need me."

She says nothing but her breathing slows until I know she's fast asleep. I lie there for a while longer just listening to her soft breaths and the sound of my own thoughts about the baby, pending fatherhood, and the heat of the woman in control of it all next to me.

She fits right here next to me. I just hope she realizes it sooner rather than later.

CHAPTER FOURTEEN

ROSALIND

I hear the tap of her walker before I see her, yet I still know what's coming.

"Turn around, dear. Let me look at you."

I smile to myself and do as instructed. Edna demands to see my pending baby bump every day. And every day she responds the same way when she sees it's still too small to rub without possibly getting arrested.

"Ugh. I need you to hurry up and show. I have a bigger bump than you do," she complains like always.

"Give her a break, Edna." And Harriet always defends my inability to show faster. "It's her first baby. She won't grow as fast as she will next time."

I grimace. "Next time? Who says there will be a next time?"

Edna points a bony finger at Joey, who is chatting with a client at the trainer station. "You mean to tell me you don't plan to tap that again?"

"I didn't say that."

"Of course, you didn't," she agrees. "You may be young, but you aren't stupid. That is one fine specimen right there. Take advantage of his virility while you can."

I can't help but laugh. When I took this job, I expected to get to know members a bit. I did not, however, expect to have an eighty-seven-year-old woman school me on my sex life.

"I will keep that in mind. Thank you, Edna."

She pats my arm and begins the slow shuffle into the locker room, Harriet right behind her. It's then that Joey decides to approach.

"What was that all about?"

"What, Edna?" He nods. "Let's just say she's one of your biggest fans. In many inappropriate ways."

He freezes momentarily, and just as suddenly, snaps out of it, asking, "Is it weird that that makes perfect sense?"

"Not if you know Edna."

"Agreed." He claps his hands together. "Anyway, are you at a stopping point?"

Stacking the last of my towels, I open the laundry door behind me to put things up. "Yeah, sure. Let me get this all in here first."

We make quick work of cleanup and then hustle to the childcare center. Dinah agreed to let us pick her brain, and I don't want to leave her waiting.

But then we open the door into the large room and my brain seems to short out.

All I can do is stand here like a statue and cringe at the screaming.

There is so. Much. Screaming. Why are all the babies mad at the same time? And why doesn't anyone do anything about it?

I look at Dinah with a mixture of sympathy and disbelief as she does her best to calm one of the loudest offenders. And then I look over at Joey, who has the same expression of fear on his face as I can feel on mine.

Is this what it's going to be like when our baby comes? Will it scream like this for no reason? Do they ever even stop?

"I don't think we're ready for this," I grumble and shake my head.

If I could turn around and run out of this room, I would. But Joey runs faster than I waddle these days, and there's no way he's going to let me leave. Mainly because he isn't going to parent alone. That much is clear. We both have our weaknesses when it comes to this stuff, but I assume we have strengths somewhere too. And none of us will make it out alive if we don't do it together.

I just wish I knew what those strengths were, because right now, I want to throw my hands in the air and say, "Fuck this."

Another worker attends to some of the mayhem as Dinah walks over to us, bouncing a whimpering baby on her hip. "What kinds of questions do you guys have, because they can be hard to answer? Every baby is different, and we won't really know what yours is like until he or she gets here."

That doesn't make me feel better. At all. We can't even have a plan in place? This isn't good.

"What's wrong with this one?" Joey asks, gesturing to her arms with his head.

I nudge him. "Joey!"

"What? I wanna know what's wrong with this one, so we don't make the same mistake. I think this is the same one that Elliott was trying to contain the other day. He's a troublemaker. I can feel it." Joey leans closer and gives the baby the evil eye. He's such an ass. Joey, not the baby.

"Hate to break it to you," Dinah says with a weird conspiratorial grin that puts me on edge, "but this guy just doesn't like being away from his mom. He's spoiled rotten because she holds him all the time."

"So, what you're saying is, don't hold the baby all the time?" Joey tries to clarify.

"When did I say that? A baby is supposed to be attached to his parents. It's obnoxious for me, but it means he's bonded to her, which is good for his development."

"So, *do* hold the baby all the time?"

"Well, you have to put it down sometimes."

"I'm so confused," I whisper, rubbing my temples.

"Okay, let me see if I have this straight." Joey licks his lips like he's preparing for some life-altering wisdom to come out of his mouth. "What you're saying is, this… all this crying… this is… good?"

"In this case, yep."

"But you just said it's obnoxious," I argue, getting frustrated and wondering what the pros and cons are to putting my baby up for adoption. I won't, but the thought does have its merits right now.

"For me it is," Dinah says, as she wipes the baby's chin of some slobber with her finger. Ew. "Which is why I have sarcasm and a witty sense of humor to get through my days. But I would be more concerned if this little one had no feeling one way or another about his mom."

"I don't understand this at all."

"How do you have such a huge family and know less about babies than I do?" Joey asks.

"I never had any interest in the babies," I admit with a shrug. "And there were so many people who wanted to hold them, I never had to. What's your excuse, Marshall?"

"Abel never let me babysit until Mabel was older. Something about her being 'self-sufficient.' Kind of rude if you ask me."

"Considering this conversation, I think Abel made the smart choice." Dinah tosses in her two cents which doesn't make me feel much better.

I blow out a breath and silently pray for my eardrums to rupture. Suddenly, I understand why my mother goes to mass all the time because parenting is no joke. It also kind of pisses me off that I'm feeling sympathetic toward her.

"Listen, Rosalind. You don't have to understand any of it." Dinah shrugs. "It'll come. Just do what feels natural."

"Roll over and throw a pillow on my head to drown out the crying in the middle of the night?"

Dinah and I both stare at Joey for a second too long in disbelief.

"Seriously?" I ask with disbelief. "Are you just going to ignore our kid if I'm not there to fix it?"

"I was kidding," he says by way of justification, but I hold up my hand to make him stop.

"Maybe don't do what comes naturally to him," Dinah clarifies, not that I needed it. "Just go with your gut. You'll be surprised how quickly your maternal instincts kick in. I was really nervous with my first one, too. I didn't even like kids. But as soon as he was born, it all changed."

Knowing I'm not the only one who has felt like this, is the first thing she's said to make me feel better since we walked in this room. Maybe there's hope for me. I'm not holding my breath yet.

Joey finally decides his jokes aren't welcome today and asks her an honest question. "Are all the babies crying because of their moms?"

"No. One of them is teething and the other is tired because the crying keeps waking her up."

"But…" I start even more confused now. "… how do you know all that?"

Dinah shrugs. "You learn their cries."

"Learn their… they have more than one?" Even Joey looks confused again, too.

"Oh boy," Dinah says with amusement. I'm glad she finds our failure entertaining. It's really freaking me out. "You guys are going to have a rough go of it. Have you started reading baby books yet?"

I shake my head, kind of pissed off at myself for not thinking of that sooner.

"Get some."

"I actually had a couple," Joey says, surprising the shit out of me. "They were in my bathroom for some light reading when the need would arise." Dinah and I both screw up our faces in disgust. Does this man have no filter? "Unfortunately, there was a small incident that started with me dozing off and ended with a wet and unreadable book, so I tossed them."

So, no. He doesn't have a filter.

"Anyway, I realized I've never been a huge reader and decided against repurchasing. Do they have an audiobook version?"

His nonchalance in the face of this massive life change is irritating me. Or maybe it's the continual crying frazzling my nerves. Either way, I kind of want to punch him in the junk right now to ensure he never ends up in this situation again. From the look on Dinah's face, she's thinking the same thing.

"Not sure about that," she finally says. "I don't see why they wouldn't. It'll just be harder to refer back to an audiobook if you're trying to look up information."

"Man, it feels like I'm going to college again, having to buy expensive books to look up specific things. I thought I was done with that."

And yet again, my lack of education makes me feel even more behind the curve.

The only thing that makes me feel even slightly better is knowing even a high school diploma wouldn't have prepared me for this either.

CHAPTER FIFTEEN

JOEY

I am so excited for today. It's the first time I'll be training my new clients in our Strongman program, and I'm ready to kick their asses.

Because they joined just days before the holidays, we decided to wait until after the new year to begin. It gave me time to decompress after spending an awkward and exhausting Christmas party with the DiSoto clan. Awkward because it turns out Nonna is more inappropriate than Blanche, which I didn't know was possible. And exhausting because this family can *drink.* I should have expected it after all the Johnny Walker Black during Thanksgiving, but I admit to being ill-prepared for the day. Nor was I prepared to be ill the whole next day.

The good news is Rosalind was excited when I gave her a new Kate Spade purse. It wasn't Gucci, but she still practically launched herself at me when she opened it. The moment I'd been waiting for was happening, and I was *this close* to getting that kiss I've been thinking about, but Abel decided he was tired of standing and shoved his way in between us on the couch. It was an asshole move, but creepy Nonna was watching, so I got over it.

Now that the holiday decorations are all being put away, it's time to get back into the routine. The great part of running a specialty class is we don't have to work around the new gym-goers. Not just anyone can join it. You have to be a paying client to participate. I'm really hoping some of those co-workers at Cipher Systems will take a chance on me. This could be the beginning of a really great program.

Making one additional quick trip around the room, I double-check the equipment we need is set up and ready to go. Besides me, these guys will be the first ones to use it.

"Hey, man! You ready to train us?" Nicolas struts in, his normal wide smile securely in place. My goal is to wipe it right off his face with some hard work and strained muscles.

"I've got some great things planned," I say with my own grin, clapping both him and Stan on the back. Stan just nods by way of greeting before a slow whistle comes through his teeth.

"This is an impressive setup. I haven't seen equipment like this before."

I look around, excited about what I'm seeing too. It's like a dream come true to have this kind of equipment bought and paid for by my place of employment. "Even better is you guys are the first ones to use it. Well, besides me of course."

"Oh yeah, that's coming up, right? The competition?" Nicolas asks as he runs his hands over the lone squat bar. Strongman incorporates a lot of unconventional exercises, but at the end of the day, there still is a lot of strength training involved.

I blow out a breath as I consider how quickly I need to be ready. "It's only three months away. I registered a couple days ago."

Another whistle from Stan. "You ready?"

"Not yet," I admit. "But I'm getting there. I'm coming in early to train every morning, and it's a pretty great time of year to beef up my caloric intake. Those Christmas hams and turkeys were all on sale last week, which was good for me and my bank account. I need the protein to build up my guns."

"Keep it up. It'll be here before you know it."

"No pressure, right? So anyway," I say, shifting gears to get us started. "You guys get a warmup in like we talked about?"

Nicolas begins bouncing on his toes. "Ran two miles. Can't you tell? Stan sweats so much he looks like he dumped water on his head."

Stan just rolls his eyes and mutters "dickhead" as his only response.

"Well, good. I figured we'd start over here." I make my way to the back of the room where I've already set up our first exercise. "These are called Atlas stones, and I'm hoping they really challenge you in a different way."

Nicolas walks over and just stares at the equipment. "So, we're lifting a rock."

Stan snickers. "That's probably why they're called Atlas *stones*, Nick."

"I know that, asshole," he retorts. "I guess I was just expected something a little less"—he waves his hand around dramatically—"primitive."

Oh yeah. He has no idea what's coming. This is going to be fun.

"It may look basic, but I guarantee it's going to give you a workout like you've never experienced."

Nicolas looks unconvinced at this point, but he also doesn't look ready to walk out yet. Instead, he eyes me and then the equipment again. "How heavy is that thing anyway?"

"We're starting you on the light set since it's your first time."

His eyes widen and he scoffs. "The light set? Do you know how much I can bench? At least make it a challenge."

Stan puts his hand up to stop the tirade. I wouldn't be surprised if he researched before walking in today. "Wait. I've seen these Strongman competitions. When you use that word, exactly how *light* are we talking?"

"It's not bad. Just two hundred twenty pounds."

By the look on Nicolas's face, he's still making light of this. "Dude. I can bench-press that with one hand."

"Then by all means, be my guest with the stones, my friend." I gesture to them and back up enough that I'm away from him, but close enough to jump in and spot if need be. "It's right there on the floor. The goal is to pick it up and drop it over that bar onto the mat. Don't throw out your back," I add and grab him a weight belt and some gloves to help his grip.

He nods with swagger and tightens the belt around his waist. He's cocky enough that I know he's going to lose real quick. Stretching his head back and forth, his neck cracks. "I got this."

Stan snickers and leans against the wall, crossing his arms and legs. Oh yeah. He definitely did some research on what to expect.

We watch as Nicolas squats down, putting his arms as far underneath as he can and lifting. At first, it's relatively easygoing. He lifts with his knees and balances it on his thighs. And that's when the struggle really begins.

He attempts to shift his weight so he can get the stone up high enough to toss it over. Part of what makes it hard is that the bar isn't waist high. It's more at a weird height, just about chest high, so it's hard to use your back muscles to help. Add on the roundness of the stone and it becomes more than just arm strength. It's constant adjusting to keep from losing your grip, even with the gloves.

Nicolas struggles for a little longer, but I'll give him that he's determined. Finally, he gets it in just the right position and over it goes, making a *bang* on the floor when it lands. The mat might protect the floor, but it doesn't change that sound.

"Holy shit," he says through heavy breaths, hands on his hips as he tries not to hyperventilate.

"Harder than you thought, huh, hotshot?" Stan quips with a grin.

"It's not that heavy, just an odd shape. And an even odder height." He grabs his water bottle and screws off the top.

"Exactly," I say with a nod, glad that it wasn't too easy for him. "Your muscles are used to bench presses and dead lifts. But this engages your back, glutes, legs, arms, and your entire core at the same time because the stone isn't necessarily balanced. But to get it over the bar, none of that matters because it's all arm strength."

He downs half his water bottle before speaking again. "Okay, you win. That was fucking hard."

"Good. So, let's start with some sets." Nicolas's eyes widen in disbelief, which makes me want to laugh. I'm better at training these dudes than I thought I would be. "Don't worry. We're not going over the bar. We're just picking it up, shifting to a stand, squatting back down, and dropping it to the floor. You can compete against each other later if you want."

"Yeah, we'll see about that," Nicolas grumbles and takes his place behind the stone.

Stan, who is obviously the quiet one, silently positions himself behind a slightly larger stone.

We go through five sets of five, up the weight for five sets of three, and once again for five sets of one. Both of them breaking out into a good sweat and Nicolas bitching the whole time. They seem really into it, which bodes well for my long-term plans. Maybe I really can build the program.

The original goal for the day included some more indoor work, but being that it's a relatively nice day out, I change my mind. Might as well pull out the big guns for our first session.

"Grab your hoodies," I mention as they mop off. "We're heading out back."

"Like *outside*, outside?" Nicolas asks, and I give him a quick nod. "Good. There is nothing worse than working out in the heat. I could use some cooling off."

Behind the building there is a fenced-in grassy area that runs the length of the building. It's kind of a hidden gem considering we're smack in the middle of Chicago and backyards are typically no bigger than a patch or two of grass, if that. When the temperatures get warmer, quite a few of the staff members make this location the unofficial break area. It's quiet, it's out of the way, and if you can block out the traffic noise, you almost feel one with nature. Well, assuming you also ignore the workout equipment. That's the other thing this particular patch of heaven is good for—an outdoor workout, starting with tire flips.

"Holy shit," Nicolas breathes. "Where did they get a tire like this?"

I understand his reaction. This isn't just a regular tire. It's huge. Roughly five and a half feet across and taller than the average toddler when it's lying on its side.

"Believe it or not, you can get them at a regular tire store."

Even Stan looks surprised by that information. "They actually sell and install these?"

"Oh hell no. Usually they come in when it can't be used on a big rig anymore and the owner needs to dispose of it. But a tire this size"—I pat it with my hand—"costs more to dispose of than it's worth. There are several shops in Chicago that have a list of gyms who need certain sizes and weights. They give us a call when they come across it. We just have to show up with a truck, and they'll load it up and send us on our way."

Nicolas looks impressed. Not at all the cocky bastard like he was with the Atlas stones.

"That brings a whole new meaning to tire flips."

"Yep. This one is our light one. It's about four hundred fifty pounds. Care to do the honors?"

"No, thank you. I learned my lesson last time." Nicolas takes a giant step back and points to Stan. "He can go first."

Stan grumbles but doesn't hesitate to get in position behind the tire.

"Our goal," I instruct, "is to make it across the length of the field. Stan, when you get to the end, Nicolas will take over and bring it back. Each of you go one length three times. Unless you go too fast, then we'll change it to four."

Stan turns to Nicolas and asks the same question I've heard from clients a million times before. "Why did we think this was a good idea again?"

"Apparently, we got more complacent with our workouts than we thought."

"Remind me not to do that again." He squats and grunts as he lifts the tire and flips it. Stan's breath is already heavy, and we just got started.

"How'd you get into this stuff anyway?" Nicolas asks as we trail behind Stan, who continues to grunt and strain. His form is great though, so I'm not worried.

"Um, I found it a couple years ago by accident when I was flipping through some channels. The World Championship was on, and these dudes were tossing logs and pulling cars on chains. It was pretty cool."

"I've seen some clips of lifting cars before. Those dudes are fucking incredible."

I nod in agreement. "It looked really interesting, and I'm the kind of person who can get bored with my workout if things don't change up regularly, so I started doing some research on it. Seeing what kinds of things I could incorporate. It sort of spiraled from there. Just one more, Stan," I yell. "Almost there, man."

He flips it one more time with a yell and turns to Nicolas. "Holy shit. You're up."

"Harder than you thought, huh?"

Stan lifts his shirt to wipe his face with the hem, having ditched his hoodie halfway through. "I'm no pansy, but that was so much harder than I thought it would be."

"It's good though, right?" *Please say yes. My ability to buy formula may depend on your answer.*

"So good." *Yes!* "We should try and get Dan to come with us, Nick."

Nicolas bursts out laughing as he begins his squat. "That would be hilarious. He'd have no idea what hit him." With that, he begins lifting, cursing me the whole way up until the tire topples over. "I'm not gonna be able to walk tomorrow, am I?"

I can't help but smile mischievously. "That was my plan all along."

He nods and catches his breath before squatting again. "Well done. I applaud you as the mastermind behind some much-needed torture."

I'll give it to them—these guys may not be used to this kind of exercise, but they refuse to quit. Not when I add an extra set. Not when we move on to farmer carries. Not when I add weights to both ends of the barbell so they're fighting to keep the whole thing balanced while they walk back and forth.

No, they're troopers and put in well over one hundred percent.

When our hour is finally up, they're dripping with sweat and practically singing my praises as they walk out the door until next time. I make damn sure Keely hears them when they promise to bring a couple co-workers for a trial run in a couple days.

"I'm impressed, Marshall," Keely says in her normal tough-guy boss tone, her arms crossed showing off her toned biceps, stiletto tapping on the ground. "I was a little worried a Strongman class would have such a specific demographic it would be a waste of money. But it turns out it may be a niche we need to fill."

I flash her a flirty grin, but not too flirty since she's my boss and all. "I told you I wasn't the only one who gets bored with their workouts. It's fun to shake things up."

"Well, keep it up. I'd love for us to be known for having more diversity in our class styles."

I fist-pump when she walks away, thrilled by how things seem to be falling together. If the ball keeps rolling this direction, adding a baby to the mix won't be as hard as it could be.

If only I could get Rosalind on board with a Strongman-themed nursery…

CHAPTER SIXTEEN

ROSALIND

I don't make a habit of watching members work out. Unless they run weird like Bambi or are funny when they argue with their trainer, like Abel's client Rian who is apparently pissed Abel can't make her lose baby weight faster, I tend to stick to my job and ignore everyone around me.

And then Joey signed up the hottest men I've ever seen in my life. And trust me, as a stripper, you see hundreds of men on the regular, so I've seen my fair share of gorgeous guys. But these security dudes? Holy shit. My poor little pregnant body can hardly take the hormones running through me right now, and all I have is my memories. That's how aroused they made me.

I admit to feeling a little bit of guilt that I find them so attractive. I'm having a baby with Joey, so I should be lusting over him, right? In my defense, I actually have been lusting over him for a while now. And when we had Christmas at my aunt Lucia's house, there was a moment when I really thought he was going to kiss me. I was ready for it.

And then Abel thought he would be funny and sit in between us. Moment ruined.

In hindsight, it's probably good that my cousin got in the way. Making out in front of my parents probably would have been considered "tacky" and "uncalled for." Personally, I think sticking my tongue down his throat would have been perfectly called for after the gift he unexpectedly gave me, but I'm too tired to fight with my mother.

I'm also too horny for my own good. I thought by now Joey would have made some sort of move on me, but he hasn't. Not even when I sleep in his bed. I know, I know. I told him he wasn't getting any sex, but I meant that night, not forever. I was still in my first trimester then and sick all the time. Now? Now my hormones are raging. I have dirty thoughts about him often, I just don't know how to let him know without coming across desperate or slutty. Besides, he hasn't given me any indication our relationship is anything more than just two people preparing to co-parent. Without any real relief my hormones are finding fantasy-worthy material pretty much anywhere. And holy. Shit. Did they ever find them with the new clients.

I can't stop thinking about their biceps bulging as they lifted those giant-ass tires. And their tight glutes as they stretched and strained. And Joey's thick thighs as he squatted and spotted. Between the three of them, it was eye candy delight.

And yes, the glass doors really did need to be washed at the exact moment they were taking advantage of the outdoor area. It had nothing to do with the sweat sliding down the back of their necks or the abs I got a peek of when they would wipe their faces with the bottom of their shirts. Nope. None of that at all. I was just doing my job. Just… doing… my job…

I blow a breath over my face as I try to calm my body down, but really, it's impossible at this point. The three of them were just so… sensual in their manliness.

Joey walks into his bedroom, where I'm currently trying and failing to get comfortable for a good night's sleep. I've been sleeping like a proverbial baby in here for a couple weeks now, having given up on going back to my own room. I'm not sure if it's the mattress or the comfort of having him next to me, but it doesn't look like I'll be leaving Joey's room until I feel better rested. Not that my current thoughts are doing anything to make me sleepy. It doesn't help that Joey's fresh from a shower, fluffy white towel wrapped around his waist and another one being rubbed through his hair. Water droplets trail down his chest leading directly to the faint treasure trail, reminding me of exactly what's underneath.

Joey is one fine specimen of a man. And no, we may not have had the most stellar one-night stand, and I may have done my best to push away the memories of how I obtained a head injury, but one thing has remained vivid in my mind all these months later—Joey has nothing to be embarrassed about. A lesser man may actually gloat at his being well-endowed, but not Joey. He knows he's got it going on, so he has no reason to flaunt it.

"Sleeping in here again tonight?" he asks from behind the towel that he's still using to sop up the excess water from his long hair.

"Yep." I barely comprehend his question as I absentmindedly peruse his body with my eyes. His arms flex as he moves, a washboard eight-pack peeking out from behind the extra bulk he's been packing on lately. He looks… strong and powerful. And that bulge under the towel is awfully large considering he's not hard at this point.

"Rosalind." My eyes flick up to his and I know I've been caught. That cocky grin is proof of that. "Like what you see?"

I can't take it anymore. I've been trying to give him signals but he's not picking up on them. After weeks of living with him and constantly being surrounded by the faint scent of his sweat and musk, I can't wait any longer. This may be a terrible decision, but if I don't have an orgasm in approximately half a second, my entire body is going to combust.

I release the bottom lip I didn't even realize I was biting. "Get naked, Joey. Now." If that isn't obvious enough, nothing is.

It takes him less than half a second to get with the program and lose the little bit of terrycloth standing in the way of me and my good time. He launches himself onto the bed, attacking me with his mouth.

His wet hair gets stuck on the side of my face, but I don't care. His tongue immediately invades me, and while it's clumsy and awkward, a few too many teeth involved, it's also a very, very welcome intrusion. My hands are roaming everywhere, trying to feel everything at the same time, desperate to find relief from the itch I need scratched so badly.

But then he pulls away. "Wait a minute. You wouldn't let me touch you the other day when you slept in my bed. You're not even thinking about me right now, are you? You're hot for those new clients of mine."

As much as I don't want to be, I can't help the way my body feels. Still, I don't want him to get the wrong idea. He's the fantasy. They're just the final straw. "Why would you think that?"

"I saw you practically licking the window while we were flipping tires today."

Busted.

"Does that bother you?" There's no point pretending I didn't go from zero to fuck-my-brains-out. I might as well tell him the whole truth. "I mean, I'm not thinking about them. I've been thinking about you a lot. For a while. But today gave me some new ideas to play with. About all three of you." I tap my temple with my finger. "Right in here, doing dirty things to me."

Joey thinks for a second too long for my pleasure before licking his lips. "That's actually really hot."

"Then shut up and get inside me."

We work together to get my panties down my legs, and I'm so close to getting them off when a shooting pain runs through my skull.

"Son of a bitch," I shout, holding my hand just above my eyebrow. "Did we just knock heads?"

Joey rubs a red mark on his own forehead. "Yeah, sorry. I was a little excited to get you naked again."

"Okay, well, for safety's sake, don't move. I'll finish this part." I finally get the offending panties off and toss them across the room, less self-conscious about my do-it-at-home grooming-gone-wrong than I should be. But seriously, I'm so horny at this point, I don't even care that it didn't turn out even remotely close to what my expensive waxer used to do. At least I didn't have to drop a huge tip after flashing the goods, and I'm still getting laid.

Finally, we seem to be working together and he pushes inside me, just as I shout, "Wait!"

He freezes. "What?"

"Aren't you going to use a condom?"

"Oh shit," he grumbles and drops his head on my shoulder. I feel my muscles already pulsing inside me. It's making it hard to concentrate on this conversation being that he's so close to hitting the exact right spot. "Hold on!" His head pops back up. "You're already pregnant. We're fine."

I push on his shoulders despite my desire just pull him closer. "But what about diseases?"

"Oh yeah. Do you have any?"

I scoff. "That was rude. Of course, I don't. You are the last person I was with, and my OB checks for all that in my blood work. I was talking about you."

"I had to get tested for a bunch of stuff when I signed up for Strongman. They would have caught it."

"So, you're clean?"

He nods. "I'm clean."

"Then go!" I instruct and grab his ass cheeks to push him further inside.

The movement feels so good, I moan my pleasure and push off the bed, gyrating my hips faster, hoping he'll get the hint and punch the gas, too. But he doesn't.

"What are you doing?" I complain. "Why are you moving so slow?"

"I don't know how fast I can go before I'll hurt the baby."

"Oh, for shit's sake. I can't take it anymore," I grumble and push him as hard as I can until he rolls over. I go right over with him, one leg on each side of his hips and make sure he's lined up with my entrance before dropping down on him again. My head falls back and I groan at the glorious feeling before setting my own pace and moving however I see fit. "For the record, you can't hurt the baby. He's well insulated in there, so the next time you are on top, you better fuck me like you mean it, got it?"

"Got it," he breathes, and I roll my hips faster and faster chasing the orgasm that's on its way. I feel Joey begin to flex underneath me. "So, you like thinking about three men with their hands all over your body?" he growls, and the thought makes my insides tighten up. "You like thinking about the looks on our faces when we strain our muscles just knowing that's what we look like when we come?"

Holy. Shit. Who knew I enjoyed some dirty talk?

"Keep talking," I beg.

"You're wondering if those are the noises we make during sex, aren't you?"

"Uh-huh."

"Well, let me reassure you," he says and nips my earlobe, sending a zing straight to my core. "That's exactly how we sound during sex."

I'm so close I want to cry. "If you move, I will rip your face off. You hit the spot with your dirty talk, do not screw it up for me."

He freezes, except for the laugh that rolls through him. The slight movement from his chuckle does exactly what I need, and the orgasm hits me fast and furious.

I groan so loud I'm almost screaming by the time I begin to come down from my high. At that exact moment Joey cries out, "Holy shit," his neck muscles strain gloriously, hair fanned out on the pillow as he finds his own big "o." And yes, it sounds exactly like when he works out. That's going to make things uncomfortable for me at work.

Completely spent, I fall onto his chest and we roll to the side, Joey's arm still wrapped around me, panting heavily. It's the most post-coital snuggling I've had in a while, and I have to admit, I kind of like it. For whatever reason, Joey makes me feel safe. Maybe it's because my bitchy attitude doesn't seem to bother him. Maybe because he's followed through with everything he's promised since the beginning. Maybe it's just because I'm coming off the best high there is. Regardless, I make no attempt to move.

"That was amazing," Joey sighs and kisses me on the forehead. "Don't you think it was amazing?"

This is one of those moments where I must decide if I'm going to be honest or if I'm going to stroke his ego. But since I've never been one to sugarcoat things, I give him the cold, hard truth.

"I've had better."

Joey lifts his head up and looks at me in disbelief. "Seriously?"

"Don't get me wrong, that orgasm hit the spot. But we also have bruises on our foreheads and stopped to discuss STDs. You're gonna honestly say that was the best sex you've ever had?"

He lays his head back down and thinks for a second before responding with, "You're right. The ending was great, but I've definitely had a better lead-up." Taking a deep breath, Joey runs his fingers through my hair before asking the question that was also on my mind. "So, you wanna do it again?"

"Yep," I respond without hesitation and roll him to his back to get this party started.

He makes sure to go faster this time.

And the time after that.

CHAPTER SEVENTEEN

JOEY

"I got your latest box, Mom. There's some good stuff in here." I inspect one of the prepackaged meals she ordered online from my favorite grocery store and had delivered. It's a chicken parmesan dish but it looks extra cheesy. That's going to hit the spot.

"They've really upped some of their options since we moved. Of course, I had to complain that three or four choices weren't going to cut it when this is what you're subsisting on lately."

"Hey now," I argue as I stack all the containers on top of each other in the fridge. "I have my protein shakes, too."

She tsks playfully. "You are so disciplined when it comes to food. Don't let that routine get in the way of feeding Rosalind. She needs extra nutrition as she grows my grandbaby, so make sure to feed her, too."

I chuckle because it's just like my mom to send over food for me, yet still worry I'm not going to share. "Don't worry. She knows she can eat whatever her body craves whenever she needs. And she was really appreciative of the ice cream you sent over."

"Oh good. I took a chance on her favorite kind. You tell her to make a list of whatever she wants, and I'll make sure it's included."

Closing the fridge, I begin grabbing the ingredients for tonight's dinner. So, spaghetti noodles and sauce. Two ingredients shouldn't be too hard to try.

"I can tell you right now she won't give you a list. Rosalind is wildly independent, so she'll never ask. If you want to make sure she's fed, just keep guessing. That's the only way she'll accept it."

"I like that," Mom says. "You need a strong, independent woman to keep you on your toes."

"That she is." And I kind of love her for it. But I don't say that out loud. The longer she lives her, the more I feel for her. But I'm still afraid of scaring her off. Her jumping me the other night was a definite step in the direction I want to go, but I'm still determined to go at her pace. The last thing I need is my mom pushing her too hard. And it is a valid concern.

Ever since my parents found out about the pregnancy, they've been ecstatic about Rosalind and the baby joining the family. My mother immediately went into grandma mode, and while I know she's sending food as a convenience to me while I train, I wouldn't at all be surprised if the boxes kept coming afterwards for Rosalind.

"Make sure you're taking care of her, Joseph." She first-named me. She's serious now. "Pregnancy isn't all rainbows and unicorns. It can be exhausting and disorienting. And not just on your body but your mind, too. Even if she's grumpy, give her grace."

"I promise I am. In fact, I'm going to make her dinner tonight."

"You mean you're going to heat up one of those meals and put it on a plate, so it looks like you did the hard work?"

My dad did that once. It's been a running joke between them how he tried to pull one over on my mom when they were dating, but she saw right through it. Come to think of it, he's probably where I got my lack of cooking skills from.

"Nope. I'm attempting spaghetti all by myself."

She huffs. "Oh boy. Good luck with that. I'll let you go to minimize your distractions. I love you, Joey. Don't burn the house down. And take care of my grandbaby!"

"I will! Love you, too."

We hang up and I pick up the spaghetti sauce jar, ready to get dinner started.

"*Pour the sauce in a medium-sized pot*," I read out loud off the back of the label. I've tried a few times to make the dish, but since it always goes badly, I figure it might help to read the instructions this time around.

Pulling out what I think is a medium-sized pot, I shrug. It's the medium one of the only three I own, so it will have to do. Fingers crossed it works and I don't get sauce all over the ceiling like I did last time. Elliott was pretty pissed when she came home to the mess. Or maybe she was just mad that I left before it was all cleaned up. Regardless, I don't have a ladder high enough to reach this ceiling, and I don't feel like going to the hardware store to rent one so I can do the dishes.

Still, Abel is right—I need to learn how to cook at least a few simple meals if Rosalind and I are going to cut down on expenses. My mother won't have premade, high-calorie meals delivered forever. Plus, a baby can't be raised on fast food. Or I don't think it can. Spaghetti seems like a good place to start. Kids like meals with noodles, right? Also, I know what *not* to do, so I might as well roll with it and see what happens.

Once the sauce has successfully been poured into the pot and placed on the stove, I pick up the jar for my next instructions.

"*Heat sauce on medium-low to medium heat*. Medium-low? What the hell does that mean?" I grumble as I stare at the controls on my stove top. I see a large M, so I assume that's close enough. I cross my fingers, then cross my chest, not because I'm Catholic but because I need all the help I can get, and go back to my written directions. "*Cook pasta according to instructions*. What instructions? You didn't give me any!" I slam it back down on the counter with a huff.

I throw my hands in the air and drop them onto my hips, not sure what I'm supposed to do now. I need to think about how to get this part done since the stupid sauce people aren't helping anymore. I've made noodles before with relative ease in the past. No explosions or fire. How did I do it?

I snap my fingers as the memory returns. Working quickly, I grab the bigger pot I have, break the spaghetti noodles in half and drop them in, then fill the pot with water to the halfway mark.

Wait.

Was I supposed to put the noodles in before or after the water?

No matter. They'll cook just the same. Or at least close enough. Looking at the sauce, I see it's slowly heating up as the electric burner brightens and dims, automatically adjusting the temperature.

I take a deep breath and blow it out, proud of myself for getting this far on my own. Maybe this won't be disastrous after all.

"What are you doing?"

Before I even look over, a smile crosses my face. The sound of Rosalind's voice does that to me. It's a new development since our night of intense, yet mediocre sex. I don't mind it. I actually kind of like it. It's as if my body has gotten on board with us being together for the next eighteen years or so as we build a little family. Not that it wasn't already hot for her.

"I am making you dinner." I quickly move to the fridge, where I pull out a loaf of pre-buttered garlic bread. All I have to do is cut it and heat it up.

Rosalind leans over and looks in the bigger pot. "Why are there noodles at the bottom of this… wait…" She puts her finger in the water and pulls it out in rapid succession a couple of times to make sure she isn't going to get burned. Then she looks closer. "Let me rephrase. Why are there *hard* noodles at the bottom of a pot of *cold* water?"

I give her an incredulous look, half-hearted as it may be. "It hasn't started boiling yet."

"It might help if you turn the burner on."

I glance up and, sure enough, I forgot the most important part. "Well, shit."

She smirks at me, but doesn't say anything, content to get the heat going as I continue to slice the bread and place it on a cookie sheet.

"I thought you didn't cook." Rosalind leans her body against the counter, small baby bump protruding under her tank top. The sight of her growing my baby hits me like a punch to the heart and I have a weird feeling in my chest—like a swelling of pride. I try to push all the emotion and protective thoughts I have out of my mind, though, knowing it's too soon to reveal those feelings to her. Rosalind has really started letting her guard down. I don't want her to think I'm being too clingy and not giving her space. I know she prides herself on her independence.

"I don't. But I need to learn. Babies need a healthy diet, not junk food and takeout every day, right?" I say by way of explanation. Rosalind just stares at me, like she's trying to figure out if I'm being for real or just yanking her chain.

Finally, she nods slowly. "Are you always a planner?"

I shoot her a smile and wipe my hands on a towel. "I don't seem like the type?"

"Not really," she says with a shrug. "But you just seem… I don't know. Prepared for all this." Rosalind gestures down to her baby bump, and I tamp down that same excitement that comes over me whenever I think about what's growing inside. I can't wait for my kid to be born. I just hope we can be a real family before then. If not, it won't change anything for me. I have to keep remembering that. "I'm still trying to wrap my brain around it all, I guess."

I carefully place the cookie sheet in the warmer at the very bottom of the oven. "I think you already know that I'm a pretty disorganized mess most of the time. But one thing I've learned about myself is that I'm really good under pressure. The more stressed I am, the better my work is."

"So, the exact opposite of basically everyone else in the world."

"Pretty much," I agree because she nailed it on the head. "It used to drive my high school English teacher crazy that I could slack off all semester long, and then at the last minute I'd pull out a five-hundred-word essay on whatever the topic was and make an A." I shrug. "But I've since learned that the skill can come in handy in certain situations. An unexpected baby just happens to be one of those situations."

"I like how you say that," she practically whispers, eyes down as if she's embarrassed to look at me.

"How I say what?"

"That it's an unexpected baby. Most people call it an unplanned pregnancy. I like your way better."

"I never thought about it, but yeah. I think I do, too."

Steeling her spine, Rosalind pushes her dark hair out of her face and stands up straight, almost challenging me to question how she feels. "It makes it hard to figure out how I'm supposed to feel. An unplanned pregnancy sounds too detached. But unexpected baby—that's what this is. Not a bad thing, just like a surprise. A big one for sure, but just… yeah."

"You still trying to figure out how you feel about all this?"

Her lips quirk to the side like she's trying to decide if she wants to smile or cry. When she shrugs, that's all I need to see.

I look at the stove and see nothing is boiling yet. "Come on." I grab her hand and squeeze. "We've got some time. Let's go sit and I'll give you a quick foot rub."

Her eyebrows shoot up in delight, and probably surprise as well. "Feet don't gross you out?"

"I'm a trainer. No parts of the body gross me out." I lace our fingers together and lead her into the living room so she can get comfortable.

"That's funny. I specifically remember you saying something about Abel's armpit making you want to puke the other day."

"There is a difference between regular body parts and him shoving his post-workout pit in my face for the sole purpose of making me gag."

She snorts a laugh and I like hearing that so much more than her feeling insecure about our new life. "Do you purposely try to come up with the most random stories to tell, or does it just come natural?"

"What do you think?"

She sits on one end of the couch and I sit on the other, grabbing her leg to bring her foot to my lap. She hesitates for only a second before relaxing into it. "I think you don't have a filter between your brain and your mouth, and you don't really care."

I chuckle as I begin kneading the bottom of her foot. The moan she lets out does nothing to keep me focused on the important part of this conversation—the part about feelings and shit. That noise brings memories of a different kind of feelings, and it's taking everything in me to not strip her tiny little shorts off her and enjoy a much tastier dinner.

But I refrain like the gentleman I am, because she doesn't normally talk out whatever is going on in her brain. I need to take advantage of this.

Plus, I can strategically add in a conversation about my new clients at some point and see if it brings back any more fantasies she needs to work out of her system, too.

I shrug to myself at the thought. I may be a good guy, but I still have a penis that likes to be used.

"I think you're right. I used to care more about what people thought, but it got exhausting around middle school, so I made the decision to stop caring."

"Wow. That's pretty profound for a preteen."

"It was much shallower than you think. That's when my chest started growing faster than anyone else's and the rumors circulated regularly that I stuffed my bra. Pretty traumatic for a twelve-year-old. Eventually, I got tired of trying to combat all the chatter, so I let it go. Or so I thought. I guess it carried into my adult life more than I knew until you pointed it out. I didn't think so at the time, but looking back, I agree. Maybe it wasn't so much about not caring as it was about pretending to not care."

I glance up as she pinches the bridge of her nose. "Headache?"

"Just a little one. I'm fine."

"Or are you worried about how this all looks to people, preteen wisdom be damned?"

Rosalind raises her head just slightly to look at me, then lays it back down. "I shouldn't care, and I think that's what pisses me off. I was a stripper for the entirety of my adult life. I don't give a fuck who cares that I took my clothes off for money. I like money. I like things. I'm materialistic like that and I just don't care. For God's sake, my mother knew. That's the epitome of not caring what others think when you have no problem telling your mother."

"But?"

She sighs and it's filled with heavy emotion. "I don't know why I feel differently about this. I don't want people to look at me like I've done something wrong, and it bothers me that it bothers me."

"Is it possible that it's not about people judging you, but because they're judging someone other than you?" I gesture to her belly which she immediately covers with her hands protectively.

"What does that mean?" she asks with fire in her eyes, and I know I've struck a nerve.

"Maybe you're less worried about what the people you know and love think of you and more worried what they think of our baby. Like your maternal instinct or whatever is kicking in and it bothers you that people might think of him as anything less than the perfection he is."

She opens her mouth to respond, then closes it again and looks away briefly. "I never thought of that. You think that's it? Why I feel so… I don't even know how to describe it. Just, not happy about people looking at me funny."

"Why not? Up until this point, it's always been about you." She shoots me a glare. "Like it's always been about me, too," I clarify. She nods once in concession and lays her head back again. "I know it feels different for me. He's not even here yet, and I already want to protect him from anything that might hurt him. And I don't have all the hormonal flushes to make me batshit crazy like you do."

Rosalind goes to kick me playfully for my comment, but since I've got her foot in my hand, all it does is make me laugh instead.

"My point is that I don't think you're weird or crazy or anything. I think you're just being a good mom. Like I'm trying to be a good dad. Hell, I'm trying to cook, and I don't do that."

"Speaking of," she mutters and sits up, pulling her foot out of my hands. "Do you smell something?"

"Can you smell water boiling?" I lean back to sniff and see smoke on the ceiling. "Oh shit!"

Jumping up from the couch, I run into the kitchen. The sauce looks good. The water pot still isn't boiling, no surprise there, but there is smoke billowing out from the oven.

Grabbing some pot holders, I pull it open and see flames shooting from the tops of my garlic bread.

"Dammit!" I yell and try to figure out how to put this shit out. What do you throw on a grease fire?

I race to the pantry looking for baking powder or cornstarch or whatever the fuck I'm supposed to use. My eyes catch on a bag of flour that I had no idea was there. Will that work?

"Fuck it," I mutter. "Good enough."

I rip the unused package open and toss the flour on the flames. It immediately explodes back onto me with a soft *poooof* sound.

Rosalind shrieks, but I don't think she's injured. It's hard to tell through the fluffy white cloud of flour now surrounding me and every single surface of the room.

"You don't throw flour on a fire!" she yells at me. "It's baking soda!"

I point down to the oven, which is no longer on fire and remark, "It worked, didn't it?"

She coughs and waves her hand in front of her unnaturally white face. The good thing about a cloud of flour is it falls to the ground pretty quickly. The bad news is that it falls on everything else as well. Including us. This is going to take hours to clean up.

"Why did you put the bread in the broiler anyway?"

"What's a broiler?"

Rosalind eyes me like I'm the idiot she apparently thinks I am, and I grab the pot holders again to pull the now ruined bread from the oven. Tossing it on the counter, the tops are a mixture of charred black and fluffy white, and obviously no longer edible.

"It's like super concentrated heat to cook meat when you can't grill. How high did you set it?"

"How should I know? I just turned it on. Nowhere on this appliance does it label the bottom part of the oven as a broiler I shouldn't use. And why didn't you say anything?"

She turns off the stovetop heat since there's no way to salvage the rest of our meal either. The one time my sauce looks decent, and a stupid fire ruins it. Figures.

Pushing the pots off the burners, Rosalind says, "I thought you knew. From now on, how about you stick to using the microwave only."

I grimace.

"Oh god. You caught the microwave on fire, too, didn't you?"

"How was I supposed to know you can't keep the aluminum foil on the plate?"

She facepalms. I mean literally smacks her face with her palm. It's a good thing I'm hot, because I'm obviously not impressing her with my culinary skills. "Never mind. From now on, you get to use the blender. I'll do the very little cooking I know how to do, we can eat from the boxes your mom sends, and we'll eat out the rest of the time."

"Fine by me," I grumble, feeling oddly embarrassed that I can't even figure out how to warm garlic bread. There is no way I'm going to be able to warm a bottle.

"Believe it or not, you can put all kinds of fruits and vegetables in the blender to make baby food. That will be your contribution to the healthy eating of this child, okay?"

My mood perks up. "I didn't even think of that. I can make organic baby food. In fact, maybe we can all start raw eating. I hear it's fantastic for your immune system."

"Let's not get too crazy. You forget you have to be vegan to eat raw. I highly doubt you can give up your meat-loving ways simply because it's harder to catch a blender on fire."

She has a point on that one. Still, if anyone can get flames from a spinning blade, it's probably me.

"Fine. We'll try it your way. But you better hope our baby doesn't starve."

She chuckles lightly as she begins wiping flour off the counter and into her hand. "Oh, Joey. When it comes to our offspring, I'm worried about so much more than just starvation."

CHAPTER EIGHTEEN

ROSALIND

"I am going to be a grandmother, Rosalind. You need to do this for me."

I pull the phone away from my ear and roll my eyes as my mother rants and raves about why I need to have a baby shower. A baby shower I don't want to have because who the hell would I invite? My family? Sounds painful.

The other thing that's painful? Putting the phone back to my ear so I can try to end this hellacious conversation.

"Mom…"

"No. You don't get to be selfish this time, Rosalind Magdalena," she continues to berate, pulling out the big guns with my middle name.

"How am I being selfish by not wanting people to give me things? Isn't that the exact opposite of being selfish? I'm thinking of others."

"I wasn't born yesterday, Rosalind, and neither were you. This is about you not liking people."

She's not totally wrong. Typically, I don't like people. For the record, I love my family, just in small doses, which she doesn't seem to understand and it's starting to give me a headache.

"You don't have to try and convince me otherwise, because Lord knows I am your mother, so of course you don't think I know anything…"

Aaaand here we go again with the guilt tactics.

"… call one of your girlfriends who has kids and ask her. Like Abel's wife. She's a good woman. She'll tell you the truth."

"She's not his wife, Mom."

"They're married in the eyes of the Lord, Rosalind. Just like you're married in the eyes of the Lord to Joey."

That catches my attention and makes me want to vomit at the idea of a lifelong commitment. I think. Then again, we're talking about Joey and I could see myself being forever with him. I like him. A lot. I might even have the beginnings of love for him, but I'm not one hundred percent sure that's how I feel and it's not partially influenced by my womb, so I'm waiting to decide for sure. "How the hell do you come to that conclusion?"

"Jesus knows when you have relations, Rosalind. It cements your commitment to each other."

I shake my head, trying to rid myself of the biblical babble she continues to toss my way. I would never dismiss her religious beliefs. Hell, half of them I share with her. But sometimes I wonder exactly what theology she's subscribing to.

Actually, I know which one—the religion of Mom-Is-Always-Right.

Regardless, I need to get off the phone before she makes me want to drown myself in a rum and Coke. I think that might be frowned upon in my current state.

"Well, I'm glad to know Jesus thinks I'm married, because then He no longer thinks I'm a sinner." She makes a noise when she realizes her own words just backfired. That gives me about one-point-five seconds to finish the conversation. "So now that I've brushed off some of that guilt, I need to go call Elliott to talk about this baby shower thing."

Am I really going to call her? Doubtful. But at least it'll get me off the phone.

And go figure, my mother goes for it. "Yes, yes. Call her right now. I need to start planning anyway."

"I haven't said yes yet, Mom!"

"You don't have to. Elliott will help you make the right choice. Now, go make that call while I check out these decorations at TJ Maxx. Oooh! Taffeta tablecloths in pink!"

The call disconnects before I can put my foot down about anything that might include taffeta. Suddenly, it's not the idea of the baby shower that's making me break out into a cold sweat, it's the idea of my mother hosting it.

I can just see it now—blue and pink balloons, probably an ice sculpture of my protruding belly, and no doubt there will be a cake in the shape of a baby that she makes me cut the head off of. Because that's the kind of thing my mother would do and never even realize how inappropriate it is because never mind that she's a Palmer, "It's the DiSoto way." I'd rather Joey attempt to cook dinner again. Far less damage to my psyche.

I shift on the couch so I'm lying all the way down and rub my hand over my protruding bump, my GED prep book on the coffee table catching my eye. I sigh and flip the offending material the bird. I decided to bite the bullet and start studying for the test, so I spent money I didn't have on the book. Stupidly, I assumed everything I learned in high school would come right back to me just by reading up on it. It didn't. So now I'm discouraged because I probably need to take a night course to prepare, I'm pissed I don't have the money for a night course, and I'm angry that it's the first step to getting my pole fitness certification, per their requirements.

The whole thing is causing an emotional spiral to begin in my brain. If I'm not smart enough to get the equivalent of a high school diploma, how the hell am I going to be able to raise a baby? You need to know things like how to tell when they're sick and side effects of vaccines and other shit I know nothing about. Because I know nothing about anything, and I just want it all to go away.

I know I'm thinking irrationally, but the downward slope is brewing and I don't know how to stop it. It's yet another reason I'm resistant to my mother's idea.

It's not that I don't want a shower. I assume there is some baby stuff I need, and it would be helpful if I didn't have to buy it. But having a party where every woman there is doting on me and trying to rub my stomach and telling all their horrifying stories of when they had babies doesn't sound appealing at all. It actually sounds like a nightmare, especially considering Aunt Angela told me all about her five-inch-long episiotomy when I was twelve. It was her way of giving me appropriate church-approved birth control. Now that there's no need for birth control, I can only imagine how much worse the stories will be. The only thing my family loves more than spreading guilt, is spreading fear, and childbirth is the perfect topic for it.

I feel a nudge under my ribs which momentarily makes me forget that someday this thing has to come out of me, and I smile instead. "What do you think, huh? Do you think we need to have a party with all the obnoxious family to celebrate you?" Another nudge, like he's got an opinion on it. "You just want the presents." This time the nudge is fast and hard. If I didn't know better, I'd say it was an intentional kick. "Okay, okay," I say with a sigh, resigning myself to the fact that I need an ally in this because it's happening whether I want it to or not. "I'll call Elliott now. Stop kicking me."

The baby stops moving, and I know I've officially lost my first battle of wills with this kid. Figures I'd already be caving just to make my life easier. Yet another way I will probably fail as a mother.

Picking up the phone, I prepare to call the one person who knows how to remedy the control battle I already have with my child, and who I trust to give me the information I need about celebrating its arrival. Well, mostly trust. I trust her with my and my baby's life, but not necessarily with Joey's. They like to pull one over on each other too much. Eh. That's his problem.

I take a deep breath and blow it out, not because I'm nervous, but because I'm irritated. Elliott isn't the one that put me in a bad mood, so it's probably a good idea to shake it off before she answers.

Singing a couple bars to Taylor Swift's hit that I actually hate but seems appropriate in the moment, I shake my arms out and dial.

It only takes a couple of rings before she picks up, but she can't say much of anything over what sounds like mass chaos in the background.

"Hello? Hello, Rosalind?" she yells, probably because she can't hear herself over the noise. Hell, I can barely hear her over all the commotion.

"Elliott?" I yell right back, like that's even going to help. "What's going on over there? Are you at work?"

"Hello? Hold on."

I hear rustling in the background as she tells at least three people what to do, not including the child she has to calm down and send on his or her way. It's an enlightening, and frankly terrifying, two minutes of my life. Two minutes of reminders that I have no idea what I'm getting myself into when I pop.

Finally, the noise dies down and I hear the *snick* of a door closing. "Okay, sorry about that. Is everything okay, Rosalind?"

"It's fine on my end, but it sounds like you're having a rough day."

She laughs, which is the strangest reaction I've ever heard to what sounds like a hellacious day. "We had an unfortunate accident with a homework table falling over and paint spilling all over the floor. I think we've got it cleaned up—well, as best as we can without some professional help—but it was rough trying to keep all the kids out of the mess. That led to babies being mad they couldn't crawl through it and toddlers wanting to make footprints everywhere. You know, the usual after-school kid-crowd stuff."

"Uh… actually no. I don't know any of that at all, but you're not making a good case for parenthood right now." And confirming that I know nothing. Although she is making me extremely glad my shift ends at three thirty. I wouldn't want to have to clean up that room at the end of the day.

Once again, she finds humor in my fear. Holy shit, she really does fit in with the family. Maybe calling her wasn't such a good idea.

"I promise, you are going to be fine," she tries to soothe, but it's not working at this point. "Incidents like these happen, but they're few and far between. Plus, you've got some time until the baby will be big enough to create chaos."

Except… "You forget I live with Joey."

Elliott pauses. For a really long time. Before finally making this weird deflating-balloon sound as she speaks. "Yeeeeeah, so maybe you just should plan for the worst and hope for the best."

"You know that's not encouraging, right?" I glance around the living room, noting that his bachelor pad didn't come with a bunch of breakables I'll have to put away. At least there's that.

"I don't really have much encouragement to give now that you reminded me of Joey's involvement. He's babysat my kids way too many times for me to forget the tornado he leaves behind. At least he's old enough to clean up after himself. When he wants to, anyway."

"He didn't clean up all the flour in the kitchen," I grumble under my breath, remembering how long it took to make a dent in that storm and how I keep finding more white dust in the most random places. Seriously. How does it get inside a sealed refrigerator?

"What? I'm sorry I thought I heard someone call me from the other room, so I got distracted."

"Oh nothing," I lie quickly because he and I agreed to keep the fire incident between us. No sense in giving anyone a reason to pop in and check on us regularly. "So, listen, my mom wants to throw me a baby shower."

"Fantastic!" Elliott remarks immediately and my hope that she'll give me a plausible excuse to decline participating in such an irritating event are dashed.

I groan. "You think it's a good idea?"

"Of course, I do! Free baby stuff? Heck yeah! Babies may be tiny, but everything they need is expensive and it adds up."

"What do you mean it's expensive? I wandered through the baby aisle at the store the other day and a shirt was like three dollars."

"Have you not started looking into what you'll need?"

"Nope. I'm in full-on avoidance mode."

"Well, let me give you a quick rundown. Clothes can be supercheap if you get them at the right place. But that's not what you really need. Car seats and diapers and not just those basic necessities are where the money goes. The things that will make your life easier."

I sit straight up as quickly as my protruding belly will allow. Once again, I realize I still know nothing at all. "What does that mean? Things to make my life easier."

"Oh boy, you'll need a swing almost immediately because the baby will probably like the rocking motion. A bassinet to move from room to room so you have a place to put the baby down. A rocking chair was a lifesaver when it came to putting Ainsley to sleep. She refused to close her eyes if I didn't rock her for at least thirty minutes. Oh! An Exersaucer for when the baby starts to get bored on the floor and wants to move around more but isn't ready for sitting up! A Bumbo… I almost forgot that one. Bottles, probably a wrap of some sort for close contact when he's tiny, a baby bathtub and a bouncy chair for sure…"

Elliott continues to list off what seems like hundreds of items I've never heard of in my life. I can practically see the price tags in my mind and the math of how much this kid is going to cost me makes my brain want to explode. There is so. Much. And Elliott's still going.

"… a crib and all the bedding is a no-brainer, of course. Also I highly recommend a Tula…"

"Wait!" I interrupt, wishing I had a piece of paper to write all this down because there's no way I'm going to remember it all. "What the hell is a Tula and why do I need it?"

"It's a kind of front pack that can also be a backpack. You'll need it to keep your baby close to you when he or she is too big for the wrap."

"I don't even know what a wrap is! I used to eat those at Subway."

Elliott sighs and I know it's in resignation to my stupidity. Because that's how I feel —really, really dumb. How am I supposed to know how to take care of my baby if I don't even know I need these things?

My breathing picks up and I make a conscious effort to slow it down, so I don't hyperventilate. It does me no good to panic. Although maybe if I have a meltdown, Joey will take over all this and I can just sit back and play with the new baby things. Something to consider when I have some alone time.

"Rosalind," she says gently, "I can tell you hate the idea of having a baby shower."

The reminder of why I called her in the first place coupled with my newfound crippling anxiety morphs into this weird kind of anger I've not felt before. It's more intense than a strong irritation and teeters on ripping everyone's heads off, even if they don't deserve it. "I don't need a bunch of people pawing at me and telling all their childbirth war stories."

"I agree. And unfortunately, there is nothing you can do about that part." I grunt in frustration. I was hoping she'd tell me I had it all wrong and no one does that except in the movies. So much for feeling better. "But that part is less important than the presents."

I pinch that spot right between my eyes. It doesn't help with the tension at all. It never does. "I want to make sure I understand this. You want me to have a baby shower for the gifts? Like, not for the people or the celebration but for the presents?

That is the exact opposite of what my mother has been preaching to me about my selfish behavior for probably fifteen years."

"I feel like you're just making excuses," she says with a chuckle. I'm glad one of us thinks this is a hoot. "But think of it this way… if you don't know what you're going to need, you won't go out and buy it. On the other hand, all these women who have done it before can anticipate what's coming and get you everything, so you're prepared. It cuts down on having to figure it out later. You just have to listen to a few war stories to hit the jackpot. You get the additional bonus of making all these women happy at once for allowing them to have a party."

As much as I hate to admit it, she's kind of right. Maybe someone will get me that Tula thing, so I don't have to shell out the cash for it, too.

"Tell ya what," she finally says, breaking the silence since I can't seem to figure out how to respond to all this. "How about I call your mom and offer to help co-host it."

I gasp. Coming to the shower is sacrifice enough. But co-hosting? With *my mother*? That's just above and beyond.

"You'd do that?" I whisper, still in disbelief and not wanting to speak so loudly that she realizes what she's offered and change her mind.

"Of course, I would." Her words hold no hesitation in them whatsoever. It's good to know the DiSoto clan doesn't overwhelm her like they do me sometimes. "I'll tell her it's so I can get the addresses for all our work friends' invitations and to help coordinate gifts. Which is true."

Except that part will take less than half an hour. Tops. Even if she gets sidetracked by a rogue kid who breaks out of her room. "You know I don't have many work friends, right? Basically, you're it. And kind of by default because you're living with my cousin."

It sounds like she takes a breath through her nose and I have the bad feeling I just offended her. But it's true. Women don't usually like me, so I never went out of my way to make friends at the gym.

"I think you underestimate how much people like and appreciate you at work." I hear Elliott's words, but I'm having a hard time understanding them.

"But… all I do is clean up after people," I argue with that self-depreciating tone I'm getting used to. What happened to all my confidence? I think it disappeared the first time I had to help unclog a toilet in the men's locker room. Nothing humbles you more than having to wear a face mask and gloves to clean up someone else's shit.

"Rosalind, you do your job without complaint or being rude to clients. You work hard and chat with people. The elderly ladies talk about how cute you are all the time," she says with a chuckle. "You're better with people than you think you are. And the women at work like you more than you know. In fact, Tabitha was asking me the other day what you needed for the baby so she could start shopping."

"She did?"

"Of course, she did! You're part of the family now in so many ways."

I bite my bottom lip as I let her words sink in. This news is just mind boggling. I had no idea people at work cared about me like that. I have a hard time believing it. It was never that way at my last job. There was an element of sticking together at the club because you just can't take your clothes off in front of strangers without having each other's backs at least a little bit, but it wasn't ever really like a family. Girls would rotate in and out on a regular basis and let's face it—we were all there for the money. Competition for the regulars who dropped the most cash in the G-string was pretty fierce. This new thought process of caring about your co-workers is very different.

Clearing my throat, I'm grateful to Elliott for letting me sit on my thoughts for a few minutes. There is so much to think about these days, half the time I can't figure out what I'm processing before it poofs right out of my brain and onto some other topic. Hell, even my keys keep going missing. I found them in the freezer yesterday. I still don't know why I put them there.

"Okay, fine. I'll have a stupid baby shower," I say resigning myself to my fate.

"Yay!" Elliott yells, but I cut her off.

"Do I have to do anything for it?"

"Just tell us a date that works for you and go get registered as soon as possible."

"Register? Like you do for a wedding?"

"Yep. Same exact thing. But you do it for baby items. You can do it at just about any big box store. It mostly depends on which one you want to shop at, so just pick whatever is most convenient for you."

I sigh again, still feeling overwhelmed by this plan. But if I have one thing to cling to right now, it's that Elliott knows what she's doing. She's successfully raised a kid that's still alive, she runs the childcare center at work, and she's willing to work with my mother. At this point, she's the best ally I have in my new, strange life.

"Okay. I'm due May fourth, so just tell me when you want to do it, and I'll be there."

"Oh, a Star Wars baby. Fun!"

"Yeah, well, as long as no one shows up with any R2D2 shit, I'll even pretend to smile at this thing. And won't punch anyone who touches my stomach. But that's the best I can offer."

"Great! I'll get with your mom, and we'll get it all sorted out. It's going to be okay, Rosalind. I promise you won't regret it."

Funny—I already do.

CHAPTER NINETEEN

JOEY

Rosalind went ahead and moved into my room. We never talked about it, it just sort of became this unspoken thing that she was more comfortable with me than without. It may actually be my very comfortable bed, but I'm choosing to believe it's my company. Or my ability to scratch the itch her pregnancy hormones have kicked into overdrive. Or the foot rubs I give her after scratching said itch.

Either way, about a month ago, I had a lightbulb moment: Rosalind doesn't like talking about her feelings very much. It makes her so uncomfortable she avoids it at all costs. She also doesn't like asking for what she needs. She'd rather do it on her own until she hits a certain breaking point, and then she bowls over anyone who gets in her way. When all of that hit me, I also realized I was tired of pretending she wanted her own space. I took a chance and made the decision for her with no fanfare or heartfelt emoji eyes. Just matter-of-factly moved her clothes into my closet.

I half expected her to throw my clothes in her old room and kick me out of mine, but the only reaction she had when she found them was a slight raise of her eyebrows after which she promptly tromped down the hallway. I was a little nervous for a few minutes, but then she reappeared with what had to be all her undergarments and various other items from her dresser. After shoving all my stuff into two of the drawers, she settled her stuff into the other two, slammed the drawer shut, and climbed into bed. She never said a word as she did it, but the intention was clear—she had moved in to stay. And I had figured out a huge piece of the puzzle that is Rosalind Palmer and her lack of relationship skills.

All that complete, it appears we have an actual room for the baby. It still needs to be decorated, but I think we've both been in avoidance mode on that part. Me, because I'm not good at decorating and don't want to make any decisions without her. Her, probably because she's overwhelmed. More than once I've caught her with a deer-in-the-headlights look when anything remotely close to pregnancy, childbirth, or being a parent comes up in conversation. She doesn't think I notice, but I do. I just don't say anything about it knowing once a deer unfreezes, they run. I don't want Rosalind's "fight or flight" to kick in.

Just the other day, Abel was bitching about having to help his girls do their science fair projects, and I swear Rosalind turned green. I made quick work of figuring out where the nearest trash can was, in case I needed to grab it to catch her barf.

Fortunately, the conversation moved on to something else and the moment passed. But the look on her face kind of haunts me, to be honest. I knew this massive life change was going to be hard, but I don't think I fully appreciated exactly how much fear Rosalind is hiding until then. Just another piece to the puzzle I'm fitting together.

Unless it's too important to avoid, for instance, making sure I know when doctor's appointments are, I try sticking to non-baby topics, like the fact that the Strongman competition is one month away.

Fortunately for me, the event happens to fall on the same day as Rosalind's baby shower, which she keeps referring to as the "Day of Judgement for having premarital sex."

Knowing there will likely be a few extra rosaries tossed her way that day, I'm more excited than I should be to have a valid reason for not going. Not that I needed one. I'm almost positive Elliott said no men were allowed. And even if she didn't say that, it would still be my excuse. Ask for forgiveness instead of permission, right?

With so many things coming up in the next thirty days, the one thing we haven't been able to avoid is baby shopping. I tried really hard to get out of it. I'm pretty sure Rosalind did too, but I put in extra effort to stay home. I hate shopping for myself when I have opinions on what I want, and since I genuinely don't care what color comforter the baby has, this is extra painful. Plus, he still won't show us his genitals, so it's not like I can shop for appropriate toys anyway. Call me misogynistic if you want, but I'm allowed to dream of my little boy being a football player and my little girl being a princess, and I'd like to know which one I should be investing in right now. Until they're old enough to tell me otherwise, I'm just going with the kinds of toys I know. So, excuse me for not wanting to shop for baby items I'm not even going to get to play with… I mean buy.

"Whhhhyyyyyy do I have to come with you to do this?" I whine for the umpteenth time, as I follow Rosalind through the sliding doors of whatever store this is. I didn't bother looking at the sign. As soon as she said "baby store," I had a single moment of pride for her ability to face the music before my brain melted.

"Because this is your baby, too, so you get to suffer right along with me," she reminds me yet again. "And because we have less than two months until this kid gets here, and we have nothing except the baby Yoda plush you found at the corner store and the baby blanket Nonna knitted for us."

"That was for the baby?" I'm trying to figure out how the yarn monstrosity could possibly have been intended for a seven-pound child to use.

Rosalind looks over her shoulder at me, brows furrowed. "What did you think it was for?"

"Honestly, I thought she forgot to stop knitting. It's so big, it can go on a king-sized bed and still drag on the floor. Seriously, Rosalind, that thing is huge. If we wrapped the baby up in it, we'd never find him again."

"That's why we put it away until the baby is old enough to use it."

"Better hope he turns into a giant eventually. And that we don't have moths while we wait." We round a corner and I realize we're walking straight through the store, not even stopping to actually shop. "Where are we going anyway?"

"The lady on the phone said the place to register is in the very back. Oh, see?" She points to a "Baby Registration" sign dangling from the ceiling.

"We don't need to register for a baby. We already have one."

"Nice try, but you still aren't getting out of this. We're registering for the baby shower. Now, take a seat while we wait for the nice lady."

Rosalind and I both drop into identical black leather office chairs. The desk in front of us seems really out of place amongst what is likely hundreds of cribs of all shapes and sizes and even more options in baby décor. There are elephants and giraffes and clowns and whales, standard stripes and checkerboard, and what I think might be called gingham, but I'm not that well versed in patterns and fabric. It is equally impressive and overwhelming that we have to choose from all these options. My great-great-grandmother didn't know how good she had it when she shoved her babies in a drawer and called it a crib.

"Hi! Are you guys here to register?" a chipper voice asks as the owner of said voice carefully lowers herself into the chair across from us. She is blonde and buxom, and I'm ninety-nine percent sure Rosalind is already contemplating throat punching her because of how big her smile is.

"Yeah, um, I have an appointment. Rosalind Palmer?"

Miss Chipper, who has no ring on her finger, so I feel confident in calling her that, begins typing away on her computer. "Oh yes. Right here. Baby Palmer-Marshall."

Surprised and oddly delighted, I turn to Rosalind. "You put my last name on the registration?"

In the surly tone she almost always uses when she's uncomfortable, she gives me the answer I should have expected. "I already told you, you're not getting out of this. And if you ever try, I've already got a paper trail with your name on it."

I laugh out loud because she's just so damn amusing when she acts all tough and pissy. Not that I doubt for one second she'd drag my ass to court and take me for everything I'm worth if I ever tried to ditch our kid. But still, she's funny.

Miss Chipper on the other hand, is slightly less amused. She actually looks a bit afraid. Oh well. Maybe her fear will get us out of here faster.

Clearing her throat, she begins pulling supplies out of the desk drawer. "Have you ever registered with us before?"

"No. This is our first time of registering anywhere, actually," Rosalind says, using a much kinder tone on her than she did on me.

"Okay. Well, here is a list of instructions on how to use the scanners." She slides a paper and pen across the desk. "If you'll read through that and sign at the bottom. Basically, it says you won't break the scanners, and if you do, you'll pay for them." Her eyes shift over to mine quickly as if I'm the one she needs to worry about. I've never once dropped my weapon during laser tag. This doesn't look much different.

"Sounds reasonable," I chime in, ignoring her rudeness. "Are they hard to use?"

"Oh no. Just point and shoot. But you'd be surprised how many people have a hard time figuring them out."

I actually wouldn't. Harriet and Edna couldn't figure out how to speed walk around the track the other day without running into each other. No way would they figure out a scanner gun.

Once the paper is signed, she hands us the scanner and, suddenly, shopping doesn't sound so daunting after all. Rosalind grabs a map of the store and we head on our way to put some items on our registry.

I put my arm around her and pull her close. "I wonder if we could play laser tag in the aisles," I whisper in Rosalind's ear, so Miss Chipper doesn't overhear. "That sounds way more fun than deciding which of these cribs to get."

Rosalind laughs and I love knowing I got her out of her head long enough to make it happen. "I agree, but we've been delaying this trip for a month. Getting one more phone call from my mother bitching about how none of her friends know what we want isn't worth putting it off any longer."

I grunt my response understanding her concern. I was the unlucky recipient of Mona's wrath when Rosalind finally had enough and gave her my phone number as well. Looks like we're stuck shopping.

"I don't get why there are so many cribs to choose from." I run my hand across the cherrywood hand railing of a baby bed that looks good enough to me. Maybe we can just scan this one and move on. "Aren't they all basically the same?"

"I have no idea. I finally tried looking online to interpret all the different options, but I could never make heads or tails of any of it, so I gave up. The only thing I do know is we don't want this one."

"Why?"

She holds up the price tag.

"Fifteen hundred bucks?" I accidentally yell. "Holy shit! Is this thing made of gold?"

I turn as a throat clears behind me. Miss Chipper's face is pinched, and I've clearly done something wrong. "Mr. Marshall, please remember this is a children's store."

I shake my head slightly, not understanding what she's trying to say and not in the mood to read between the lines after having such a shock to my system over what kind of racket these baby bed companies have going on.

She huffs and rolls her eyes. "Please watch your language. Some of our patrons don't want their kids exposed to those kinds of words."

"Oh shit, sorry," I respond and immediately realize I did it again. "I mean, oh shoot."

She gives me a tight smile and goes back to her work. Rosalind, on the other hand, is not trying very hard to hide her enjoyment in the situation.

"Ooooh…. You got in troubllllllle."

I fling my arm around her shoulder again and pull her as close as her belly will allow. She doesn't resist, only laughs and falls in line with me as we head to a less surveilled part of the room, which I admit to liking a lot. I don't need eyes on me while I gasp over these prices. "You hush. You are just as much to blame."

"What? What did I do?"

"You shouldn't have flashed me that price tag. Miss Chipper is lucky I didn't drop an f-bomb."

"Miss Chipper?"

"That's what I was calling her in my head before I was reprimanded. I'm kind of wishing I picked a different nickname now."

Rosalind slaps me lightly on the chest and proceeds to drag me around the store, looking for things we'll need.

We spend close to an hour trying to figure out what is an actual necessity, what's going to get shoved in a closet only to be forgotten about, what half the stuff actually does, and what color any of it should be. That one ended up being easy—we decided on green. It seems the most gender neutral but isn't ugly. That was the only easy decision.

And still, after sixty long minutes of reading boxes and instructions, we have officially registered for a stroller, a car seat that very well may be the wrong size, and pacifiers.

That's it.

Our baby is never going to survive with us as parents.

We end up back at our starting point—in the middle of zillions of cribs.

“Well, I’ll never get that hour of my life back,” Rosalind says as she drops her bag on the floor, carefully contorts her body into a bending-over position so she can riffle around inside it, and pulls out a hairband. She has no idea how hot I find it when she pulls her hair up into a messy bun. Not only does her dark hair contrast nicely against the creamy skin of her neck, but it also makes her boobs stick out with her arms raised like that. These days, they’re bigger than they were. I have no complaints.

I bet Miss Chipper would have a stroke if she knew about the visual images going through my brain right now in her kids’ store.

Dropping her hands to rub her belly once her hair is secure, she adds, “Do you feel as annoyed as I do by all this crap? Can’t there just be one option of everything to make it easy?”

“Or maybe an aisle that labeled ‘you will definitely need this’ next to the aisle marked ‘you might need this, so come back later if you do.’”

“Ohmigod yes. That would make things so much easier.”

“I still have no idea what crib we need to zap, but after looking around at all this themed stuff, can we agree on one thing?”

“What’s that?”

“No clowns. None. Ever. We are not scaring our baby that way.”

Rosalind laughs and replies with “agreed” before reaching down to grab her bag off the floor. At least I thought that’s what she was doing until she suddenly peeks over the headboard and belts out, “Think fast!” then points the scanner right at me in laser tag fashion.

On instinct, I dive for the floor, then do what’s supposed to be a ninja roll away, but I’m sure it looks more like a belly flop. Safely hidden behind something that is labeled a 3-in-1 convertible bed, whatever that means, I quickly stand and shoot at Rosalind who attempts to ducks down with a shrieking laugh. She fails miserably.

I do another ninja roll-slash-duck walk and secure my position behind what I think is either a changing table or a cart for tools in the garage. With this many drawers, it could go either way. I listen momentarily, trying to decipher where Rosalind is, when I hear soft footsteps and I know I’ve got her.

Standing quickly, I point the gun right at her, a smile on my face. A smile that drops almost immediately when I realize it’s not my baby mama, but Miss Chipper. And she is not amused. But in true professional form, she pastes a very fake smile on her face and slowly takes the scanner out of my hand.

"I'm more than happy to help you two decide what items you'd like to add to your registry. It's part of my job to make sure our customers have a…" She pauses and searches for a word that accurately reflects her thoughts without coming right out and saying we're annoying the shit out of her. "… productive experience. Why don't we start right where we're at and build your nursery from here?" Turning away from me and to face Rosalind, who looks about at shell-shocked as I feel, she asks, "Do you know if you're having a boy or a girl?"

Rosalind just shakes her head, no words coming out of her mouth.

"A surprise baby. Those are always fun." Miss Chipper seems to relax a bit, which is great for her, but not so good for Rosalind, who has gone from carefree to so tense her glutes are going to be hard as rocks if she doesn't stop clenching so hard. "Now, what kind of theme have you decided on?"

"No clowns." Rosalind and I say it in unison. I smirk at her because I can't help feeling like we're starting to get on the same page. It's us and our baby against the world. Or at least against small retail tyrants.

Miss Chipper sighs deeply and with clear exasperation. I'm almost positive when she clocked in this morning, she wasn't planning on spending half her day with a couple of clueless parents-to-be.

She should have just left us to our laser tag. Instead, she escorts us around the building, pointing out items we will likely need and giving us the merits of each one. Who knew there were different-sized bottle nipples depending on how old the baby is? I sure didn't.

Judging by the look on Rosalind's face, she didn't either and it's really shaken her. I squeeze her shoulder in support and she gives me a pained smile, then nods at whatever Miss Chipper has said.

For most people, this would probably be fun, but for us it's creating a whole new level of stress. I make a mental note to grab come chocolate-drizzled popcorn from the store on our way home for Rosalind to munch on while I give her an extra-long foot rub tonight. It's the only thing I can think of that may relax her again.

I just hope this trip ends up being worth it.

CHAPTER TWENTY

ROSALIND

Six weeks.

That's all I have left of my life as I know it.

That's actually not completely accurate. The life I loved since I was eighteen years old—one that included an awesome apartment, a regular stylist, waxing, nails, massages, shopping for whatever I wanted whenever I felt like it—all the things that made me *me* ended the minute I peed on a stick that turned bright pink. Sure, quitting my job and moving in with Joey were sacrifices I was willing to make and would again if needed for my child, but those are probably the only good things I've done as a mother so far.

The longer I'm pregnant, the more I realize I'm ill-equipped, under-prepared, overwhelmed, and downright bitchy as I prepare for yet another major life change. It honestly is taking everything in me these days to not fall into a pit of despair. I don't know if that's hormones talking or a sign of depression, but the one thing keeping me going is Joey.

Never did I expect that a man I met at a strip club, one who shoved money in my side string and dropped me on my head during sex, would end up being my rock through the most difficult time in my life. He hasn't only followed through with everything he promised, he also seems to know me better than I know myself sometimes. It's like he can anticipate when I'm going to start freaking out and knows exactly how to calm me.

Yes, I am referring to his foot rubs, and yes, they are that magical. Or maybe it's the intent behind them. I don't know what I would do without him and that terrifies me. Every day I fall for him a little more and I don't know if I'll survive without his stupid jokes and wide smiles every day. No one has ever cared for me the way Joey has the last few months, including anyone with the last name Palmer or DiSoto.

It's not that my family doesn't care. They just like to talk in circles, lovingly berate, and add a solid dose of that famous Catholic guilt before pitching in to help when there is a problem. This very hands on, anticipating my needs before they come up, jumping in to make my life easier that Joey does without a second thought, is brand-new behavior to me.

It scares the crap out of me because I like it so much. I'm already preparing for my heart to be stomped on in the future. I know the statistics. Relationships that start the way ours did typically don't go well.

But here in the present, I have to focus on the bigger problems. I get to spend the next six hours in a childbirth and parenting class. Not my idea of fun, but something Joey felt we both needed so we could be prepared. His motto seems to be "knowledge is power." My motto remains solidly in the "ignorance is bliss" area.

Yet somehow, he convinced me to agree (probably while pressing that sweet spot on my arch), and so here I am, waddling into a classroom in the office wing of the hospital. Standard blue carpet is on the floor with standard dark blue plastic chairs placed in uneven rows.

"This is going to be a really uncomfortable six hours," I grumble and rub my lower back. In the last two weeks, I've gone from being the cute pregnant lady to the one everyone is afraid is going to pop at any moment. The old ladies at the gym ask me regularly if I need to sit down and rightly so. My poor feet can hardly take walking around work every day and I have to fold towels while sitting now. It's really boring not being able to see over the half-wall to watch everyone work out. It's way more entertaining to watch Bambi as she runs.

"Oh, we won't be in these chairs all day," a very excited-sounding redhead who looks all glowy and shit says as she turns around to look at us from one row ahead. "I'm Jenna." *Jenna* reaches out to shake my hand. From the pearls around her neck to the perfect-length pink nails, she screams psycho PTA mom. She is perfectly polished and perfectly coifed, and I get the feeling she'd be clutching that necklace she's wearing if she caught wind of how our baby came to be. She reminds me so much of my mother, down to that half-shake thing with her fingers, that she immediately puts me on edge. I already think I don't like her. "This is my husband, Phil, and this is the third time we've taken this class."

Phil never turns around, which means he can't see my eyebrows shoot up in disbelief. Let's face it, I'm trying not to judge her, but I'm definitely judging how many times she's taken this class. I shouldn't, I know, but I can't help it. Three times in this class is something my mother would do. It means there are some major control issues happening with this one and she is definitely going to take a turn to crazy town at any moment. Fortunately, my wispy bangs hide my forehead, so Jenna doesn't know exactly how judgmental I'm being.

"We'll start in the chairs for about an hour, but then we'll move to the floor for breathing exercises."

I look around and, sure enough, there are giant pillows scattered around the room, most against the walls. I hope someone sanitizes those. I've learned the hard way exactly how disgusting people's hygiene habits can be.

Joey seems to have the same questions I do about our newest acquaintances, because he asks what I'm thinking. "Why have you come three times?"

Jenna giggles and smacks Joey's knee. My eyes narrow and I feel a sudden wave of jealousy of her touching my man. I guess technically I don't know if he's my man but considering we're all partnered up in this class for a reason, was it necessary for her to touch him? This is not making me feel any better about my immediate response to this woman. His question wasn't funny, although I'm guessing her answer might be quite entertaining, especially with the mood I'm already in and we haven't even taken roll yet.

"You can never be too careful when it comes to childbirth," Jenna explains and picks up a giant binder that she starts flipping through. Control issues confirmed. "We have a very detailed labor and delivery plan with lots of activities to keep us entertained and motivated. Oh, like this one—Soduko! But we still struggle a bit with some of the breathing techniques, so we want to make sure we have them perfected before the big day." She giggles and pats her belly, and I can't help but wonder why she thinks giving birth is going to be such a good time. Is she expecting this is going to tickle?

Did I miss that part of the brochure? Honestly, I hope so. I'm not looking forward to the pain.

It appears to be my lucky day because the instructors calls us to order, effectively halting the conversation. Jenna giggles again, smiles, and puts her finger to her lip saying "Shhhh!" before shrugging in delight.

I can't help it; I mimic her movements and do it right back to her because I'm feeling bitchy and my back is killing me and don't want to be here. I'm trying very hard to not just leave. Joey nudges me to get me to stop, but I turn and shrug as if to say, "What else am I supposed to do when sitting behind Mona #2?" He tries not to laugh and even focuses his attention on the instructor.

"Good morning, class," the woman at the front says, opening her arms wide in greeting. "My name is Babbette, and I'm so glad you're here as you journey through pregnancy, ready to bring new life into the world."

"Babbette?" I whisper in Joey's ear and he nudges me again, but I catch the smirk on his face.

"Childbirth is a wondrous and beautiful event and there is much to plan for. But before we begin that part of our pilgrimage…"

A giggle at her choice in words accidentally escapes, and I quickly cover it with a cough.

"… I want all the dads and partners to grab one of the small tables you'll find against the wall and set it up in front of you and the new mommy. Go ahead," she encourages as all the men and a couple of women begin wandering around the room grabbing the tables. "Be careful now. Don't pinch your fingers or set it on your toes."

It takes a few minutes for all the tables to be set up and the chaos to settle. Well, except for the one couple whose table keeps collapsing. The two women can't seem to figure things out, and one of them, who I assume is the grandma based on her age and how much she resembles the very pregnant woman next to her, gets flustered and appears on the verge of tears.

Babbette and her long, flowy skirt quickly flutters to their side and attempts to help but her dangly bracelets keep getting in the way. The entire situation amuses me way too much but is quickly over once Phil finally jumps in and saves the day. And by that, I mean he slides the brackets that no one else seems to notice into place.

If nothing else goes right when his baby is born, at least any tables are sure to be sturdy.

Once all is settled, Babbette instructs all the partners to grab a basket from the front of the room. Inside are two baby dolls, a couple of diapers, and blankets.

Joey and I place the dolls on the table and wait to figure out what she wants us to do. Jenna, on the other hand, is rocking her doll like a real baby and cooing at it. I look at Joey with one eye raised in question and he just shakes his head. I'm starting to think she may be cuckoo. I just wonder if it's only when she's pregnant, or if she's like this all the time.

"Since most of you are new, let's start with an icebreaker of sorts," Babbette begins. "Before we get started with the hard parts, we're going to ease our way into parenting with arguably the most important part of taking care of your baby—diapering. I want you to lay your baby on the table—just pretend this is a changing table—and open the diaper. Make sure the Velcro tabs are in the back next to the baby's bottom. If you need to, lay the diaper next to the baby so you can see where the back of the diaper is."

She walks us through the process, step by step. Joey, the overachiever, gets it quickly and on the first try. I, on the other hand, pinch my skin and get my sleeve stuck in the Velcro. Now I have a baby dangling from my arm.

"That's it. I quit," I grumble and rip my fake child off my sleeve and toss it on the table, leaning back and rubbing my back again. Jenna gasps at my unmothering behavior, but I don't have it in me to care. I'm too frustrated and in too much pain. "As soon as this baby is born, I'm giving you full custody and leaving since I'm clearly a danger to it."

Joey laughs through his nose and reaches for my doll, probably to fix my mistake—again. "Because you didn't do your first diaper perfectly? Don't you think that's a little over the top?"

"No. Maybe."

"It just takes practice."

I scoff and cross my arms because come on. "And when have you practiced?"

"I am training for Strongman," he says like that has anything to do with child-rearing. "I have incredible forearm strength and dexterity."

I laugh despite wanting to argue that point. He does find my G-spot pretty easily. And he's currently in the process of swaddling both dolls. Even I have to admit his fingers are oddly agile for this activity.

"Fine. Then you get diaper duty. Every time."

"Okay. You have to breastfeed, so it's the least I can do."

I hold my hand up to stop him. "Whoa. What do you mean I have to breastfeed?"

He places both dolls back in the basket now that they're warm and cozy and probably already planning his father-of-the-year party. Honestly at this point, he sort of deserves it. "I was doing some research on formula and discovered the benefits of breastfeeding far exceed bottle-feeding. Everything from bonding to nutrition to brain development."

I drop my head back and roll my eyes. "Okay, Dr. Spock. I'm taking your baby books away."

"What? Why?"

If I was feeling a little more confident, I'd probably laugh at him looking like I threatened to kick his puppy. But I'm not, so I don't.

"Because it's making you think you have a say over my body."

"But…" Gotta love him, he looks genuinely confused. "It's not about you. It's about the health and well-being of our baby. Our lives are never going to be the same."

I open my mouth to respond, but I notice Jenna turning her head ever so slightly, and I know she's pretending not to eavesdrop. That's just flat-out rude.

"I'm already donating my vag to this endeavor. I'm not donating my boobs, too, no matter how many baby books you read and how many times it's in the giant binder of perfect baby births."

Jenna's back stiffens and her head whips back to face front. Ha! Gotcha, Nosy Neighbor.

"But…" Joey starts before I interrupt him.

"No buts. Now practice changing your diapers again, Daddy-O, so you're ready when the time comes," I say with a clap on his shoulder. "I have to pee. This kid seems to think my bladder is a damn pillow."

I push away from the table using Joey's shoulder for leverage and cringe when I have to use my other hand to help me balance as I stand up. Joey looks at me like he wants to offer help, but wisely knows to keep his big mouth shut right now.

I waddle to the little girls' room down the hall and thank God I'm alone to do my business. Pee is pee unless you're this pregnant. Then it comes with gas and possibly a rogue hemorrhoid. I honestly don't know why high school health classes don't teach about this part of pregnancy in their sex education classes. Seems like knowing you'll have a lump sticking out of your butt for the rest of your life might be a massive deterrent from sex in high school. I'd imagine it wouldn't just work on the girls, but the boys too. They talk a big game, but really, they freak out easily when it comes to girls and their bodily functions. Flash a tampon box in their direction and you'll see what I mean.

Damn. I should be a high school teacher. One trip to the bathroom and I've already cut the teen pregnancy rate in half.

When I finally get done in the stall, I make slow work of washing my hands. I could say it's because I'm being extra careful with germs but, really, I don't want to go back into that room.

I know Joey craves all the information and wants to be as prepared as possible for our baby, but things like this only seem to be highlighting everything I don't know. It feels like a giant neon arrow is over my head pointing down and flashing "Keep an eye on this one. She's a hazard to her baby."

It doesn't help that I can see the physical changes every time I look in the mirror. I used to be beautiful. My skin was spotless, my hair was always done, I was curvy in all the right places and tiny in others. Quite frankly, I was a bombshell.

Now, all I see is random acne that breaks out daily, dark circles under my eyes, hair that almost never comes out of its messy bun, and hips that have very obviously spread. And let's not forget that I'm growing skin tags under my arm. Yet another perk no one bothered to tell me about until it started happening. And even then, it's only because I happened to run across it while flipping through some of Joey's bathroom reading material. I thought my body was just going whacko. Turns out, I'm one of the lucky pregnant women to grow shit on my skin.

I sigh deeply as I stare at my pallid complexion. "It'll be worth it in the end. It'll be worth it in the end," I say to my reflection. "Right?"

Not wanting to look at myself anymore, I shake my hands off and grab a paper towel. As much as I'd rather stay in here, at some point Joey will wonder where I am. The thought of him sending either Jenna or Babbette to find me hiding out is enough to make me cringe. It's better to go back to class.

By the time I get there, the tables and chairs have all been stacked and pushed to the outer perimeter of the room. Everyone is sitting on the floor, which sounds even less comfortable than those plastic chairs, and the partners are leaning against one of the giant pillows, pregnant moms lounging between their legs.

I crinkle my nose because, while I understand the reason to sit in this position, it's way more public display of affection than I care for. Especially when you're not positive how to refer to the guy sitting at your pillow. Six weeks from having my baby and I have no idea where I stand with his father. I sigh. Just one more thing I should probably figure out at some point.

Not wanting to be called out for my inability to follow instructions, I quickly find Joey and totter my way to him. Putting my hand on his shoulder for support, I lower myself to the ground, him trying to figure out where to put his hands to help me. It's awkward and ineffective, but I still make it eventually.

"Hey. You were gone for a long time," he says with concern in his eyes. "You okay?"

What he means by his obvious scan of my belly is if the *baby* is okay. But I don't correct him.

"Fine. Just a really big hemorrhoid problem."

His face scrunches up in disgust.

See? Squeamish animals they are. Sex education would be a breeze for me to teach.

"What did I miss?" I whisper as we get into the correct PDA position, which is not as uncomfortable as I thought it would be. Leaning against his chest actually relieves some of the pressure on my back. I have to give it to Babbette—she knew what she was doing with making us lounge this way.

"Babbette couldn't figure out how to get the VCR to work, so not much so far."

"A VCR?"

"Yeah, I didn't know what it was either. From what I can tell, it's like one of those old-school eight-track tape players from the seventies."

I shrug because his guess is as good as mine. My mother always complains about how fast technology changes now, so I couldn't know anything about a VRC or whatever he called it.

"Thank you, Phil, for helping me get that set up." Babbette claps lightly and smiles at Phil whose face I still haven't seen. He always seems to be facing the opposite direction. Weird. "The miracle of childbirth is a beautiful thing, but there are many things to consider as you decide which choices are right for you. For instance, you may want to hire a doula. You may decide to avoid any and all drugs and give birth naturally."

I snort a laugh because that is *so* not going to happen. Joey chuckles behind me and shushes me in my ear.

"You may find clothing irritating when you are in hard labor and opt to only wear a sports bra or even nothing at all."

"That's a thing?" I whisper mostly to myself. Apparently, I'm louder than I realized because now Jenna is looking at me like I'm the bad kid and needs to be sent to the principal's office.

"But the first step to deciding these things," Babbette continues to drone on, "is to know what to expect during labor. This movie will give you a glimpse into the journey so you can begin to make plans. Phil, can you please hit the lights?"

Quickly, I look over but, once again, the phantom of the childbirth class keeps his face hidden from me. Until suddenly, he doesn't. And that's when I realize who he is.

I shake my head when he catches my eyes and his widen. Old Phil is a regular at The Pie Hole. His spending ways are practically legendary in the dressing room. No wonder he's been keeping his face hidden. He doesn't want me to call him out. He scurries over to Jenna and kisses her on the cheek, keeping his eyes on mine in a silent plea to keep my mouth shut. Rest assured, Phil, I've got bigger things to worry about than how much baby money you've dropped on your favorite dancer, ironically called Baby on stage.

The room goes dark and the movie begins like I expect—an outside view of a hospital with the sounds of a woman in labor in the background. And that ends up being the only normal thing about this movie.

It cuts away to the room where the woman in question is butt-ass naked and writhing around on the bed.

"Wait," Joey says quietly behind me. "Did Babbette accidentally turn on some porn?"

An understandable conclusion since her birthing partner is also shirtless. I just have no idea why. To make matters worse, at that exact moment, the woman rolls onto her back and spreads her legs. I'm sure the intent is for us to see the head currently squeezing out of her, but that's not the part that's most noticeable.

"Huh," Joey says. "By the size of that bush, I think we can definitely assume VCRs are from the seventies."

I can't help it. I laugh. I laugh loudly. I laugh until tears are streaming down my face, and I'm afraid I'm going to fart.

Babbette cocks her head and furrows her brow, obviously not understanding my humor. Jenna is glaring at me with what amounts to loathing, but I can't stop.

"Sorry, sorry." I wave my hand in front of my face. "Don't mind me. I laugh when I'm nervous."

That answer seems to pacify the instructor. Crazy train over there is another story, but frankly, I'm shocked she's sitting through this movie for the third time. Although if Phil is as big of a perv as Joey, and I know from experience that he is, I suddenly understand why she didn't get any resistance from him.

"Listen," I whisper to Joey. "I've already made a decision about childbirth."

"Great. What do you want to do?"

"Just knock me out and wake me when it's over."

Joey laughs again and wraps his arms around me, squeezing me a little tighter. I don't hate it. Actually, I really like it. Even in public. "Hate to tell you, but that's not the way it works."

"Fine. Then you make all the decisions until you give me the drugs. Then we can decide."

"I haven't done this before, but I'm pretty sure that's still not the way it works."

I huff in response. "Fine. But at the bare minimum, please make sure I'm groomed to perfection and don't look like that."

I point up at the screen right as the baby is pushed all the way out. Again, that's what I should be focusing on but, instead, all I see is the umbilical cord still dangling out of her and her lady bits looking like they just went through a meat grinder.

My jaw drops open and I know my eyes are as big as saucers. That is what I'm going to look like when this is over? All stretchy and swollen and disgusting?

I better take advantage of Joey's oral skills sooner rather than later because there is no way he'll ever go down on me again once that happens.

And no matter what he says, one decision is set in stone from this point on—I am *not* giving up my fabulous boobs, too.

CHAPTER TWENTY-ONE

JOEY

Today is technically my easy workout day—cardio and some light weights—but I have too much pent-up energy for that. I should take the break and enjoy it. Rest is a vitally important part of health and being at your best. But I need to sweat out the mental energy and my three-mile run on the track upstairs didn't do it for me. There's too much on my mind that I can't seem to make heads or tails of. Too much to process.

Wiping my face with the hem of my white tank, I take a deep breath and prep myself to do more farmer carries. I squat down and grab the barbells, one in each hand and slowly stand up making sure to hold my core tight. Sounds easy until you add in the fifty pounds of weight on each end of the barbells. Both of them weigh a total of roughly a hundred and forty pounds and teeter back and forth with my movement. That's the key to this exercise—keeping the barbell balanced while I walk back and forth as quickly as possible. In competition, the weight and how far you can go both count towards your success.

Abel tried to make fun of me for this exercise one time until he tried it. It was hard not to laugh whenever the front of his barbell hit the ground, making him stop short.

Scratch that, I laughed hard, and had no problem with him knowing it. He almost rammed the back end into his face, and if there wasn't a clip keeping the weights in place, they would have scattered all over. It was one of those times I wish I had been shooting a video because I could watch it over and over. Serves the fucker right. He may have a plaque hanging in the weight room for his success in squatting the heaviest amount of weight, but we both know who's actually stronger. I just prove it in non-traditional ways.

Seems like I'm doing a lot of things the non-traditional way right now. And therein lies my emotional problem—Rosalind.

I'm worried about her. I'm worried *for* her. I know she's struggling with pending motherhood, but it feels like her negative feelings go deeper than that, and I don't know how to help. It's as if she's falling into some sort of depression. The thought had crossed my mind a couple of times over the months, but I dismissed them as being part of her standoffish personality. Then we went to the childbirth class and something Babbette said made me realize I may be handing this whole situation all wrong.

After the childbirth/porn video our instructor kept referring to as a "beautiful documentation of our journey," she started talking about postpartum depression and what it looks like. Anxiety, mood swings, insomnia, fear—all signs of depression after the baby is born, but it hit me that they're also signs of depression in general. They are also all things that seem to be getting worse as time goes on.

I do my best to let her know I'm not going anywhere. I rub her feet every night, I get her favorite takeout, I try to make anything to do with the baby fun and light, even stopping for ice cream after every doctor's appointment, but she seems to be pulling into herself more and more.

Part of my problem is I don't know her very well. Sure, I know she loves daytime talk shows and the finer things in life. She is wildly independent, a lot on the bossy side, and has a huge family that she loves, even if they overwhelm her. But those things all seem surface level. I have no threshold in which to gauge any changes in behavior and, truthfully, that kind of scares me. What do I really know about her beyond her previous employment and that she's having my baby? Almost nothing. And that's a scary realization. We're going to be part of each other's lives for at least eighteen more years. She's going to help me raise my child. She's going to be equally responsible for this child's health and well-being, but is she up to the task?

I don't think she's a psychopath or anything, but there are still the unknowns rolling around in my brain, and the more she holds it all in, the more uncomfortable it makes me feel. The more it also makes me worried she'll take a nosedive into a serious depression postpartum. And I have no idea how to make it better.

Instead of wallowing in my thoughts, I'm out here carrying barbells and trying to shred my muscles to the point of pain so I can concentrate on that and not my worries. I need some time to let my own thoughts rest. Maybe that'll help me sort it out.

I hear the door open and slam closed behind whoever has joined me. I doubt they're here to work out. Probably a staff member taking advantage of this beautiful spring day. I'm surprised none of the classes have moved out here for a change of scenery yet. It's only a matter of time.

"Isn't today supposed to be your light day?"

Ah. Abel. Makes sense. He knows me better than just about anyone, so I'm sure he's trying to figure out what's wrong with me. Of course, I'm not going to tell him. That's too easy, and it's way more fun to keep him guessing. I may have lots of thoughts and feelings right now, but that doesn't change the fact that I'm a smart-ass at heart.

"Okay, stalker," I grunt as I slowly lower the barbells down to the ground. "Super weird that you know my workout schedule."

He saunters over and inspects the weights I'm using, probably curious about how much I can carry. I know. I'm impressive.

"I've worked with you for years. It's not hard to see the patterns of behavior when you rarely deviate from them."

"Well, I'm changing things up today. You could join me if you want. Make a real man out of you."

He holds his hand up. "Pass. I trained Trevor this morning, and you know how he likes me to work in some sets. My quads are already tapped out for the day."

"Suit yourself. But a little creativity in your workout wouldn't hurt." I wipe my brow again and look around the small yard, trying to decide what I want to do next. "Do you happen to know if any of the sleds are free inside?"

Abel gives me a concerned look. "Okay, now I know you being out here alone is more than just deviating. What's wrong with you?"

I easily avoid his gaze by taking the barbells apart so I can put each piece away. "Why does something have to be wrong? My comp is in less than two weeks. I need to get in some extra workouts to prep."

"I'm calling bullshit on that. I've seen you train for Strongman. Hell, I've helped you work out for it. You have never added sleds as part of your training."

Flashing him a cocky grin, I refuse to admit my weakness. "Just because I have a competition doesn't mean I don't want to look my best, too. A little fine-tuning of these glutes will get me ready for bathing suit season. The bend and snap isn't just for the ladies." I wiggle my ass at him just to make him gag.

"I have absolutely no idea what you're talking about, but I also don't appreciate you planning on showing your ass to any woman besides my cousin."

I must flinch at the reminder of her because Abel's demeanor completely changes to one of compassion.

"Ahh. So that's why you're out here beating up your body. Woman problems." I could deny his hunch, but I'm already tired this conversation. It's why I came out here to be alone—so I could feel how I feel without anyone asking me about it. Looks like it was a short-lived solution. "How's she doing, anyway? For real. Not the same non-answer answer she gives me every weekday."

"She's giving you non-answers?" This news surprises me and is also a little concerning. I would feel better knowing she's talking to someone, even if it isn't me.

"Her standard answers are 'fine,' 'any day now,' and 'we don't know yet.' I can see it in her eyes that she's struggling with something but can't get anything else out of her. And now you're out here on your easy day… what's really going on, Joey?"

I drop my head and put my hands on my hips. As much as I don't want to have this conversation, reality is Abel knows Rosalind better than I do. Maybe he can give me some insight as to what's happening, or at least some advice on how to help her. He's also been through a pregnancy before. If nothing else, maybe he can tell me what's happening is normal.

"I don't know," I finally admit, blowing out a frustrated breath. "She refuses to read any baby books and she barely made it through our childbirth and parenting class the other day. At one point she left claiming she had to pee, but she was gone way too long for me to believe her. I was afraid she ditched the class."

Abel laughs. "I won't pretend to know for sure, but trust me when I tell you everything down in this general vicinity"—he waves his hands in front of his own genitals—"is going haywire for her right now."

I cringe. "She said something about a hemorrhoid, but I thought she was yanking my chain. Could she really have that? In her butt? I thought only old people got those."

Abel shakes his head. "Old people and pregnant women, my friend. May had a really bad one. She bitched about it the whole time she was pregnant with Mabel. Maybe you need to grab some Preparation H on your way home."

"Maybe," I say absentmindedly because I don't remember anything unusual in that area last time I went down on her. If she does have that issue, I'm kind of glad I missed it. My gut, though, tells me that would be an easier fix than what I'm actually dealing with. I guess I need to level with Abel. "Between you and me, I'm starting to wonder if she's going to bail on us at some point. Like I'll come home one day, and she'll just be gone. Maybe not until after the baby is born, but I just feel like I need to prepare myself to be a single dad. It's that bad."

Abel's jaw clenches, but I'm not sure if it's in anger or concern. "Rosie? She won't do that."

"No one calls her that."

"Whatever." Abel rolls his eyes and I can tell the gears in his head are turning. "Okay. Real talk. What are you doing to make her feel like she's not alone in this?"

"I give her a foot rub every night. And I big spoon her when she falls asleep."

His eyebrows rise ever so slightly. "I had no idea you guys had become that physically intimate."

I shrug. This is old news to me. "Her bed was making her back hurt, so she moved into my room. Plus, her hormones are making her uncomfortably horny—"

"Hup, hup, hup, nope." He holds his hand up to stop me. "I want to know nothing about my cousin's sex life. You knocking her up is weird enough. I need no details. Have you maybe cooked her dinner?"

I refuse to admit to the outcome of this very scenario knowing Abel will never let me live it down, so I just answer with, "You know what happens when I cook."

He nods because likely he's still finding spaghetti sauce in random places from the last time I tried to feed his kids. "Maybe order her favorite takeout?"

"That's the thing, man," I say as I walk to the bench next to the wall and plop down on it. Rubbing my hand down my face, I shake my head in frustration. "I've done all that. I've made it a priority to do everything I can to let her know she's not in this alone. I'm here and I'm not going anywhere. This is my family. *She* is my family now. But no matter what I do, I can't seem to help her out of whatever funk this is. And it's getting worse."

"But have you told her that?"

"What?"

Abel sits next to me and rests his elbows on his knees. "Let me ask you a question—how do you really feel about Rosalind?"

"Hey, you used her name!"

"Don't tell her. It's too much fun pissing her off."

I chuckle because it is fun. She's damn cute when she's feisty. "Can't argue with you there."

"Really," he prods. "If your life depended on it, how would you answer my question? Do you like her like a friend? Are you in love with her? Are you just tolerating her because of your kid? What?"

I pick at the callouses marring my hands as I think about how I really feel. I know for sure I don't just put up with her. How could I? She's funny and tough and sexy as hell. She's smarter than she gives herself credit for and her dreams are unique and interesting. And she tolerates me and all the things I'm terrible at, which is basically anything outside this place.

"I don't know if we know each other well enough to say it's love yet."

Abel nods slowly. "Valid point. What else?"

"But I like her, Abel. Really like her. Beyond just being a cool co-worker I chat with during the day. I mean I love hanging out with her at home. I love that she's working on her future and the things she wants to accomplish, even if she doesn't know I found her GED study book. I love that she's going for it. I love her pissy attitude and the way she can put me in my place with just a look. She's entertaining and… she's so fucking beautiful. And not just on the outside. Just look at how much she's sacrificed for our baby. Not everyone would do that."

Abel, if anyone, knows exactly what I'm saying. His ex, May, left him and his daughter to live with her manager boyfriend. Never mind that she wasn't a model at that point, or at this point either actually. Regardless, her family got in the way of her dreams, so she got rid of them. It was traumatic on everyone at the time. Thankfully, Elliott showed up and they got a second chance at being a happy, healthy, two-parent family. Again, with the non-traditional in this family. Are unusual situations genetic?

"Think about that for a second." Abel breaks my thoughts. I'm hoping he has some words of wisdom. "Rosalind has always been fiercely independent and worked her ass off because she loves spending money."

"Nothing wrong with that."

"Nope. But in the last few months, she's quit her job that makes bank, moved out of her fantastic apartment she loved, sold all her Gucci and Prada shit to buy diapers, and last week had to clean shit off the wall in the family bathroom attached to the pool."

"What? Someone shit on the wall?"

"I stopped asking questions a long time ago. People are cagey sometimes. And Rosalind is the one bearing the brunt of all that right now. What have you done?"

I admit that question is kind of offensive. "Did you not hear me? Everything I can think of from foot rubs to playing laser tag at the gift registry."

Abel barks out a laugh, likely because he knows how that ended. "You got banned from the store, didn't you?"

"Pretty close. Miss Chipper wasn't so chipper after all."

"Somehow, I'm not surprised." He sniffs and this smile falls from his face. "I'm not suggesting you aren't doing a lot. What I'm saying is your life hasn't changed much at all. You live in the same apartment, you have the same job, you're still training for your dream competition. You've given up half your bed and a few hours of your time. That's very different situation than the massive changes she's going through, one right after the other. And if I know women, and I think I do…"

I cock my eyebrow at him, but he ignores me.

"… I live with three of them. I know a few things. My guess is Rosalind is feeling like she gave up everything but isn't sure for what. Yes, it's for the baby. But how does she know you aren't going to bail on her? You've been so focused on the baby, you haven't told her how you feel about *her*."

"But… she hasn't told me how she feels about me either."

He cocks his head. "So, she can scare you off?"

I roll my eyes. "I'm not going to be scared off. You know me better than that."

"*I* do. But does *she*? She's lived with you what, four months? Five? That's not a lot of time to build trust in a relationship. It's a start, but remember, these circumstances are different. There's a lot more at stake and she has a lot more to lose if things go south. Add in hormones, an aching back, maybe a hemorrhoid…"

As much as I hate to admit it, Abel has a good point. I've been trying so hard to help her feel comfortable with the idea of being a parent, I've forgotten she also needs to feel good about *us*.

"I need to take her on a date."

Abel smiles and nods. "You should have taken that first step a long time ago. Make your intensions toward *her* known."

"Yeah," I say with a nod as ideas begin running through my thoughts. "She needs to know how I feel about her. Thanks, Abel. For once, you have some advice I can actually use."

He shoves me and stands up. "Let's clean all this up. You need me to help you stretch out all this shredding?"

I shake my head and follow him to the abandoned equipment for cleanup. "Always trying to get me lying down with my legs up, aren't you?"

He laughs and smacks me upside the head—the true sign of manly love.

CHAPTER TWENTY-TWO

ROSALIND

This couch has become my favorite spot in the apartment. It really might not be as comfortable as I think, but it's the first place to drop after climbing all those stairs to get home. I knew when I moved in that it would be rough to climb them every day, but I wasn't thinking about how hard it would be with a giant heavy basketball sticking out of my abdomen. Not only is my balance off, my back aches from carrying the extra weight. I freely admit to having to stop and get my breathing under control at every landing. I wonder what our landlords would think of us adding one of those fancy chairs to ride up every day. After the baby is born, I could use it to carry groceries instead. I'll have to pitch the idea to Joey.

Regardless, I'm here now enjoying some trash TV and veggie straws that have become my snacking obsession over the last couple weeks. I'm comfy, my taste buds are happy, and I'm not moving unless this place catches on fire or I have to pee. So that means I have about thirty minutes until I move, and not because I foresee any flames.

The door flies open just as Maury is about to announce who the father is.

"Hey!" I yell as I continue to shovel this faux potato goodness in my mouth. "I wanted to know who got her knocked up."

Joey glances over at the television and then back at me. "You know those are reruns, right? You can probably google it."

"It's not the same." I toss the bag onto the table and lick my fingers off. I refuse to miss out on any of the salt. "How was work, anyway? Got any new old-lady stories for my listening pleasure?"

Joey's little-old-lady class has become the highlight of my day. Not just the funny anecdotes he comes home with, but because they constantly fawn over me whenever they're headed into the locker room. I'm not sure why it feels different when the elderly rub my belly than when anyone else does it, but I don't mind their wrinkly hands. Maybe I just like old people. These ladies in particular are ancient enough that they have no filter and give zero fucks about it. If those are the required traits of age, I'm going to be the most entertaining elderly woman ever someday.

Joey lifts my legs and sits down on the opposite end of the couch, immediately placing my feet in his lap and starts rubbing my calves. One thing I've learned about him over the last few months is he really likes to touch me. Not in a sexual way, although I'd be lying if I said he didn't like doing that, too. But, in general, he's just a touchy person. My shoulder, my back, my forearm—he's very physically affectionate.

"There weren't any old-lady fights today," he says. "But Edna did ask if I'm servicing you appropriately, so your body is ready to give birth."

I snort a laugh, because of course she did.

"And did you tell her you are making sure to fuck me with your fingers, tongue, and giant cock every night so I can sleep?"

"Uh, no. I don't trust her not to ask details about my performance."

"Don't worry. I'll let her know I'm a very satisfied woman." I attempt a flirty grin, but I might have veggie straw crumbs around my mouth. By his reaction, I'm either successful in my seduction, or he's hungry and wants to lick my face.

"Stop looking at me like that. I have plans for us this evening, and I don't want to get distracted by your fantastic body."

I want to focus on what he just said about me being hot, but I have bigger issues. "What do you mean *plans*?"

I didn't realize it was possible, but with the way he shrugs and the slight bite of his lip, he looks almost shy. "I was hoping to take you on a date."

“A date?” I wasn’t expecting that at all. My heart does a little pitter-patter, but I don’t want to get ahead of myself either.

“Yeah. Just you and me, getting to know each other. Doing something together that doesn’t have anything to do with this third wheel right here.” His big hand sprawls across my even bigger belly and he rubs. I know Joey loves this baby more than anything, but I appreciate him wanting to get to know me, too. The thought of it makes me happy. Giddy even. It also terrifies me because what if he doesn’t like what he sees? Also, the idea of walking those steps again makes me kind of want to retch.

“I can’t go on a date with you.”

His looks crestfallen. “Why not?”

I go with the easier-to-explain excuse. “I make one trip up and down those stairs every day. I refuse to do more.”

“I can carry you.”

I have no doubt he’ll follow through on that promise, but it’s more than that. I close my eyes because I don’t want to admit the truth, but I have to.

“I don’t have anything to wear,” I say quietly, embarrassed to even say it out loud. A few months ago, I would use that same excuse and it meant everything in my closet bored me or I was PMSing. Now, it means I genuinely don’t have any appropriate clothing to wear unless I’m at work, and even that’s stretching it.

“What do you mean you don’t have anything to wear? You get dressed every day.”

“I wear a uniform, Joey. Yoga pants are stretchy and work shirts can be sized up. Nothing else fits except these sweatpants that I stole from your drawer.” My eyes stay glued to the television. Not because I’m watching, but because I don’t want to see the look in his eyes. I’m not sure if it’ll hold pity, judgement, or confusion, but I don’t want to take the chance.

“Huh.” He moves my leg back and forth as he inspects the material. “I knew they looked familiar, but they look so much better on you I didn’t recognize them.”

I furrow my brow at him and shake my head. I don’t think I’ll ever understand how Joey’s mind works.

“Change of plans,” he continues, “let’s go on a shopping date.”

"What?" I push away from him and sit up. If he's determined to go out, I might as well make sure it's somewhere good and he's officially captured my attention. "What do you mean a shopping date?"

"Let's go to that maternity store in the mall I've always avoided walking past."

"Avoided…? Wait. You avoided it because you didn't want to get someone pregnant by proxy, didn't you?" I deadpan.

"Listen, science changes regularly, and someday, they could say it's possible. You never know until it happens, and I didn't want to get stuck having a baby with a random stranger."

I nod slowly. "Makes sense. Don't walk by the maternity store but have sex with a stripper. Solid plan." I give him a hearty and sarcastic thumbs-up. "Worked great."

"Listen, I was in my early twenties when I was a bit hyper-focused on my bachelor life, okay? Early thirties Joey is older and wiser and, well, already knocked up a stranger. Turns out it's not so bad." I can't help but smile at his ridiculousness. He has this way of always easing my anxiety just by being himself.

He nudges me and smiles. "So? What do you say? Wanna go on a really strange date with me?"

How can I say no to that?

"Ohmigod that feels so good. Right there," I groan, throwing my head back against the headrest.

"Careful," Joey chides. "You're going to give me a complex."

I giggle and turn to look at him, flipping through a health magazine as the nail technician shaves a boatload of calluses off the bottom of his heel. It looks like painstaking work and not something I would ever want to do.

Then again, I got to fish a turd out of a public pool the other day, so I have no room to judge.

"Don't worry, babe. Your foot rubs are still the best." My technician looks up and I shake my head and mouth *yours are better*. Her eyes crinkle behind her mask, and I know she finds the whole situation amusing. But how could she not? A very pregnant woman and her super-hot bodybuilder boyfriend getting matching pedicures? You don't see that every day.

Also, I'm not sure if he's technically my boyfriend, but I'm making a conscious effort to not miss out on all the enjoyment of this evening by focusing on things like the word "boyfriend" and where this relationship may or may not be going.

This date is unlike any other I've been on. All my past dates started with me getting dressed up and sexy before going to the standard dinner at a fancy restaurant, maybe dancing or drinks afterward. But tonight, I left the house in the stolen sweatpants, followed by Joey spending over an hour with me at the maternity store. I tried on item after item, looking for anything that would make me feel less fat and dumpy, him finding some reason to compliment every single thing I modeled for him. Then when I found some things that will work for the next few weeks, he didn't even blink while handing his credit card over to the cashier. Just dropped the cash and smiled when he saw the pleased look on my face as I caught a glimpse of myself in one of the full-length mirrors.

I may have fallen in love with him at that moment. I definitely fell in love with this dress.

It's a strapless number covered in red flowers inside black and white designs. The silky material feels soft against my skin and its formfitting but not clingy down to my knees, so while it shows off my bump, I feel pretty. Sexy even. I, for sure, feel more like myself wearing it and that provided more relief than I was expecting.

Joey drops his magazine on his lap and looks over at me. "You've never called me babe before."

I shrug coyly. "Maybe I just saw a side to you tonight that makes you deserve it."

Not that he doesn't always show me he's all in. But I was starting to wonder if that meant all in for the baby, but "we'll see" for everything else. Everything else being me. But tonight, he's made *me* a priority, not just the baby. It's like he figured out I was losing myself and he knew exactly how to help me find her again.

"You mean I wasn't doing enough before?"

My eyes tip up in a half roll. "You did. You do. This just tipped you over the line to deserving of a nickname."

"Does that mean you're enjoying your date?"

I sigh in contentment because I haven't felt this peaceful, possibly ever. "It's been perfect."

"Good." He reaches over and grabs my hand, entwining our fingers. "Do you want to get something to eat when we're done here?"

He rubs his thumb over my hand, making goose pimples dot my arms. If he sees them, he doesn't say anything.

"Can we get takeout instead and go home? I have to work in the morning, and I'll never make it if I don't get to bed on time."

"Oh really." He waggles his eyebrows up and down which makes me roll my eyes all the way this time. My thoughts went there too, but I'll never give him the pleasure of admitting it. Instead, I try half-heartedly to push him away, but he grabs my hand tighter and laughs. "I'm just kidding. We'll stop by the Thai place you love after we're done here."

"Sounds like a good plan." Unfortunately, that plan means the world's best foot rub comes to an end. It sucks, but it's actually the worst part of the night so far. Everything else has been perfection.

In what feels like record time, we've left the mall, climbed into Joey's truck that he almost never uses because public transportation is way more effective, and I've got my favorite dinner sitting on my lap, the smell making my salivary glands work overtime.

Pulling into our parking spot, the one that is rarely vacant, Joey gets out and rounds the car, opening my door like a true gentleman.

When he takes the food off my lap and grabs my hand to help me out, a shiver runs down my spine. How is it that these small things—opening doors for me, holding my hand, knowing my favorite foods—all make me want to jump his bones right here on the front steps? I've never been the kind of woman who gushes when a man shows her some attention. Hell, I'm usually the one who demands to be treated like a queen or I won't show you the time of day. It's a little disconcerting. I don't like not knowing if these feelings are because my hormones are jacked or if I'm becoming emotionally mature, which sounds insane in and of itself.

But I push that out of my mind. There's no reason to ruin what has been the most enjoyable night I've had in a long time, because who doesn't love shopping?

"You gonna be able to make it up the stairs in those shoes?" Joey glances down to my new strappy wedges that are way more comfortable than most of the sneakers I own.

I blow out a resigned breath as I look up at how many fucking stairs we have to climb. "I can do it. It's just going to take me some time. You go ahead."

He does. Taking two steps at a time, he races up to the apartment leaving me behind.

"Well, that was rude," I mutter to myself as I grab the railing and drag myself up the first rung. "You didn't have to show off all your agility and shit. And you better not eat all the drunken noodles."

At least he's out of eyesight, so he can't see how winded I get. Or so I think for about five seconds before he comes racing back down the stairs again.

"Are you purposely trying to make me feel like a loser that can't make it home without huffing and puffing?" Seriously. I've barely made it five paces and he's already back down again.

"No. I was putting the food down quick, so I could come back and do this."

He leans over and picks me up in his arms, making me squeal.

"Put me down!" I demand as I wrap my arms around his neck and hold on tight. "You're going to drop me!"

"Does no one pay attention to what I train for every day? Don't answer that," he adds quickly. "All of you are going to be surprised when the videos of me winning hit the gym website."

I can't help the giggle that bursts out of me, although I'm not positive it's because he's funny. It may just be a default reaction to my fear of being dropped.

"Yeah, laugh it up. But you weigh almost nothing compared to the sandbags I've been lugging around."

"Comparing your pregnant baby mama to sandbags? Such a charmer," I joke, feeling a little more comfortable when I realize he's right. I've seen the equipment he uses. Hell, I sanitize most of it. And they do weigh more than me. Even with my thirty-five-pound weight gain.

Joey stiffens, and not from muscle use. I'm pretty sure I just said something wrong, I'm just not sure what.

We reach the apartment in a fraction of the time it would have taken me just to get up the first flight, which I'm grateful for. I'm hungry, and yet I'm a little rattled by Joey's sudden silence. It feels like I need to address that before we start eating, which admittedly is a bit weird for me. This emotional maturity and putting someone else's needs first is really starting to get annoying.

As soon as my feet touch the ground, I turn around and meet Joey's eyes with mine. "What's wrong? What did I say?"

He scratches his chin and tightens the man bun on his head before answering me. "I don't want to call you my baby mama anymore."

"Okay," I say confused. "What do you want to call me? Mother of your child, or something more proper?"

He shakes his head and puts his hands on his hips, obviously uncomfortable with this conversation. It immediately puts me on alert, and yet, we just had a great date, didn't we?

"What if I called you my girlfriend? But only if you want," he adds on quickly.

I know my jaw drops wide open, but I couldn't stop it if I tried. A myriad of emotions runs through me—shock, disbelief, excitement. But the most prominent feeling is happiness. Well, and fear. I wouldn't be me without a healthy dose of unnecessary and irrational skepticism to go along with everything else.

If I wasn't in such a state of shock, I'd explain all this to him. But instead what comes out of my mouth is, "What?"

He steps forward and grabs my hands, linking our fingers. "I like you, Rosalind. Really like you."

"I really like you, too."

"And not just because we're going to be parents together."

I suck in a breath, overwhelmed by his words and how they're making my heart beat faster and stronger. Is this what a real relationship feels like?

"I love how strong you are, even when things are uncertain. And how you gave up everything for our child, and even for me in a way. I want to take care of you and make you happy. And yes, I even want to make you come as often as possible."

And he's back. There's the Joey I recognize. The one who makes me laugh.

"I know this is sort of a backward way of doing things, but if our paths had crossed in a different way, I'd still be totally into you. Do you maybe want to be my girl-friend, no matter how immature and odd that sounds?"

It takes me just a moment of absorbing his words before I launch myself at him, as close as I can get with my belly in the way. My arms wrap around his neck and I kiss him with such force, such passion, he's knocked off-balance momentarily.

We are a mess of lips and tongues and hands roaming as I pour all the emotions I can't seem to express verbally into this kiss.

He finally pulls back just slightly, his lips still against mine. "Is that a yes?"

"You know my default mode is still bitch right? The snark is strong over here."

"I'm counting on it," he breathes before getting right back down to it.

As we kiss, he guides us toward the bedroom, disrobing as we go. My new dress ends up on the floor somewhere in the hallway. Joey's shirt lands in the doorway. The rest of our clothes are scattered about as they are tossed aside in our haste to get them out of our way.

Joey finally lays me on the bed gently, careful not to lie on top of me, and clasps our hands together above my head on the mattress. He pauses momentarily to look into my eyes before pushing slowly inside me and it occurs to me as he moves—this isn't just fucking. This is making love. And we finally got it just right.

CHAPTER TWENTY-THREE

JOEY

The day I have been waiting for is finally here. My very first Strongman competition is about to begin, and I can't tamp down my excitement. How can I? I've been training for this day for so long, the energy coursing through me is almost overwhelming in the very best way.

I glance around the gym and try to absorb every second of this experience. The roar of the crowd. (A small crowd anyway. This is a local competition.) The menacing looks on the other competitors' faces. (Menacing is a stretch. No one looks like they want to pummel anyone else.) Stan and Nicolas walking toward me.

Stan and Nicolas walking toward me?

"What are you guys going here?" I ask immediately, reaching out to shake their hands. They both slap me on the back in camaraderie as well.

"You've been talking about this day non-stop for weeks," Nicolas says as he looks around the room, probably taking everything in like I am. The meet is being held in the weight room of a local competing gym, but they did a nice job of clearing out all the equipment to make room for today's events. "We wanted to see what it's all about."

I turn to look at Stan. "He was talking smack about how he could take on anyone here, wasn't he?"

Stan chuckles. "You know it. The man never learns his lesson."

I shake my head and put my hands on my hips. "I guess I need to get some bigger tires, then, since he's already mastered them."

"No!" Nicolas practically yells, putting his hands up. "I talk a lot of shit, but we both know I'm a pansy. Please do *not* get bigger tires."

I gotta give it to him—at least he's honest.

"So, is your woman here, or did she decide there's too much testosterone in one small area for her taste?" Funny how Nicolas can twist any conversation from working out to women. That takes some talent.

Also funny how I can feel the goofy grin on my face. "My woman." Yeah, she is. "Nah. She's actually at her baby shower today."

"Oh man, you got lucky you had an excuse to miss that," Nick adds. "We got stuck going to Rian's shower before their baby was born. I don't know who cried more, Rian because she was so sick of people trying to touch her stomach or Carlos because he's become a huge puss since she peed on that stick."

My eyebrows rise in question. "That doesn't happen to everyone, right?"

"I don't have any idea," Nicolas admits. "Our office isn't exactly full of your average everyday people. I wouldn't worry, though. You're getting a big dose of manliness right here."

"Are you doing all these events?" Stan asks, and if I'm not mistaken, I see a bit of awe on his face. He's not the only one. I've done a double take or two since I walked in. Some of these guys are beasts. They make my Cipher Systems guys look normal sized in comparison.

"Nah. Since it's my first one, I'm only doing a few events. Get myself acclimated to the environment. Test out my body when I'm adding adrenaline. Set a bar for myself. Just see how it goes, ya know?"

"Smart," Nicolas says with a nod of his head. "But I don't see any Atlas stones anywhere."

"They're probably still in the back and haven't been rolled out yet. They need a dolly to move them." Both men nod in understanding. "But I'm not doing that event today. I'm doing the farmer's carry, the overhead log lift, and the max keg press series."

Stan cocks his head to the side. “You’re going to lift an actual log over your head.”

A broad smile crosses my face just thinking about it. “I hope so. We’ll see if I can get it up.”

“Jesus, Joey. Don’t say things like that in a crowded room,” Abel quips as he joins our little group, shaking hands with the other guys in greeting.

“Yeah, you’re super funny, DiSoto. Especially since your cousin didn’t have any complaints about my abilities to get it up last night.”

Abel grimaces. “Why do you always have to bring Rosie into it? I don’t need to know this shit.”

“No one calls her that.” I shrug. “But you walked right into it this time.”

Stan and Nicholas nod in agreement.

“Listen, we just wanted to come over and say hi,” Stan says. “But we’re supposed to be in the spectator area, so we’re going to head that direction. Good luck, man. And don’t hurt yourself. I may have extra motivation for next week’s session after watching this, and I need you in tip-top shape.”

“Noted.”

After the obligatory back pats and hand slaps, they leave Abel and me to prep for my first event—the keg press series.

There are three levels I have to complete to be considered successful, all in sixty-second increments and all progressively harder. First up is lifting a two-hundred-pound keg as many times as I can in one minute.

“You ready?” Abel asks me as he helps me get on my wrist bands.

“I think so.” As nervous as I am, I’m feeling pretty good. Confident in the training I’ve been doing and excited to see if I can accomplish this feat in front of a crowd.

“Good, good.” He tosses me a peanut butter sandwich, giving me a quick protein boost. “I have a question though.”

“Shoot.” I rip open the baggie and shove a bit in my mouth, watching closely as the first competitor gets in position. He’s a huge, burly man who is carrying a ton more weight in his gut than I am. He takes several deep breaths before leaning over to begin. Here we go.

"I was talking to some guy at the sign-in table."

"Uh-huh." I'm only half listening as I chew, trying to keep my nerves from getting the best of me. This guy may be chunky, but he's got great form. Lots of control and hits his marks quickly.

"When I told him who I was here with, he laughed and called you 'Cinnamon.'"

"Yeah." Holy shit, he just did seven presses in one minute. No way I'm beating that score, but damn that was a good set.

"Joey."

"What?" I turn my attention to Abel who is still babbling about food or something. I have no idea, but I'm a little irritated he's pulling me out of my zone.

"Why did the guy at sign-in call you 'Cinnamon'?"

My shoulders sag as I finally register what he's asking. "Fuck me. I was hoping he'd drop it."

Abel furrows his brow and I sigh, knowing full well he's not going to let up until I tell him.

"He decided I needed a Strongman nickname. Like other athletes have."

"You mean like WWE."

"That's what I said. It's stupid. But he was adamant, and I just wanted to check in, so I told him to do whatever he wanted. I guess he thought that meant he needed to start promoting it as well."

"Okay, so he's a strange bird. But why 'Cinnamon' in particular?"

I really don't want to tell Abel. He's never going to let me live it down. But I also need to focus, so I'll let him have his fun. This time.

"It's because of my hair."

Abel cocks his head in question.

"A man bun?" I wave my hand around the lovely locks in question because I may not want a nickname for it, but I still can't deny I've got a great mane. "Like a *cinnamon* bun?"

It finally registers on Abel's face only he doesn't laugh like I thought he would. "That's… kind of stupid actually."

"I agree." I turn my attention back to the next competitor, knowing my turn is coming and that I need to refocus.

Abel crosses his arms over his chest, staring the same way I am. Finally he can't take the silence any more. "You know I'm never going to let you live that down, right?"

"I've already made peace with that."

"Good. Good."

Just a few short minutes later, my name is called, along with the stupid-ass nickname that I ignore, and I take my place.

Visualizing the form I need to use and the muscles I need to concentrate on, I take three deep breaths. Then, I lean over and lift.

Grunting and straining, I do my best to ignore the people around me who cheer every time I lift the keg. Every part of my body is screaming with effort as I pay attention to not just my movements, but the judge noting when I hit my marks.

Sixty seconds seems like a lifetime and yet it goes by in an instant as the first part of my first Strongman event comes to a close. I finally drop the keg and smile, proud of myself for a job well done, regardless of the outcome. I felt good. I felt strong. I just hope the judge felt the same.

Looking over at the results, a cheer comes from my friends and I "whoop" in delight. Five reps in one minute—not the best score we'll see today, but a solid start for a newbie, and I move on to the next round.

"Nice job, Cinnamon," Abel yells as he slaps me on the back and squeezes my shoulder.

I want to be irritated by him using that name, but I'm so pumped now, I can't even find it in me to care.

CHAPTER TWENTY-FOUR

ROSALIND

The day I have been dreading is finally here.

My baby shower.

Logically, I know everyone has the best of intentions, and I'm appreciative of it. Hell, the gift pile alone is pretty impressive. But I've been here for a whole seven minutes, and yes, I am watching the clock like a hawk praying time will move a little quicker, and I already want to bolt. Unfortunately, there's nowhere for me to go. I was kicked out of my apartment this morning so it could be set up for the party.

The bad news is that meant I had to shower and get ready in the gym locker room while I waited for the text that I was allowed to return home. The good news is at least I don't have to lug a bunch of gifts up all those stairs. Let my family and the other random guests do the hard part. I admit that's the only reason I agreed to let them invade my living room.

Stepping foot through my front door, it's clear after my mother banned anyone from helping her with decorations, she put in a tremendous amount of effort to make this day perfect. There are balloons covering the ceiling and beautifully decorated craft tables offering activities ranging from writing me notes on a card to decorating a onesie I'm sure the baby will never wear. It's all very charming. Sickeningly charming. It makes me want to hug her for her effort and barf from the cheesiness of it all. My feelings are very conflicting which doesn't help my already anxious mood.

Plus, if one more person asks when Joey and I are going to get married, I might be the only third trimester inmate in county lockup.

"Fucking Joey, leaving me here by myself for this shit," I grumble under my breath when I see the itinerary for today. Yes, there is an actual printed itinerary that includes a list of games we're going to play and when I get to finally eat. This baby is hungry already.

"Did you see the cake yet?" Elliott sidles up to me and whispers the question in my ear as she wraps her arm through mine and walks with me to the refreshment table.

"Oh no. Tell me it's not a red velvet cake shaped like a baby. I don't know if I can stomach the crime scene once it's cut open. Even if it's delicious."

Elliott giggles lightly and the sound of it give me a bad feeling. "I think you'll wish for one of those after seeing what your aunt Natalia got instead."

I groan. "Natalia was in charge? We are totally fucked, aren't we?"

"Umm…" She bobbles her head back and forth. "That's one way to put it."

We quickly make our way to the cake table and my hands immediately go over my mouth as I gasp. "Ohmigod, what was she thinking?"

It's a baby alright. Only it's so much worse. The cake is designed to look like child-birth. In particular, a closeup of the exact moment the baby's head comes out of its mom's hooha. It is way too lifelike, and even worse, the naked lady in the childbirth porno has nothing on this icing bush.

"I am not eating fake pubes!" I whisper yell to Elliott, who gives me a sympathetic look and pats my arm.

As if it couldn't get worse, my mother approaches before I can get the horrified look off my face.

"Isn't it incredible?" she breathes, staring at this shit-show in awe. "So much atten-tion to detail."

"You knew she was doing this, Mother?" I try not to shriek, but I'm barely hanging on, waiting for Nonna to tell me this is a lifelike version of when she had my mother or something equally as disgusting. Even the thought makes me want to gag.

"Of course, I did," she answers, like this isn't the tackiest and most inappropriate cake choice they could have made. "It's a beautiful cake for the beautiful event childbirth is."

"It is a *vagina*, Mother. That you want me to eat."

She gives me a mom-glare, as if I'm the one that's crossed the line. "Don't be crass, Rosalind. Now stand next to your cake so I can take your picture."

I'm sure my eyes are wide when I whip my head around to look at Elliott, a silent plea for help.

She pats my forearm again and mutters, "The good news is she doesn't know how to upload that picture anywhere. And she lost the connector to the printer."

She's got a point. Small miracles for that.

"I'm so glad Joey isn't here."

Elliott smirks. "We will never, ever speak of this in front of him." I nod, eyes still wide. "Now turn around and smile for your picture."

I'm not sure it was a smile that crossed my face, but whatever it was, it has stayed in place for the last two hours as I've been poked, prodded, and questioned about everything from baby names to nursery decorations to whether or not I've been doing Kegels to build up my vaginal muscles for birth.

Women have absolutely no filter when it comes to this stuff. I'm sure some women feel a connection to others by sharing their battle stories of peeing on their doctor during birth or whatever, but I'm not one of those women. I don't need to be part of that clique. In fact, at this moment, I kind of want to run away screaming and never have anything to do with any of these people again.

Thank goodness we don't have another major holiday for at least seven months. Surely by then, someone in the family will be engaged and my "miracle" will be long forgotten. One can hope.

And if not, I'm going to throw Abel under the bus and tell everyone I found little blue pills in his cabinet. Uncalled for? Absolutely. But these are desperate times and I'm ready for them to be o-v-e-r.

Elliott pushes some torn wrapping paper off the couch and plops down next to me, having finally escorted the last person out the door. Mom and Lucia are in the kitchen doing dishes and talking loudly about the shape of my hips and how that will determine what gender the baby is. Nonna has apparently had enough and is lightly snoring in the tacky chair I let Joey keep across the room.

"Cake aside, that wasn't too bad, right?" Elliott asks as she slips her shoes off and gets comfortable. Or at least as comfortable as she can while she absentmindedly folds wrapping paper to throw away later.

"Forty women wrapped their arms around my waist to see if their estimated measurements of my size matched the amount of toilet paper they took off a roll. How bad do you think it was?"

She tries to hide her amusement, but I know she's laughing on the inside at my humiliation. It isn't enough that I'm as big as a house, let's accentuate it by measuring with *toilet paper*. Awesome.

"Okay, fine. Most of the party sucked for you," she acquiesces. "But at least it's over, and now everyone will back off for a while."

"Lord, I hope so." I lean my head against the back of the couch and close my eyes. The shower may be over, but it's just one more step closer to the big day, and I'm still not sure I'm ready.

Elliott, sensing my mood, nudges me. "Rosalind? What's wrong? I know this wasn't necessarily fun for you, but it seems like something else might be going on."

I sigh deeply, feeling more comfortable discussing this with Elliott than anyone else. Maybe it's because she's a single mom, too, in a similar situation to mine. Not quite a family, not quite not, but making it work nonetheless. "I'm just overwhelmed. I feel like I can't do anything right. I have a job that makes zero money. I don't know how to put any of these presents together." I gesture to the boxes that surround the room. "I don't know how to do any of this."

"None of us do," she says with a shrug. "We just figure it out when the time comes."

I scoff. "Okay. You're like the perfect mom."

"I have never been called that before by anyone. Especially my own mother."

I have a hard time believing that. Everyone at work is always saying how amazing she is. "Please. I'm sure Abel has told you before."

She leans forward slightly and furrows her brow. "Have you met your cousin? He's too busy trying to irritate me because he's ornery than whisper sweet nothings about my parenting style."

That elicits a laugh out of me. "Okay, now that I believe. But he thinks it."

"Maybe," she says with a shrug. "And I admit, sometimes I give myself a pat on the back if I feel like I had a parenting win, but most of the time, I'm winging it. And even then, I get it wrong a lot. The other day, Mabel kept telling me her foot hurt while we were walking to school. But she tends to be a bit of a whiner in the morning, so I assumed she was just being her normal difficult self and brushed her off. By the time she got home that afternoon, she was limping."

"What was wrong?"

"She had this huge blister on her big toe. Her feet had grown, and her shoes were too small. It rubbed her raw over the course of the day. I had no idea and felt so bad. I could have at least given her a Band-Aid and gone out on my lunch break to pick up some new shoes, or made Abel do it, but nope. I told her to quit whining and sent her on her way. Major parenting fail. My point is, we're all just doing our best, and I know that's what you'll do too."

I nod and try to absorb her words, but it does little to make me feel better. However, I make a mental note to check how big my baby's feet are on a regular basis. I suppose that's something.

"What? Why does that make you look even more sad?"

Tears well up in my eyes and I curse these damn hormones for making me emotional over stupid shit. "What if my best isn't good enough? What if I get it all wrong?"

"Rosalind," she says gently while squeezing my hand. "As long as you aren't abusive or neglectful, right and wrong are relative."

A lone tear slides down my cheek and I feel the word vomit coming. "But I don't want to breastfeed because I refuse to give up my boobs, too. And I can't get diapers on a doll right and they don't even move. I don't like cooking for myself, let alone for a baby. I miss working out on my pole. I can't do this."

Now that the words have started coming out, I can't seem to stop. I blather on and on about every mistake I can possibly make and everything I've given up. Elliott just sits there and takes it like the champ she is.

Until she suddenly jumps up from the couch and walks across the room without saying a word. That was kind of rude when I'm having an emotional moment but whatever.

She returns quickly and hands me some cards. "Read these."

Taking them from her, I realize they're the notecards all the guests used to give me their best baby advice. I roll my eyes because these are the same women that "oohed" and "aahed" over a cake shaped like a vagina. Dear Abby, they are not.

"I appreciate everything you've done, but I don't think these are going to make me feel any better."

I go to hand them back to her, but she pushes my hand away.

"Just trust me. Read."

Huffing, I decide it's probably easier to do as she asks. Maybe we'll get a laugh out of them.

Looking at the first one, I read out loud. "Breast or bottle doesn't matter in the end. They all end up eating dog food at some point anyway."

My eyes whip up to Elliott's. She raises her hand. "Guilty. I had the worst time keeping Ainsley out of the dog food when she was a toddler. I thought she was going to grow some fur. She actually used to growl at the dog to keep him away from the bowl while she was eating."

"Ainsley? Your Ainsley?"

"Told you. Not perfect. Keep reading."

I flip to the next card. "There is no such thing as spoiling a baby. If you want to hold her, hold her. I wore mine until she was two!" Dropping the cards in my lap I ask, "How do you wear a baby? I keep hearing this, but I have no idea what it means."

"You got this fancy Mobi wrap right here." She grabs one of the boxes off the floor to show me the picture of a baby wrapped up in a piece of green fabric. Low and behold, it looks like the mom model is wearing the kid model. "Or you can opt for a Tula when the baby is bigger, which is not quite like this but same concept. Or she might like exploring and not want to be held. You'll know when the time comes. Babies have this ridiculously loud way of telling you what they want."

I look back down at the cards to read another one. "Call me when you are ready to install some of the babyproofing items. Those things are brutal on your fingers, but since mine have already gone through the sting, save yourself."

That one makes me laugh. Dinah is funny sometimes and I just know she wrote that. I put it aside to cash in later because I'm no dummy.

"Only use non-toxic chemicals around the baby. If you need some, I'm more than happy to show you the ropes." I look up at Elliott and flash her the card. "She attached her business card."

Elliott snatches it out of my hand and throws it over her shoulder. "There's always one in the group. She means well, but when you're already feeling overwhelmed, it can be a little obnoxious."

I continue reading card after card from women I know and love offering words of advice—most of it about caring for myself and my mental well-being. It's like they've been there, and they know what I'm going through, even if they aren't the best at having boundaries.

And then I read the final one.

"Feeling overwhelmed is normal. So is feeling stressed. Never hesitate to ask for help. Forget taking a village to raise a baby. It takes a village to support our moms! We are your village." More tears well up when I realize who it's from. "Joey's mom wrote that," I say quietly.

Elliott nods. "I know. She may not be here in town, but she wanted to be part of this. She's fallen in love with you because Joey has."

I scoff again and wipe away a stray tear. "Joey isn't in love with me."

"I wouldn't be so sure. He may not have said the words yet, but his actions certainly support the theory."

I think about all the things he's done over the last several months, all the promises he's kept, all the accommodations he's made, all the sacrifice he's had, and a warm feeling floods my chest. He may not love me yet, but I will concede that he could be well on his way. And I don't mind it at all. I think I might be on my way to loving him, too.

"Speaking of," I say, deterring the conversation because there have been way too many truths revealed in the last ten minutes and I'm starting to get itchy, "I need to check my phone. He's at his competition and said he'd text with his results if he had a second."

"Oh, that's right. I hope he won." Elliott grabs my bag off the floor and hands it to me so I can search through it and find my cell. I kept it safely hidden in my purse just in case someone saw it and decided I needed my own pictures to remind me of this special day. Newsflash: I don't.

"He isn't expecting to even place. He more wants to test himself out and see where he should set his goals at." Finding my phone, I pull it out and swipe over the screen. Sure enough, I have four texts from him. "Oh good, let's see how he did."

I read them out loud so Elliott can get an update, too, because I know she's as curious as I am.

"Keg lift is over. Got five presses on my 200, two presses on my 225, and almost two on my 250." The words are followed by a picture Abel must have taken of Joey straining as he lifts a keg over his head. His face is red and contorted in a grimace, a few stray hairs have fallen out of his loose bun and are stuck to his face, every muscle flexed. He looks like Thor in that *Avengers* movie when he puts all his effort into swinging his hammer.

And now my hormones are raging again. I can only hope my libido will still be this high once the baby is out of me.

"Does that mean he won, or what?" Elliott asks.

I shrug because her guess is as good as mine. "I have no idea, but there's a picture, so I guess it's good?" I flip the phone around so she can see.

Her eyes light up and I know she's as impressed by his effort as I am. "Wow. I had no idea he was so… powerful."

I smirk at her choice of words because, yeah, I know my boyfriend is hot, and quickly shoot off a reply to him.

Me: That is amazing! I'm so proud of you! And you look hot in that picture.

His reply is almost instantaneous.

Him: Wait until tonight and I'll show you what else I can lift with. **eggplant emoji, kissy face**

A laugh escapes me because I should have known that's the response I would get. My phone vibrates again with another message.

Him: Hope you're having fun at the shower. I want to hear all about it tonight and see all the pictures! **heart**

No way is he seeing pictures of my event. He may almost love me, but this mama needs her sexy times, and somehow, I just know seeing the cake will ruin the mood.

CHAPTER TWENTY-FIVE

JOEY

I smooth my hands up her thighs and grab her hips so Rosalind can ride me like the cowgirl she is.

Really.

Her long hair is down around her shoulders, a straw cowboy hat on her head that she holds onto as she slowly rocks forward and backward. I have no idea where the hat came from, but I'm not one to turn down a little role play, which makes this even hotter.

Her soft body moves as she continues with her pace, chasing the orgasm that is sure to make her scream. My eyes stay locked on her swaying breasts, full with dark areolas and hard nipples. Her stomach round with my baby, and I can't help but put my big hand on it, still in awe at the things her body can do.

Her rocking increases and she begins moaning my name. "Joey," she groans, and my spine begins to tingle.

"Joey," she says again with more urgency, and I know she's right on the edge.

"Joey!" she yells, only it's not with pleasure. Her movements are rough and almost painful. Things start getting weird and I'm not sure what's happening.

"JOEY!"

I startle awake to feel Rosalind shaking me frantically. "Joey, get up!"

"Well, that was a total letdown." Pulling the sheet back, I look down apologetically. "Sorry, Little Joey. Maybe next time."

"Joey!"

I rub my eyes and prepare myself to climb out of bed and get whatever she needs. It's been happening more and more lately. A glass of water, a cracker, I never know what urgent request will come in the middle of the night. It doesn't bother me, but I'm short on sleep lately. It doesn't help that my body is still trying to recuperate from my competition yesterday. Maybe that's why she was so close to finishing before I woke up.

"Good morning, Rosalind. Do you need some ice cream?"

She opens her mouth to answer but pauses, like she's considering it now that I brought it up. But then her face contorts, and I know exactly what's happening. A sudden rush of fear runs through me.

"Can I eat ice cream while I'm in labor?" she cries.

I try to scramble out of bed, but my feet are all tangled in the sheets and I fall to the floor with a loud *thump*. Rosalind groans and I pop up immediately knowing my eyes are probably as wide as saucers. "You can't be in labor. You aren't due for almost three weeks."

It's impressive how she can grimace in pain and shoot me the evil eye at the exact same time. It's a talent really. "Tell that to my contractions."

Contractions? Oh shit. "Okay. Get in the car." I start thinking about what I need.

Pants. I need pants.

"Call the fucking doctor first," Rosalind snaps at me.

I grab my phone off the dresser and scroll through looking for the doctor's number, but my brain can't seem to fire on all cylinders right now. "Where is it? Where is it? Where is this fucking phone number?"

"Ohmigod, give me the damn phone." I slap it into her hand, and she points at me with the other. "You, go get me ice cream while I make this call."

Remembering everything we learned in our class, I crinkle my nose in concern. "Babe, I don't think you should be eating right now."

If her head could spin around, it probably would at this exact moment. "I wouldn't want it if you hadn't said anything, so go," she says through clenched teeth.

Knowing I need a moment to pull myself together, I forgo this argument and race to our small galley kitchen. I open the freezer and pull out her favorite kind. Weird that I can remember what ice cream she wants but can't remember the name of the doctor while we're in crisis. I'm useless already.

As I take a deep breath in through my nose and out through my mouth, I try to slow my heart rate while I think about everything I read in the book. We have bags packed for us. We have a bag for the baby. I have the list of people we need to call. I think we're ready. I just need to stay calm for Rosalind. She's doing okay now, but the more intense this gets, the more she needs me to be her rock.

I can do this. My girlfriend and my child are depending on me.

My child.

Holy. Shit. This just became real.

I move my arm to put the ice cream away and catch a whiff of myself. Okay, maybe I need to shower first. No reason to gross my baby out during our introduction.

I head back to the bedroom and Rosalind is walking around the room, hand on her back, moaning softly. I rush to her and hand her the ice cream.

She glares at the bowl like it makes her want to gag. "What is that for?"

"You said you wanted it."

"I'm in labor. I can't eat that."

I can't seem to keep up with her mood swings already, but I have bigger things to worry about. "What did the doctor say?"

"He said Dr. Walters isn't working today, but someone will meet us at the hospital ASAP. Especially since my water broke."

"Your what?"

She gestures over to the bed and I look. Sure enough, there is a large wet spot like she lost her bladder or dumped a gallon of water all over. Right about now, I'm thanking my lucky stars I thought to discreetly change out our old mattress pad for a waterproof one a couple weeks ago. It's going to make cleanup a whole lot easier.

"Okay. We just need to grab the bags, but I think we're ready to go. Let me just jump in the shower first."

"You're going to shower?" she screeches.

"Babe. I kind of stink."

"This is not the time to be worried about vanity." She moves closer and pokes her finger in my chest. "I am in pain and this baby is coming and…" She pauses, sniffs, and crinkles her nose. "Ohmigod, you're revolting. How did that happen? All you did was sleep. Go wash that off."

"I was sweating in my sex dream. I'll make it fast!" I yell as I race to the adjoining bathroom.

Ten minutes later, we're on the road to the hospital. Right about now, I'm feeling pretty good about not selling my truck. For a couple years, Abel has pressured me to unload it, saying it wasn't worth the money I spent on insurance every month. Of course, he had no issues borrowing it to move Elliott into his house. And now, I have no issues taking my girlfriend to the hospital in a private vehicle I'm in control of rather than the L, which may not even have a full line of trains running at this time of night.

Rosalind begins breathing deeply and I place my hand on her thigh, probably more to center myself than anything. "It's okay, babe. I'm right here. We got this."

Her breath hitches, and as I anticipated, her emotions are finally catching up with the moment, anger dissolving into tears.

"I can't do this," she whispers and cries softly. "I don't want to do this."

I grab her hand and squeeze, keeping my eyes on the road and praying we don't hit any red lights. "You don't have to do this. *We* have to do this. And we can. I know we can, okay? Because we're doing it together."

Her sobs grow stronger. "I'm so scared, Joey. There's so much that can go wrong."

"But there's so much that can go right, too. That's what we're going to concentrate on. A quick labor, an easy delivery, and a perfect baby that we're going to raise to the best of our ability. Okay?"

I feel rather than see her nod, so I keep talking.

"It's going to have your eyes and my glorious hair." That makes her giggle, which is what I was going for. "And most importantly, it's going to be healthy and happy and love us just because we're the parents. Okay?"

She takes a deep breath and nods, before squeezing my hand tighter and moaning in pain once again.

I'm praying everything happens just like I said because suddenly those are the only things I want.

CHAPTER TWENTY-SIX

ROSALIND

Fuck being pregnant. Fuck being in labor. Fuck these nurses and the doctors and the fucking epidural that didn't seem to take.

I told them, TOLD THEM, the medicine wasn't working, but did they believe me? No. No, they did not. And now, I've been lying here for damn near two hours having full-on labor pains because the damn nurse won't call the anesthesiologist in to fix it.

Thankfully, that stupid blonde bimbo is gone, and I have a new nurse. We'll see if this one is playing with a full deck and takes care of me and spends less time on her computer.

"How are you feeling?" This nurse is a brunette, so I'm hopeful. Does her hair color make much of a difference? Probably not, but right now blondes are dead to me. "Give me a pain level between one and ten."

"A fucking eleven," I snap at her. "My epidural never took."

"It wore off already?"

"No. It never took," I say slowly so she understands my desperation. "I haven't had any relief at all."

"Oh no. That's not good. Did you tell your other nurse?"

I want to snap at her and say, "No. I thought I'd wait for you to start your shift." But I'm trying to be nice, so I stick with, "Sure did. She rolled me over on my side and told me gravity would help." The nurse gets a weird look on her face. I narrow my eyes because I know, *know* I was played by someone who was just too lazy to care. "She was lying because she's afraid of the anesthesiologist, isn't she? I know he was a dick, but I can take him if I have to."

Nurse Brunette pauses momentarily, then pats my arm. "Let's see how far along you are and then we can call him back if it's not too late." She leans in a little closer and adds, "I'm not afraid of him either."

Knowing we're finally getting somewhere with this mess relaxes me just enough to not want to throat punch anyone. Until Joey opens his stupid mouth.

"Too late? Why would it be too late? What does that mean?"

"We only have a certain window for epidurals, so getting another go at it is going to depend on how far along her dilation is." The nurse, whose name is apparently Heather if the information on the marker board is correct, grabs some gloves and moves the sheet to just above my knees. "Are you okay with him being in here for this?"

"He's the one who did it. He deserves to see all the grossness," I grumble. "Maybe it'll keep him away from me for a while."

Out of the corner of my eye, I can see Joey shaking his head but wisely keeps his mouth shut. This has already been the longest five hours of my life, and I have a bad feeling this is just the beginning.

"Okay then. You're going to feel some pressure." And then Heather shoves her entire hand inside me. Hell, she may be elbow deep with how much "pressure" that is.

"Holy shit," I yell. "Please tell me you can call him to fix this."

She moves the sheet back down and I roll to my side, trying to breathe through yet another contraction.

"You're about eight and a half centimeters, so I'm sorry but it's too late now."

My head pops up off the bed. "What do you mean it's too late? It's already in. There is already a needle in my back."

"But it needs to be redone completely. By the time he finishes with the patients before you, the baby will probably already be here."

Rage fills me. "You document on my chart that I told that shitty nurse to call him. I told her. She denied my rights to have a proper epidural. I'm not paying for pain relief when I didn't get any!"

Joey begins stroking my hair as my breathing hitches. "Hey, hey, hey. Calm down. It's okay."

Overwhelmed and in pain, I begin to cry. "It's not okay. I can't do this, Joey. It hurts so much, and I didn't want to have a baby, and I'm going to be a terrible mother, and I can't do this. I didn't know it would hurt so bad."

"Babe, listen. It's going to be okay."

"How can you say that? You don't know."

"You're right. I don't know. The only thing I know is how to be a personal trainer. And the biggest lesson I've learned there is that you can't have the benefits of the hard work if you don't allow yourself to feel the pain of it."

"What benefits? Losing my figure? Losing sleep? Losing my job?"

"Gaining our baby. Who you are going to fall madly in love with the minute he or she gets here."

"But what if I don't?" And just like that, I finally get to the crux of my own issue. I'm terrified. Not of labor or delivery, although they aren't fun right now. I'm afraid I won't love my baby. That I don't have the same maternal instinct as anyone else. That I'll be like Abel's ex-wife and ditch my kid for my own selfish dreams. That I'll put the same look on my baby's face that Mabel's mom puts on hers.

I don't want to hurt my baby. More than anything in this world, I want to do right by her. What if I can't?

"Look at me." Joey gently tugs on my chin, so I look up at him. Pushing the sweaty hair off my face and wiping the tears off my cheeks, he says the words I need to hear. "The fact that you're so worried means you already do."

Just like that, my tears stop as I think about what he just said.

I'm worried because I already care.

I'm worried because I don't want to do it wrong.

I'm worried because I feel protective.

I'm worried because I love him. Or her.

I blink rapidly as a lightbulb seems to go off in my brain. "You think?"

"I know. Rosalind, you aren't going to be like your mom. Or Dinah. Or Elliott. You're going to be like you. And that's what this baby wants more than anything."

In between contractions, I reach over and kiss him on the lips, nothing salacious, just with genuine appreciation. "I love you."

The words pop out before I can stop them, but I can't find it in me to care. Take it or leave it, that's up to him. But this entire conversation is the most honest I've been with anyone, including myself.

"I know." He smirks and I shove him, making him laugh. "I know because I love you, too. And we're going to be the world's worst parents, but as long as we love our baby with everything in us, it won't matter."

Just like that, another contraction hits and his sweet words don't hold as much meaning as they did. "As long as I don't rip your face off first for doing this to me. Holy shit, that hurts."

And it continues to hurt every forty-five seconds for the next hour. Yes, an hour before the on-call doctor, Dr. Chan, finally moseys his way on in to check on me. As if my insides aren't being ripped out of my body. What is it with everyone taking their sweet-ass time today? Don't they see I'm in crisis?

"Hello, Rosalind," he says with a smile I want to rip right off his face as he washes his hands. "Let's see how far along you are. You're going to feel some pressure."

Once again, someone takes fisting to a whole new level, making me cry out in pain. "Yep. It's time to push. You didn't get an epidural?"

My nostrils flare and I swear flames shoot from my eyes, but since no one flinches, I guess I'm not as dangerous as I feel.

"It didn't take," Heather says while sliding a thermometer over my forehead. "Doctor Chan." She shows him the results and he frowns.

Apparently, Joey noticed the exchange, too. He squeezes my hand a little tighter. "What? What's wrong?"

More people come into the room, bustling about as if they belong. A high-tech baby bed is moved in and the head of my bed is raised up. Lights come from out of nowhere and equipment is moved around.

Dr. Chan begins putting on a gown and a mask, new gloves. This is really happening. I'm about to have a baby. "Rosalind, you have a small temperature, but we're going to try to get your temp down before we start pushing."

"Is that bad?"

"Probably not. It's not uncommon for something like this to happen. Easy to treat, so there's nothing to worry about."

"But the baby will be okay, right? I mean, he's already almost three weeks early."

"Three weeks is still considered normal, so I have no doubt he'll be fine." He looks at the monitors. "Heartbeat is in normal ranges. Contractions steady. So far, so good for both of you."

I look over at Joey, eyes wide in fear.

"Hey," he says softly. "It's okay. We've got you. I've got you."

A cool washcloth is immediately on my forehead, another one around the back of my neck. It does nothing to ease my concerns about this new obstacle. But the one thing I have no doubt of is that Joey's got me. Not just now, but for forever.

CHAPTER TWENTY-SEVEN

JOEY

Despite how calm everyone is on the outside, myself included, on the inside, I am freaking out. Not because the baby is almost here, but because of this fever thing. Of everything I imagined going wrong, losing Rosalind was not one of them. Suddenly, I feel like there is a real possibility she could be very sick, and I'm kicking myself for not calling her mother when we got here.

Granted, Rosalind made me promise not to call because the idea of her mother fawning all over her during labor and refusing to leave during delivery had her in a panic. I honored her wishes, but I'm concerned it was the wrong move on my part.

I'm also terrified for myself and our baby.

I refuse to let my doubts show, though. No matter what happens, in this moment, Rosalind needs me to be a rock, so that's what I will be.

"Let's go ahead and try a couple of pushes," Dr. Chan says gently, which does nothing to make me feel better or to take the look of agony off Rosalind's face. "Joey, you grab her leg under the knee to hold it up while Heather does the same on the other side."

"Ooooooh…." Rosalind groans and it makes it even harder to tamp down my fear.

"Does that hurt?" I ask, not wanting to cause her any more pain than she's already in.

"Everything hurts," she says with a moan, eyes closed, some stray tears sliding down her cheeks. "Just do whatever it takes to get this over with."

"Here comes another contraction," Dr. Chan says, as if the look on Rosalind's face didn't already tell me that. "On the count of three, lift your head and chest up and push down like you're going to the bathroom. One, two, three…"

Rosalind does as he instructs, grunting as she pushes with all her might. From my angle, nothing seems to happen, but he seems pleased.

When she runs out of steam, she lies back down and I wipe the tears from her face. She opens her eyes and looks at me, practically pleading with me to make this better for her. My heart feels like it's being ripped apart with the guilt that there's nothing I can do for her in this moment except hold her hand.

I rest my forehead against hers and whisper, "I love you. You are so strong."

She nods and takes a deep breath, trying to regain her strength like only a woman who is creating a miracle can do.

"One more time," Dr. Chan encourages as Rosalind's expression turns into a grimace once more.

She sits up and we go back to our positions, holding her in place as she yells through the push.

When the contraction is over and she rests, Heather runs a thermometer over Rosalind's forehead. I try not to pay attention, instead focusing on the things Dr. Chan is saying about the baby progressing. No one seems to be on alert, which gives me hope that maybe everything will be okay. Hope that is replaced by fear again with Dr. Chan's next words.

"Rosalind, there's nothing to worry about, but your temperature is still over a hundred, which means you may have a little bit of chorio."

My heart feels like it stops. I know chorio isn't uncommon, but she hasn't been in labor that long. She shouldn't have it after only five hours. That part is the most concerning.

Focus, Joey. Stay calm. You're her rock.

"What does that mean?" I ask.

"What is chorio?" Rosalind adds. "Like an infection?"

"Exactly. An infection of your amniotic membranes." Dr. Chan is so calm. I'm so very impressed with how he doesn't seem to be freaking out about everything that has gone wrong so far. "It happens sometimes. When your water breaks, it allows some bacteria different access to your body, but it usually doesn't happen this fast. You're the exception to the rule."

I refuse to think of how that bacteria could have gotten in her, so instead I ask, "What happens now?"

He looks up, a serious expression on his face. "The biggest issue here is we don't want the baby to get the infection. So, when he or she is born, they're going to have to spend a couple days in the NICU. Just to get some IV antibiotics as a precautionary measure."

"What? NO!" Rosalind yells, her mama bear roaring to life, to hell with the pain she's in.

"Hold on, babe." I grip her hand tighter, as much to get her support of me as me giving it to her. "Let's hear what he has to say, okay?"

She looks at me, eyes wide, the overwhelming fear evident on her face. "They can't take my baby, Joey. They can't."

I stroke her hair back and hold her gaze. "They're not, honey. The baby isn't going anywhere without us, I promise. This is about making sure the baby doesn't get sick, okay?" Her eyes are still full of fear. "I'll go with the baby when he's born, okay? I can do that, right?" I ask the doctor.

He responds with a reassuring, "Absolutely."

"See? The baby won't be alone. I'll be right there. I won't leave his side. We got this."

Rosalind bites her lip and nods, squeezing her eyes tight just as another contraction hits. I coach her through pushing again before turning back to the doctor when we have another lull.

"You were saying, the baby goes to the NICU?"

"Just for a couple days. We'll have him on an IV and will give him precautionary antibiotics, just to ensure he doesn't get an infection."

"What about Rosalind? Is she going to be okay?"

"Chorio is nothing to ignore, but it's relatively easy to treat in these situations. Rosalind"—he turns to speak to her directly, which I appreciate—"you're also going to be treated with IV antibiotics, so you won't be discharged for at least three days as well."

"Will I still get to see my baby?"

"Absolutely. The bright spot to your epidural not kicking in is you'll be able to go see him probably within the first hour he's born. Just as soon as you're cleaned up and ready. You don't have to wait for the numbness to wear off."

"Okay," she says through a deep breath and I know she's prepping her body for more pain. "Okay, I can do that."

Heather hands the doctor a pill.

"Before you have another contraction, though, I need to give you a suppository of Tylenol to try and get your fever down. You'll feel a little pressure in your rear entrance." I turn my eyes away as he sticks his finger where I've never been allowed before. "There. Done. Once that takes effect, you'll feel better."

"I hope so because here comes another one," Rosalind groans and the doctor encourages her to push again.

And just like that, she gives birth…

To the Tylenol.

I try really hard not to laugh and by the looks on the doctor's and nurse's faces, I'm not the only one. Unfortunately, Rosalind notices and looks around at all of us.

"What? What happened?" She catches my eye and understanding seems to dawn. She knows me too well. "I just pooped out that Tylenol, didn't I?"

The room erupts into some much-needed laughter. Surprisingly, even Rosalind smiles. I kiss her on the forehead and hope she understands none of us are remotely grossed out. Only relieved the tension has dissipated.

"My fault," Dr. Chan says. "I should have known better than to give it to you right before a contraction. Let's try that again."

"Can't you just use my IV or something?"

"It would be nice," Heather jumps in as she hands him another pill. "Unfortunately, Tylenol doesn't come in IV form, so in certain scenarios, this is our best option."

Once again, I avoid watching the whole process. I may not have a problem watching my baby be born, but there are still some things a man doesn't need to see. Fortunately, though, this time things seem to stay put.

We continue holding her legs when she pushes and wiping her brow when she relaxes. I am in complete awe of this woman and how hard she's working, with very little complaint. Well, there's complaining about how much it hurts and a few random threats to rip my nuts off, but overall, Rosalind just seems to tap into the strength I didn't know she had.

It takes only five minutes and as many pushes before I see a head full of dark curly hair popping out.

"Holy shit," I breathe, amazed by what's happening in front of me. I look over at Rosalind, who is panting heavy, eyes closed. "Do you see that, babe? Look."

Her eyes peel open and she glances down as Heather holds up a mirror so she can see. "Yeah, that's weird," she croaks out, voice thick with exhaustion, before relaxing and closing her eyes again.

"Just one more push, Rosalind, and your baby will be here," Dr Chan instructs. I swear I can see the smile on his face, even with the mask in the way. "Are you ready?"

"Yeah." She takes a deep breath, bends her body forward, and grabs on to the back of her knees. Then she holds her breath and pushes.

With that last burst of adrenaline, the most amazing thing happens—my life completely upends. As I watch my baby come into this world, I realize everything I have read, everything I have listened to, every plan I had in place is completely irrelevant. Nothing matters except that my baby is healthy and happy and feels loved. Nothing.

"Holy shit, Rosalind." My hand grips hers tighter as emotion overwhelms me.

"And you have a bouncing baby girl," Doctor Chan announces proudly, and my knees go weak.

It's a girl? It's a girl! I have a daughter. A beautiful little girl who is making it very clear she is unhappy to be out in this cold room.

"Wow, has she got a set of lungs on her," I remark with a smile, still enthralled as I watch the doctor and nurses work. I'm not sure what to do except sit here and hold Rosalind's hand.

"Do I get to hold her?" Rosalind asks, her eyes following our baby's every movement. "I don't want her to miss me. She needs me."

Dr. Chan looks up from where he's still working at the end of the bed. "Of course. We'll have a few minutes before we have to take her to the NICU. But first, I need one more big push from you so we can get the placenta out. Then we'll bring her over."

"Can I…?" I clear my throat which has suddenly gone tight. "Can I go look at her?"

"Of course, you can!"

"Take pictures!" Rosalind demands.

I fumble with my phone as I stand up, but quickly make my way to where she's being weighed and measured and begin snapping random photos. Her cries have turned to whimpers and I don't know how to help her, so I just do what comes naturally… I talk.

"Hey, my little princess. You don't need to be sad. We didn't leave you."

A nurse smiles behind her mask. "She recognizes your voice."

"Really?"

"Yep. See how she turns her head your direction whenever you talk? Try again."

"Hi, baby. We're so happy you're here." Sure enough, just like the nurse said, there is definite head movement. I'm shocked and am surprised my entire body didn't just turn into a puddle on the floor. Especially when her whimpers stop. I did that. I made it better for her just by talking to her. For the rest of my life, I just want to make everything better for her. "That's right. I'm your daddy. You're safe with us, baby girl."

"She's not clean yet," the nurse says as she rubs a towel over my little girl, getting the gunk off of her. "But let's get her wrapped up so she can see her mommy before the NICU team gets here."

It takes just a few seconds, but suddenly, she's handing me this little bundle of baby and I know I'll never be the same.

"Good morning, little one. Actually, it's not morning, but it feels that way, doesn't it?" I sway and bounce gently as I talk. "Do you want to meet your mommy? She's right over here."

Rosalind reaches up and I guide the baby down to her chest, where the two of them seem to snuggle right into each other. I immediately take out my phone again to document this moment. I have never seen anything more beautiful in my life.

"We did it, Joey," Rosalind says through her tears. "We made this. Can you believe it?"

With Dr. Chan's nod, I put one leg up on the bed and curl in next to them, the three of us making our own little bubble of happiness.

"She looks like you," I breathe, barely comprehending how something so beautiful came from the worst one-night stand ever. I've never been so grateful for a bad decision in my life.

Rosalind kisses the baby's head and we stay like that for as long as they let us, the three of us a family.

CHAPTER TWENTY-EIGHT

ROSALIND

I can't believe my baby girl is already twenty-four hours old. It took forever for her to get here, and she's already growing up right before my eyes. And yet, she still doesn't have a name. I guess in my attempt at denial of all things motherhood, we forgot she'd need one of those. Especially if she decided to come early.

"What do you think of Arabella?" I ask Joey, as I stroke a finger down her perfect cheek. They're plump and rosy. And they move when she dreams of sucking in her sleep. She is an absolute doll, and when I look at her, I swear my heart almost explodes. I'm so grateful she is healthy enough that she doesn't have to spend all her time in the NICU and can be in here with me when she's not attached to antibiotic fluids. I may have only been a mom for a day, but I don't think I could stand being away from her.

"It's pretty. Do we call her Ari or Bella or Arabella? That's a mouthful for a little one."

He sits down next to us and gazes down at her. He's been doing that a lot over the last day. Not that I blame him. It's hard to look away from perfection. All six pounds, fourteen ounces of her.

"I don't know. Maybe we can just try them all out as we go and see what fits?"

Joey nods in agreement. "We've got time. Besides, she'll probably demand we call her something random when she gets a little older anyway. Like when I was five and I made everyone call me Batman."

I laugh quietly, trying not to disturb the baby. "And they did? They called you that?"

"I refused to respond to anything else. I mean *refused.* My mom finally gave up and decided it would be easier to let my kindergarten teacher break me of it."

I shake my head in amusement. "Arabella it is. What do you think of that, little one?"

She lets out a little squeak and I take that as a sign of approval.

"Speaking of my mother," Joey adds. "What do you think of her middle name being Renee?"

I look up at the man who is already the world's best dad and smile. "I think your mother would be honored if we name her first grandchild after her."

He nods, and if I'm not mistaken, I see some wetness in his eyes. But that's Joey for you. He's a nut and says what's on his mind, but he also has the biggest heart of anyone I've ever known. I have no doubt that all the fears and concerns I had were for nothing. Joey will never stop fighting for our happiness and health. Never.

A quick rap on the door has us both looking up to see Elliott poking her head in. "Is it safe to come in?"

"Yes, please," I call out and Joey hops off the bed to greet our first guests.

Well, second guests. My parents were here the moment Joey called my mother and they finally left about an hour ago. Only because our latest nurse saw the look on my face and made up a story about us needing our rest since we are still considered "high risk" due to the chorio. I have no idea if there was any truth to it, but it got us a small reprieve from the hovering, so I'm grateful. Now, if only she would quit texting demanding updates. I really hope Joey's mother is more tolerable when she gets here in the next few days.

Elliott heads straight to the sink to wash her hands while Abel grabs Joey in a man hug. Words are exchanged, but I'm not sure what. I'm sure it's all congratulatory since Joey wipes his eyes as they pull apart.

"Go wash your hands," Elliott demands of her boyfriend as he gives me a quick kiss of congratulations on my cheek and makes a face at the baby. Elliott pushes him out of the way and sits down next to me, oohing and aahing over the newest love of my life.

"Rosalind, she's so beautiful," Elliott gushes, and I can't say I disagree with her. "She looks just like you. Look at all that dark hair. Are you just in love?"

"Yeah. I am. I didn't expect it to feel like this, but it's just so intense."

"I understand that." Elliott carefully pets my daughter's dark hair, and I appreciate how gentle she is with her. I know babies are hard to break, but this one is mine. I don't want to risk it. "Does she have a name yet?"

"We just decided on it. This is Arabella Renee Marshall." Elliott gasps in approval. "We're still trying to decide if she'll go by a shortened version of her name, but Batman over there says we've got time."

Abel looks at Joey quizzically. "Batman?"

"Never underestimate these guns." Joey flexes his muscles at his best friend who laughs and engages in conversation about the joys of fatherhood and what it takes to raise a little girl.

"There's time for all that," Elliott says. "It's amazing how sometimes they just tell you what they want to be called." She tears her eyes away from Arabella to look at me. "And how are you now that she's here?"

Isn't that the hardest question to answer? I'm ecstatic. I'm terrified. I feel strong. I'm afraid. I'm confident.

"Mostly, I'm in love."

"With her or him?" She quickly tilts her head Joey's direction.

"Maybe a little of both, but I was referring to her." I smile and then screw up my face as I resituate myself on the bed.

"Still sore?"

"A little," I admit. Now that I have battle stories, I see the appeal in sharing them. "Apparently, I didn't need any stitches, so hopefully everything will heal quick."

"You are so lucky. I had way too many stitches. It was hell to use the facilities."

"Worth it though, right?"

Elliott nods vigorously. “Absolutely. I’d do it all over again for Ainsley. Not that I’ll do it again. And don’t you ever let Abel know I said that.”

“Is he pushing you for another one?” This is news to me.

“Nah. It’s a running joke, but neither of us wants that. We’re happy exactly the way things are.”

I nudge her with my shoulder. “So, no ring anytime soon?”

She shrugs. “Maybe someday, but I think we feel less pressure with the way it is right now. Who knows? If it were to ever happen, it would be a quick ceremony at the courthouse, so people get off our backs.”

“You mean the girls?”

Elliott giggles and pinches the bridge of her nose. “Someone at their school was a flower girl a couple weeks ago, so now that’s all they talk about. Maybe we can dress them up for Halloween and call it a day.”

“You know that’s not going to cut it with those two. They’re never going to back down. The two of them together is always trouble.”

“I know.” She looks back down at my angel and coos. “I’m hoping little Arabella here will distract them for a while.”

“We’ll do our best.”

“You really do look better,” Elliott adds reassuringly. “Except for the IV pole you’re attached to, you look physically good. And like you’re starting to get the feel of this whole motherhood thing already.”

I sigh because there are so many thoughts and emotions still running through me. “It’s weird because I’m still scared, ya know? There are so many things that could go wrong. I mean, look.” I hold up Arabella’s little arm that has an IV port sticking out of some sticky gauze that’s been wrapped around to secure it in place. “She’s not even a full day old, and she’s already on an IV to keep her from getting sick. And what we have is mild. There’s just so many things to be worried about. Will that ever go away?”

“Never.” From her tone, there is no room for argument on this one. “Every age carries their own concerns. The trick is you eventually learn how to balance out the fear of something going wrong with the joy of knowing that it’ll be okay in the end.

And as long as she's happy and healthy, all you need to do is enjoy raising her to be the best little person she can be."

She makes sense. "I guess I just had it in my mind that I needed to make things perfect for her. That if I didn't do it exactly right, it was wrong."

"But what does exactly right mean? Ainsley likes doing her hair in the morning. Mabel doesn't. Are either of those things wrong?"

"No."

"Ainsley pops out of bed first thing in the morning. I have to drag Mabel's covers off her to get her to even budge. Are either of those wrong?"

"No."

"I think people forget that this little one right here"—Elliott looks back down and smiles—"she's her own person. She has her own ideas and her own opinions. She'll have her own favorites and her own goals. Besides the obvious ones, the only 'wrong' you can do is to try to make her be *you*. Just let her be *her*, safely and appropriately, and you've done exactly right."

"You make it sounds so easy."

"It is easy. The hard is because it's constant for a while, and you do it on very little sleep. But once you get through those years, you'll see it gets easier."

In all the times Elliott and I had these conversations, it's been hard to wrap my brain around what she meant. But now, while I look at my little girl snuggled safely in my arms, content and happy, I finally understand what she means. And this time, I believe her.

CHAPTER TWENTY-NINE

ROSALIND

6 months later

"How was she for you?" I ask Dinah as she lifts my baby off the floor and hands her to me. I can't believe she's already old enough to sit by herself. As soon as Ari sees me, her arms and legs start kicking rapidly, a gigantic smile on her face.

It's really the best feeling in the world when she looks at me that way.

"She was perfect like always."

Once she's in my arms, my sweet girl snuggles right into my neck, legs tucked under her body as I kiss on her curls. If you had told me six months ago I could love someone like this, I would have told you to stop hitting the sauce. But it's true. I love her so much my heart physically aches sometimes. I didn't even know that was a thing until now.

As it turns out, a lot of my fears were exacerbated by what my doctor now thinks was some pretty normal depression. Whether it was hormone related or situational is unknown. What we do know, however, is that after Ari was born, it turned into post-partum depression. Joey is the one who caught it and brought it to my doctor's attention. After discussing and shedding a bunch of tears in the doctor's office that day, all it took was a mild anti-depressant to get me back on the road to feeling better.

It also secured my trust that Joey doesn't just love Ari. He loves me, too—enough that he notices my downward spirals, even if they're so subtle I don't see them myself.

Several months later, I'm grateful. I can't imagine still suffering in silence. It's much nicer enjoying motherhood, even when it's exhausting.

Handing her over to Dinah again, Ari lets out a squeal of displeasure. "So impatient like your father. Hold on, my love." I turn around so Dinah can help me secure the baby on my back. "Did she eat?"

"And had a diaper change," she says with a small grunt of effort as she holds Ari to me and lifts the Tula into place. "She's ready for a nice long nap."

"Awesome. Thank you so much, Dinah. You have no idea how much I appreciate you," I say as I adjust the top knot on my head. Ari's latest trick is to grab a whole handful and yank when I least expect it. It's not fun for either of us and she doesn't need to be exposed to those words quite yet. Not that her daddy doesn't say them on the regular but hey… we can still be ladies even if he is a scoundrel.

Okay, fine. I'm the one who usually uses those words. And someday, she can use adult words, too. But maybe not as her first words.

"It's no problem at all, really." Dinah finishes adjusting and helps me get my arms in the straps, so Ari is safe and secure for the next couple hours. "I wish all the babies were as good as she is."

I laugh because I know exactly what she means. From the beginning, she has been a good sleeper, a good eater, and almost always in a good mood. I feel like God knew how terrified I was and cut me a break. I also know lightning never strikes in the same place twice. "This is why I'm not having another one for a long time. I know exactly how lucky I am."

Probably noticing a mommy here, a little one with brown pigtails toddles up to Dinah, arms out for balance.

"Oh my gosh," I exclaim. "Is that Rian's baby girl? She's walking!"

Dinah scoops her up into her arms. "Can you believe she is thirteen months old already? Seems like only yesterday Carlos was freaking out about decorating the nursery. Now, he's freaking out about her college fund."

I can't help but laugh. "Sounds like you've got a good daddy, Baby Evelyn. Don't you?" I coo at her, making her smile. She really is a cute baby. Looks like her mother.

"Yeah, she's got him wrapped around her little finger, and she knows it, too."

Just then, a couple of monsters race by.

"Cooper! Ryder!" Dinah yells. "I'm not going to tell you again to stop running!" She looks over at me and rolls her eyes. "I gotta go. See you in a few hours."

I wave as I walk out the door, ready to spend some time folding clean towels.

Ever since I got back from my maternity leave, the gym has been really supportive and family friendly to us. The childcare center isn't licensed as a daycare, so they can only keep kids for a couple hours at a time, but it works in our case.

I go to work alone in the early morning. A couple hours later, Joey arrives and drops Ari off with Dinah. Two hours later, Dinah helps me strap the baby to my back and I do the low-maintenance work while Ari naps, her little head leaning in to listen to my heartbeat. When she wakes up a couple hours later, Joey is in between clients, so he straps her to him while he focuses on paperwork and has his lunch break. Then back to the childcare center for an hour of playtime until I get off. My mother says Ari is going to be spoiled from being carried around all day, but I don't care. My baby, my rules.

Plus, it has been a godsend to not have to pay for daycare. It freed up the money we needed for me to take that GED class, which I passed with flying colors and awarded me the equivalent of a high school diploma. Training for my fitness certification starts in a couple months.

So yes, Elliott was right—baby wearing has been a life saver. All three of us feel like we're bonding, even if we're working at the same time. Who says I can't multitask?

I know Ari will eventually be too old for this, and we'll have to find help watching her, but I also know my mom, and at some point, she's going to cave and want to spend a few hours a day with Ari. How can she not? She's the most beautiful baby in the whole world.

I feel a small tug of some pressure behind me and immediately smile.

"How're my girls doing?" Joey asks as he strokes Ari's head. He's still standing behind me, so I can't see him, but I know exactly what kind of adoring expression he's sporting right now. He gets it every time he looks at her. And sometimes when he looks at me. It makes me remember all the naughty things he still likes doing to me at night.

Even with the stretch marks and the pooch that doesn't want to go away, Joey still finds me sexy and lets me know with his tongue on a regular basis. And he always makes sure to tell me how much he loves me with his words, too. Someday when he finally asks me to be a Marshall, I'll be ready to say yes.

"Dinah says she was great as always."

"Even after getting her six-month shots this morning?"

I snort a laugh and snap a towel out. "You had a worse time with her shots than she did, Joey. It was almost embarrassing seeing a grown man cry for longer than his baby."

"She was in pain."

"She was pissed," I argue back. "You better get that under control because she is going to figure out really quick how to turn on the waterworks to get what she wants from you."

"And she can have whatever her heart desires."

I roll my eyes, but I'm not upset. There are worse things than having a baby daddy who loves your child so much you have to fight him not to spoil her. "You better win the lottery, then."

"I'm still waiting on Abel to get me those numbers."

"What?"

"Nothing. Just an inside joke." He makes his way in front of me and leans against the half-wall I'm using to sort and organize. "You'll be interested to know I have a new client."

"Yeah?" I'm always interested to know how his clientele is shaping up. I'm proud of how much effort he puts in and people seem to love training with him. He deserves it.

"Does the name Scott Adleberry ring a bell?"

My arms stop moving mid snap and my jaw drops open. Everyone knows the name Scott Adleberry. "The quarterback for Chicago Squalls. A legend among men and a god on the field? That Scott Adleberry?"

He purses his lips, not doubt wondering if his new client will star in my latest fantasies. "You don't have to be so excited, but yes. That one."

"He's your new client?"

Joey nods smugly. "Called and signed up this morning."

"Holy shit, Joey. That's… I'm at a loss for words."

"As you should be. And now that I'm sure I sparked more inappropriate threesome fantasies"—I playfully snap a towel at him, which he easily dodges—"I was thinking, I could grab some Thai takeout on my way home, we crack open a bottle of wine and have date night on the living room floor." The waggle of his eyebrows tells me "date night" is actually a front for some hanky-panky. Not that I mind, but I have to keep him on his toes.

I smirk and snap another towel. "I hate Thai food."

"What? That's all you ate when you were pregnant."

"And I'm not pregnant anymore. My taste buds changed."

He looks utterly confused by this revelation. "So. Weird."

"I won't argue with you there. But how about we get Cajun food instead? There's a new place about half a block down from us that smells amazing every time I walk by."

"It's a date." He looks around quickly, probably to make sure Keely isn't lurking anywhere, then leans in and kisses me slowly and with feeling. It's the kiss of two people who aren't in lust, but in love and building a life together. I'll take this kind of kiss over any others.

"Get a room," someone says behind me and we pull apart, only for Joey to break out into a smile.

"Stan, my man, you're early," he says, and they do some weird manshake greeting I will never figure out.

"Thought I'd bring a couple new people from the office with me to try out the class. Do we have room? It's getting pretty full in there."

"Sure. We've got someone new joining us but we'll make it work," Joey responds and turns to me. "I'll see you later." He gives Ari a quick kiss on the top of her head and turns back to his client.

I watch as they walk away, discussing Atlas stones or log raises, I'm not even sure.

The one thing I am sure of, though, is I am so blessed to have this life. A year ago I never would have imagined I'd have the most precious baby in the world, the best boyfriend a girl could ask for, a job that makes sure we're a happy family, and a kind of joy I've never experienced.

I am truly the luckiest woman in the world.

The End.

ACKNOWLEDGMENTS

A comedy of errors in the time of pandemic
based on a true story, and exaggerated for effect

Once upon a time, there was an author who had an idea for a book. It would be fun. It would be zany. It would be a little weird because the characters would be a little weird, but that's what the author liked about them. The story started strong and funny and the author happily wrote all her words every day, and even kept her house somewhat clean. She and **Karin Enders** would discuss the ins and outs of Strongman competitions, as Karin is somewhat of an expert, and things were falling into place. The author almost felt like she was a Disney princess singing through her day.

Then, like the plot twist from a dystopian novel, a pandemic ensued for the first time in over one hundred years. Suddenly, schools were closed, toilet paper was missing, and children were home during work hours. Mental health/motivation started to fall apart. It was a rough time for everyone.

The author was determined, however, to write a romantic comedy and powered through, even though she wasn't feeling funny at all. She was feeling exhausted and overwhelmed. Still… she wrote.

Bad idea. (maybe. We'll see at the end of the story.)

When she finally wrote "the end", the author was so happy to be done that she cried. Immediately, she sent it to her beta readers **Hazel James**, **Aly Stiles**, **Marisol Scott** and **Brenda Rothert** who all read it, then stared at the author for a beat too long before collectively saying, "Um, your characters are kind of crabby."

This is not at all what the author had in mind, but recognized she herself was feeling kind of crabby, so maybe she accidentally transferred her own feelings into those of Rosalind and Joey. Oops.

Slightly discouraged, the author went through the words with a fine-toothed comb and made her characters a little less, well, rude. They are, afterall, flawed. But there is good in them as well.

Satisfied the second draft was much better, the author sent it to **Andrea Johnston** who was delighted at Rosalind's tough exterior and the general nature of the book. She also suggested some more changes.

Six weeks later than intended and after writing an entirely different book in the meantime, because she is an author after all, the second draft was finally sent off to editing with **Erin Noelle**. The author breathed a sigh of relief. Prematurely.

Erin's assessment was comprehensive and as detailed as an ER doctor's. Basically… this book needs some major surgery.

The author wasn't overly surprised as the pandemic had turned off her romcom mood in a very strong way. She was, however, also still cranky and immediately turned to **Karla Sorensen** to complain.

Karla cocked her head from the clouds because she is, in fact, that tall, and said, "I'll give you until tomorrow to whine about it, and then you will suck it up and work." The author complied. Sort of. She also contacted **Brooke Nowiski**.

Thinking she would get some sort of sympathy, the author dramatically threw herself on the floor, with weeping and gnashing of teeth. Brooke merely tapped her foot, crossed her arms, looked at the petulant child and said, "Are you done yet?" before putting on her sexy cat suit, cracking her sexy whip, and pulling out the tequila, all while wondering how she got stuck with this emotional mess of an author and making a mental note never to give said author her phone number.

Once she was done flailing, the author got up off the ground, brushed herself off, and did a massive overhaul. It took a week or so, but she sent it off to **Hazel James** and

Nicole McCurdy who provided much needed feedback on the good, the bad, and the ugly. That final feedback was exactly what the author needed to finish up the story.

It was then sent to **the author's mommy**, partially because moms always say things like, "I'm so proud of you even if it sucks!" And partially because oddly enough, this mom has an eagle eye for proofreading. Go figure.

The moral of the story is, life sometimes sends you lemons. Sometimes it sends you things even worse than lemons. And when that happens, things will go off-kilter. Words won't come like they should. Things won't fall together easily. But if you surround yourself with people who can tell you exactly what you need to hear, whether it be "I'm proud of you" or "Suck it up, buttercup," you can get through anything. For that, this author is so very grateful to the women in this story.

She is also considering sending Brooke more tequila.

The end.

ABOUT THE AUTHOR

Mother, reader, storyteller—M.E. Carter never set out to write books. But when a friend practically forced a copy of Twilight into her hands, the love of the written word she had lost as a child was rekindled. With a story always rolling around in her head, it should come as no surprise that she finally started putting them on paper. She lives in Texas with her four children, Mary, Elizabeth, Carter and Bug, who sadly was born long after her pen name was created, and will probably need extensive therapy because of it.

Find M.E. Carter online:
Website: http://www.authormecarter.com
Facebook: https://www.facebook.com/authorMECarter/
Goodreads: https://www.goodreads.com/author/show/9899961.M_E_Carter
Twitter: @authormecarter
Instagram: @authormecarter

Find Smartypants Romance online:
Website: www.smartypantsromance.com
Facebook: www.facebook.com/smartypantsromance/
Goodreads: www.goodreads.com/smartypantsromance
Twitter: @smartypantsrom
Instagram: @smartypantsromance
Newsletter: https://smartypantsromance.com/newsletter/

ALSO BY M.E. CARTER

The Hart Series:

Change of Hart

Hart to Heart

Matters of the Hart

Matters to Me

Matters to You

Matter of Time (coming July 8, 2021)

Texas Mutiny Series:

Juked

Groupie

Goalie

Megged

Deflected

#MyNewLife Series

Getting a Grip

Balance Check

Pride & Joie

Amazing Grayson

Little Miss Perfect (Exclusively inside the Getting a Grip Duet box set)

-

Charitable Endeavors

(written with Andrea Johnston)

Switch Stance

Ear Candy

Model Behavior

Better than the Book

Beyond the Lyrics (Coming Fall 2021)

Cipher Office Series

(Penny Reid's Smartypants Romance Universe)

Weight Expectations

Cutie and the Beast

Holiday Reads

(written with Sara Ney)

Kissmas Eve

New Year's Steve

Stand Alone Novels

(written with Sara Ney)

FriendTrip

For a complete updated list visit: www.authormecarter.com

ALSO BY SMARTYPANTS ROMANCE

Green Valley Chronicles

The Love at First Sight Series

Baking Me Crazy by Karla Sorensen (#1)

Batter of Wits by Karla Sorensen (#2)

Steal My Magnolia by Karla Sorensen(#3)

Fighting For Love Series

Stud Muffin by Jiffy Kate (#1)

Beef Cake by Jiffy Kate (#2)

Eye Candy by Jiffy Kate (#3)

The Donner Bakery Series

No Whisk, No Reward by Ellie Kay (#1)

The Green Valley Library Series

Love in Due Time by L.B. Dunbar (#1)

Crime and Periodicals by Nora Everly (#2)

Prose Before Bros by Cathy Yardley (#3)

Shelf Awareness by Katie Ashley (#4)

Carpentry and Cocktails by Nora Everly (#5)

Love in Deed by L.B. Dunbar (#6)

Scorned Women's Society Series

My Bare Lady by Piper Sheldon (#1)

The Treble with Men by Piper Sheldon (#2)

The One That I Want by Piper Sheldon (#3)

Park Ranger Series

Happy Trail by Daisy Prescott (#1)

Stranger Ranger by Daisy Prescott (#2)

The Leffersbee Series

Been There Done That by Hope Ellis (#1)

The Higher Learning Series

Upsy Daisy by Chelsie Edwards (#1)

Seduction in the City

Cipher Security Series

Code of Conduct by April White (#1)

Code of Honor by April White (#2)

Cipher Office Series

Weight Expectations by M.E. Carter (#1)

Sticking to the Script by Stella Weaver (#2)

Cutie and the Beast by M.E. Carter (#3)

Weights of Wrath by M.E. Carter (#4)

Common Threads Series

Mad About Ewe by Susannah Nix (#1)

Give Love a Chai by Nanxi Wen (#2)

Educated Romance

Work For It Series

Street Smart by Aly Stiles (#1)

Heart Smart by Emma Lee Jayne (#2)

Lessons Learned Series

Under Pressure by Allie Winters (#1)

CPSIA information can be obtained
at www.ICGtesting.com
Printed in the USA
BVHW070619030321
601494BV00004B/278